You
Better
Not
Get
Old

by Yomi Akinode

Previously published as 3 Score & Ten (2023)

Printed in the United States of America

First Printing: 2024

ISBN-13: 979-8990607705

Table of Contents

1

Chapter 24 – Now what?

Chapter 1

Disillusioned, Goram Naphtali, a successful Dotcom Venture Capitalist and an Israeli Congressman in the Knesset, quit Congress in protest due to the slow, lackluster approach of the Israeli government in handling the grave threat that Iran as a country posed to the safe existence of the state of Israel.

Weeks later, his father, ridden with dementia, died in a terrorist bombing, and months after the loss, Goram had a first-hand experience of a terrorist bombing while having lunch in downtown Tel Aviv.

Continents away in the United States, a pretty rookie FBI Agent of Scandinavian stock, Berlin Yords, trapped in the ingrained notion of good physical attributes as detrimental to effective criminal policing in the highly competitive FBI culture, took on increasingly dangerous assignments to prove her mettle, consequently sustaining endless life-threatening bodily injuries.

Meanwhile, Goram established *NBT*, Neshema Biomedical Technologies, to research gerontology, concentrating on dementia. He then bolstered those activities by inaugurating the Endless Love Foundation to keep his father's memory alive.

Still restless, Goram was coerced by a radical Rabbi into joining a cabal of powerful industrialists bent on fulfilling a flawed biblical tenet that, if left uncorrected, would pose grave risks to the existence of the human race. This action collided between the disillusioned venture capitalist and the relentless FBI Agent.

Chapter 2

Post COVID-19, Goram Naphtali addressed Congress, announcing his resignation from the Knesset...

"In 1973, I was too young to bear arms at Yom Kippur but old enough to hide my mother when the bombs came.

"All 6' 5" of me was too tall to be stealthy as a Mossad spy, but now I am too stubborn not to fight the only way I know and can.

"So, I support Mother Israel with all I am, whenever and wherever. Hence, I retire today as a Knesset member to forge ahead and find more effective avenues to support my Jewish people.

"I leave you with my most worrisome fear of Iran becoming nuclear-capable within a decade. But first and foremost, my immediate task after leaving this laudable body and loyal colleagues is to vigorously pursue all avenues and sciences available to eradicate dementia in honor of my late father through the 'Endless Love Foundation.'"

Goram walked out of the auditorium with a loud ovation and appreciation for his decade-long service as a lawmaker.

***

Outside the hall, Goram pulled out a cell phone and called his Jordanian caretaker at Eilat village, his ancestral orchard farm. "I'm coming to the farm in two weeks."

"Yes, Sir, Mr. Naphtali. We're always ready for you. Will you be using the motorcycle?"

"Yes, but don't touch Sheba; she's mine."

The caretaker chuckled. "Just checking, Sir."

***

Goram walked into his Eilat lounge on Friday night carrying luggage and files. He opened a hidden wall safe behind a gun rack, tossed in the files, and entered the bedroom, collapsing heavily on the bed.

The following morning, he walked onto the veranda at dawn with a steaming mug. He sat on a wooden deck chair, seemingly at ease, and surveyed the farmland as he read the latest news on the war against Iran.

He put down the newspaper, sipped, and picked up a local journal for the valley. He chuckled periodically at items that tickled him.

He looked up to a sudden rattling at the right side of the homestead, with tall trees shading the home. Two squirrels were chasing each other up and down the trees. He returned to his reading. Then, moments later, he lifted the mug. It was empty.

"That's it then," he muttered.

He walked off the deck towards two sheds and unlocked the large sliding door in the first shed. He rolled out an old black motorcycle he called *Sheba*. He failed to kickstart the antique cycle and rolled it toward the back of the house.

"Every damn time Sheba."

He opened a small door, revealing a well-tooled bike garage. He brought out a series of tools to work on the vintage monster.

It was well into the afternoon now. Sweaty but self-satisfied, Goram successfully kick-started the bike.

"Sheba's back."

He rode through the orchard toward the pump house. He smiled as he parked next to the red pump lever and playfully tried to pump it before riding off.

Next, he stopped at THE CIRCLE and revved the bike multiple times, remembering the family scrambling into the bunker tunnel during the war.

The horror of the 1973 Yom Kippur War experienced on the farm flashed through his mind as a nineteen-year-old hiding with his family in the bunker tunnel...

"Please help Mama..." Goram wailed at his father...

Goram shook his head to ward off the sudden, intrusive memory. The bike stalled, and he couldn't get it to restart. He began to roll the machine towards the house.

"Just as well, Sheba."

***

Refreshed, Goram returned to a sports arena in downtown Tel Aviv.

A Rabbi sidled up to Goram, the center of attention at the annual commemoration of his father's *Endless Love Foundation* for advancing studies in age-related ailments, specifically dementia. After shaking hands and "kissing babies," he faced the Rabbi to shake one more hand.

"It's a pleasure to attend one of these things and finally witness it myself," Rabbi Chosky announced.

"Thank you, Rabbi. Your presence is a blessing, and you are welcome for the great cause."

The Rabbi paused for a long while, and Goram spoke.

"Do you have a question, Sir?"

"Yes, I'm just not sure you'll view my query as laudable."

"Oh?"

"Believe me, Congressman, today and here is not the right venue."

Intrigued, Goram paused to face one of his assistants hovering behind him. "I'll be right with you."

He turned to face the Rabbi, who shoved a business card at him. "I shall be leaving now, Mister Naphtali."

Decades earlier, the 25-year-old Chosky had lived in an apartment with a family of four named the Cantors in Tel Aviv.

During a Palestinian terrorist missile attack, he saved teenage Lewis & Anna Cantor but not their parents from the devastation. He looked after the kids for weeks until their uncle, Levi Straus, living in the United States, came to collect the new orphans.

Levi took the kids to live with him in Los Angeles while he managed his famous landmark, a rare bookstore on Hollywood Boulevard...

Goram turned the business card over in his hand, noted an inscription, THE ORDER, put it in his jacket pocket, and watched the Rabbi walk away. Goram then followed the assistant to the podium.

"Attention, great ladies and gentlemen. Before his untimely demise, several months prior, my father began to look at me as a total stranger after so many years of sharing dinner table wines, Matzoh ball soup, and Challah..." The audience lapped it up with hand claps and approval murmurs.

He continued, "Your support and contribution today will go a long way to enable this foundation and find a cure for a humbling disease such as dementia. Our latest venture, Neshema Biomedical Technologies, NBT, has the science and the brain trust to confront this dastardly enemy." The room exploded in extended clapping.

As the evening tapered and the large arena was nearly empty, Goram stood with his two confidants, Avnar Barak, his bodyguard and majordomo, and friend and colleague paleontologist Erman Erturgu, Ph.D., all three nursing drinks and talking about the just-concluded event.

***

The trio carried the evening over to Goram Naphtali's home and retired to the lounge. No sooner were they inside than Erman, who predated Avnar working for Goram, complained, "Why does he have to carry that thing around?"

"Necessary evil, Professor," Goram said lightheartedly as he walked off to escape the pitty-patter-friendly fight brewing.

Avnar brandished the gun from his holster in his absence, playfully goading the academician. "Guns don't kill people. People kill people," Avnar professed.

"Sure, Brainiac!" Erman retorted as Goram reappeared, squelched the impasse, and beckoned them to follow him further into the home.

Goram opened the door to the staircase leading to a sporty basement room and clicked a hidden wall button that opened into another cove. The gentle hum of air circulation was audible in the secret room, with vast art collections clearly labeled and arranged. Goram took turns bragging about each of his collections.

Avnar, an avid "antiquer," as he calls himself, was taken by the pink lotus lamp rumored to be the most expensive lamp sold at Christie's auction house in New York. Erman, the forever cynic, was less impressed.

When he entered the cove, he slipped on gloves from a glove box on a side table and carefully inspected the lamp with critical eyes. He returned the item to its location, saying nothing. Goram and Avnar looked at each other and smiled knowingly.

Goram then moved the party back upstairs to the lounge for the rest of the evening.

***

Two weeks later, Goram cuts the ribbon in front of a new glass building on the outskirts of Tel Aviv.

His new venture capital fund will research gerontology here, focusing on dementia. The facility will be headed by a young American erudite, John Jacobs, Ph.D., who graduated at the top of his biochemistry class at Harvard, all thirty-two years of a scion of serious, intellectual, and focused disposition.

Goram called him to the temporary stage for the opening at the entrance lobby of the new company.

Though only twenty-five people were present, they were the power brokers in politics and businesses across Israel, mostly from Tel Aviv and Jerusalem, including his former Knesset friend and colleague, House Speaker Josef Matursky.

"Please welcome a gifted young man, John Jacobs. I call him JJ because, at his interview, he insisted I always call him by both his names. We negotiated, and I won. Now, I call him JJ."

The room burst out in contagious laughter as JJ approached the stage.

"My boss, the great Goram Naphtali, will never know whether I liked to be called JJ because…" He allowed the sentence to hang—someone from the audience filled the gap.

"…Pay your bills?"

JJ deadpanned and then continued.

"Gerontology is a catch-all for a nasty neuro-debilitating condition with dementia as one of its manifestations that sneaks up on people, especially as we all age. NBT–Neshema Biomedical Technologies Inc.–will evolve a lasting efficacy to the ailment.

"Please, give me time to lay out a not-too-technical introduction of our challenges."

JJ turned on a large screen behind him, and details about dementia scrolled through slowly as he paused and briefly explained each section…

"The most common form of Dementia is Alzheimer's disease, which is neurodegenerative with no cure and accounts for 60 to 80 percent of cases. It is caused by specific changes in the brain, such as trouble remembering recent events that occurred minutes or hours ago.

"Difficulty remembering more distant memories, walking, talking, or personality changes come later. Family history is the most important risk factor, as having a first-degree relative with Alzheimer's disease increases the risk of developing it by 10 to 30 percent.

"Vascular dementia is a general term describing problems with reasoning, planning, judgment, memory, and other thought processes caused by brain damage from impaired blood flow to the brain, developing after a stroke blocks an artery in the brain.

"Still, strokes don't always cause vascular dementia. A stroke's effects on thinking and reasoning depend on severity and location, and this type of dementia can also result from other conditions that damage blood vessels and reduce circulation, depriving the brain of vital oxygen and nutrients.

"Lewy Body Dementia, LBD, is associated with abnormal protein deposits, called alpha-synuclein, in the brain. These deposits, called Lewy bodies, affect chemicals in the brain whose changes, in turn, can lead to problems with thinking, movement, behavior, and mood.

"Fronto-Temporal Dementia, FTD, most often leads to changes in personality and behavior because of the part of the brain it affects. The condition causes people to embarrass themselves and behave inappropriately toward a previously cautious person. Responsibilities at home and work, as well as language skills like speaking or understanding, may suffer.

"FTD causes are unknown, but a family history of FTD is a disposition with ten to 30 percent due to specific genetic causes and its gene-variant dependence.

"Finally, a more troubling Dementia version is called mixed dementia, mixing multiple types of dementia in the brain simultaneously at the age of 80 and older, and the progression may be faster than with only one kind of dementia...

"I have attempted to be brief while annotating the disease breadth. The 'good' news about all the information you saw on screen is available for general consumption on the intranet. Please read up on it. With that, I hand it back to Mister Naphtali."

Then, a serious audience member asked a question that drew JJ's smile.

"What's your research subject, Doctor Jacobs? After all, I don't expect you to expose people already suffering from these ailments to face further than necessary probing."

"Thank you for the question, Sir."

JJ then took the attendees through his proposed research strategies…

"The large book before you is the most important reference for the research exercise. It contains the DOE– Design of Experiments—that will statistically determine the planning, conducting, and analysis of interpreting control tests to evaluate test parameters and their outcomes.

"Please open to page 17b."

JJ waited for the people to turn their pages.

"We plan to utilize pigs for our experiments because they are mammals with all the major structures found in humans present. The differences that do exist are relatively minor.

"Our primary interest in this study is identifying areas within the central nervous system that change over time based on different applications of experimental procedures and factors we plan to introduce." He returned to his seat.

"Pigs have the same musculature, aside from locations and size, and differences in the gluteal. They have mostly the same thoracic and abdominal organs as humans. The human liver has four lobes; pigs have five. The thymus is found in the same area.

"A pig's uterus is bicornate, has two large horns in addition to the body, and the pig's central nervous system models well for size, anatomic characteristics, development, and blood flow."

JJ looked up to ensure the audience was as engaged as he was. Satisfied, he continued.

"Also important is the Sow reproductive system, which shall become significant for our process as we plan to house a backup pig farm to farrow piglets to backfill the primary experimental subjects. However, the farm will not be part of the data package for regulatory quality control purposes. The farm will be subject to similar electronic monitoring as an additional data point source."

He closed his notebook and looked up. "Questions?"

"How many subjects?" someone asked.

"24. Twelve were primary, and twelve were control. Each subject shall have a headgear containing six electronic probes inserted into the pig brain and connected permanently to monitors and recorders as they live in their pens. Daily, they will be taken out to wander outside for an hour to simulate normal living.

"Each probe shall monitor a specific area of the brain responsible for a specific type of memory, and the records will show that the pig is aged and deprived of stimulation, such as playing with other pigs, wandering around, etc. The backup piglets shall be fitted with probes once they are a month old," JJ answered.

The room murmured briefly and then went quiet for seconds until Goram glided to the stage as hostesses with drink and aperitif platters appeared in the lobby.

"The better news I'm told… also on the intranet…" He looked briefly at JJ and then continued.

"…is that there might be reversible dementia caused by people having underlying factors such as medication side effects, increased pressure in the brain, vitamin deficiency, and thyroid hormone imbalance. So please celebrate with us tonight as the hard work begins tomorrow. Thank you very much."

Goram and JJ then circulated amongst the guests.

Chapter 3

Weeks later, Goram and JJ descended the staircase to the animal husbandry area of NBT to inspect pregnant Sows in the pen in the early morning hours.

As they neared a large Sow's pen, a sudden mild electronic surge caused some interference to the electrical equipment. Ceiling light fixtures flashed on and off briefly, and electronic doors to all the animal enclosures clicked but did not open.

"I thought the electronic expansion in the warehouse was completed."

"No, two more weeks to go, and according to the IEC, Israel Electric Corporation, they need to be on-site for the upgrade."

"Why, JJ? I thought we were upgrading the warehouse server systems."

"Yes, but the new power consumption load quadruples."

"Do you need help with the bureaucracy?"

"No, we'll manage."

They both walked back up to the office.

***

After meeting Rabbi Chosky for the first time at the Endless Love Foundation, Goram welcomed the Rabbi to his office at NBT.

"Thank you for your presence at the inauguration, Sir." The Rabbi waved him off and then jumped right in.

"Have you heard of THE ORDER?"

"As a word, yes, but not what it is. What is it?"

"It's a collection of like-minded people with similar concerns as yours about aging, but approached from a rather radical angle, biblical, I might contend."

"I'm glad to hear that; how can I help?"

The Rabbi heaved a sigh and launched in.

"I want your support, financial support mostly, to bring the world's population to a meaningful, youthful, and less disease-ridden level. Can you help?"

Goram leaned forward. "Of course, but I'm not sure what you mean."

"Most global resources are dedicated to the elderly to make their lives as comfortable as possible in their sunset years. I'm agreeable to such sentiments, but not when the quality of life of those individuals is no longer merry; they are simply hanging on for the sake of hanging on to life."

"That's what we humans do. We're programmed to survive, Rabbi."

"Be that as it may, wouldn't it be refreshing always to have a relatively youthful population unencumbered with the old just living for the sake of living?"

Goram stared curiously at the Rabbi. "I'm not sure I follow or agree."

"What if I were to tell you that the bible specifically instructed us on exactly how long each of us should live?"

"I don't know what to say, but I'm still unclear about what you want from me."

The Rabbi sat back. "I want your influence and wealth to underpin THE ORDER's tenet of global culling aging, which we reference as three scores and ten."

"Culling?"

"Yes, culling, elimination, killing…" Goram flew off the chair. The Rabbi remained seated.

"Please, hear me out, Mister Naphtali." The Rabbi motioned for Goram to sit down.

"I know it's uncomfortable, unusual, and perhaps shocking to hear, but we must stop feeding the beast, or it will end our population faster and earlier than necessary. It's the single most important existential threat the world faces."

Somewhat calmer, Goram asked, "How do you propose to do what you're suggesting legally? The last I looked, killing is still murder."

"Science. That's where you, your wealth, and the company come in."

"Experiments?"

The Rabbi nodded.

"Human history is littered with inhumane experiments benefitting humankind today, the premise being…"

Goram interrupted, "With all due respect, Rabbi, it's historically documented that all those people experimented upon suffered tremendous hardship under situations neither chosen nor within their control. Why, in this day and age…"

The Rabbi raised a hand, and Goram stopped talking.

"No one can compete with us Jews regarding human suffering. Our religion has been coerced to almost demand we suffer first, attain peaceful justice later, laden with emotional scars, and then go on to glory happily. The rest of mankind is just catching up to us. Look…"

The Rabbi paused, softened his voice and demeanor, and continued.

"Before you list them, I will preempt you as I've preached these dastard occurrences to infinitum… The Nazi/Mengele experiments were devastating on twins and other young Jews, the American Syphilis trials on innocent African American men were horrendous, and the recent Uyghur castigation in China is morally reprehensible, yet, it's been proven repeatedly over centuries that to eat a pleasant omelet, a few eggs must be cracked."

Goram sat back and gave it to the Rabbi.

"It's factual that justifying sinful, painful, heartless, and experimental procedures on anyone, especially our aged population, would render us directly onto a turbo-charged vehicle heading straight into hell, regardless of purported potential gains."

It was the Rabbi's turn to sit back.

"What legacy do you prefer, Goram?"

"Does it matter?"

"Yes, it does, and that's why I'm sitting here today."

Goram heaved a sigh. "It's now widely known since its establishment that my father's foundation encouraged experiments from all avenues to find cures to slow the progress and eliminate age-related ailments."

"Be that as it may, Goram, the human biological/biochemical constitution is programmed to degenerate with age. We may extend our lives a little, but the quality of such lives is debatable.

"Would you want to live to be 100 while blind? Or be 150 while you can no longer love your wife in all ways? Or…" Goram interrupted.

"So, what exactly is Three Score and Ten?"

"You're toast when you turn 70," the Rabbi off-handedly interpreted.

"I guess *you better not get old*," Goram concluded.

The Rabbi glared, got up, and left.

***

Two weeks later, Goram's chauffeur in a black Rolls-Royce buzzed through the decorated high metal gate and parked next to a series of black Mercedes-Benz cars in Rabbi Chosky's office compound parking lot.

Goram Naphtali walked toward the plant-covered two-story building in an affluent corner of Tel Aviv. "Rabbi Chosky, please."

A scowling military-type security guard at the front desk scrutinized Goram's credentials and motioned him down a short corridor to the staircase. Goram knocked on the door at the top landing.

Chosky, short and bearded, directed Goram to a chair across the desk. They waited for each other, but Goram broke the impasse.

"Thank you for the audience. It's been two weeks since our last meeting."

The Rabbi tugged at his beard, answering, "The Knesset speaker thinks highly of you."

Goram's eyebrows furrowed, questioning.

"You know Josef Matursky?"

The Rabbi's hand gesture of humility fell flat as he spoke.

"THE ORDER, my life's work, as articulated in your office, is a profound religious entity populated with what some people call disillusioned zealots. We're not that.

"We are sickened, wary, and tired of a cadre of useless aged population robbing us of plentiful youth to combat the unwinnable war with the Arab world.

"We, the Cabal, embrace tenets rooted in the biblical suggestion of population containment achievable through three-score and ten-year human life age limits—my numerous requests to the Pope for support unrequited."

Goram sidestepped the self-flagellation. "The Palestine-Israeli détente war is killing our people."

Goram stopped talking; the Rabbi encouraged him to continue, but he didn't. The Rabbi does.

"Our group, though small in size, harbors big ideas and radical actions beyond the realms of Vanilla platitude to placate Israelis. Again, I hate to be blunt, but your wealth will primarily secure where we lead our people.

"But, a forty-year sojourn in the desert under brutal rules cannot endlessly exchange for constant terror."

The Rabbi sat back, satisfied.

Goram was prepared to leave. "Unfortunately, I have other obligations today that will prevent me from staying longer."

"I need to show you something before you leave."

Goram reluctantly followed the Rabbi.

Both descended the staircase into the basement, cluttered with books, boxes, and supplies, sporting five distinguished men:

Mukaiba Golda,

Abel Schuster,

Blau Horowitz,

Hoffman Levi, and

Abulafia Cardoso.

All dressed in black suits, they mill quietly in two groups with drinks in hand. Rabbi Chosky introduced each person to Goram.

Later, Chosky and Goram briefly discussed the situation in the parking lot.

"I lived in America for a long time, but now I'm here to continue the good work. America was great but a heathen's haven, all the same," the Rabbi confessed.

"Why did you leave, Rabbi?" Goram probed, but Chosky was evasive.

Berlin Yords's second year as an FBI Agent devolved into a personal tragedy when a misguided Jewish zealot assaulted and killed her African friend over her physical appearance by wearing a Hijab and a long robe in New York.

The investigation led to a location in Queens, the small Yom Marantz synagogue, where a radical Rabbi preached. Two years later, the radical Rabbi whipped two unstable zealots into a frenzy that culminated in the kidnapping of a young prostitute.

Berlin and her senior FBI partner traced the kidnappers to Bayonne, New Jersey, where a fierce gun battle ensued.

Her partner lost his life, while Berlin sustained massive injuries. She received multiple awards for bravery...

Goram's chauffeur lightly tapped the car horn to alert him.

To the Rabbi's relief, he watched Goram slowly back up to open the car door as he returned to the building.

For weeks, Goram couldn't shake his discussion with the Rabbi. He sent Avnar Barak to visit the Rabbi for a last look to ease his guilt, as he planned to reject the offer.

Avnar Barak, in Rabbi Chosky's office, listened attentively to the Cleric's ideas as Goram had instructed him.

"You're Josef Matursky's boy, yes?" Avnar hesitated ever so briefly.

"In a manner of speaking."

"You're not?"

"I am, yes," Avnar confirmed unequivocally.

"So, how do we go about this, young man?"

"I'm here to listen, Sir."

The Rabbi leaned forward. "Surreptitious addition of nerve Agents into the water supply for a painless demise."

He stopped talking, and Avnar remained quiet.

"Well?"

"Oh, Sir, I have no opinion. I'm here only to collect all your thoughts and suggestions and funnel them back to Mister Naphtali."

"What do you think of the idea, though? Will it work?"

"I have no opinion either way, Sir."

"What if we float a new company that caters to vacations and day trips and then engineer fatal accidents? I know it sounds cruel, but the alternative on a grand scale is nothing compared."

Avnar remained mum.

The Rabbi appeared exasperated but kept it in check.

"Okay, what if we supply free food coated with something that dissipates in case of autopsies?"

Avnar still did not offer any opinion.

"I realize the hesitation to flout Goram's directives, but you have an opinion that I wish you'd share, please."

The Rabbi waited, and so did Avnar.

A combative, silent impasse has just ensued. Chosky broke it.

"Alright, how about we invent an implantable electronic device with activation access to trigger cessation of life?" Still, no comments from Avnar.

The Rabbi finally called it quits.

"Mister Barak, I have another appointment; I will need to talk directly with Goram once he has reviewed these suggestions. Yeah?"

"Yes, Sir."

Avnar left, and Chosky watched him walk towards his car in the parking lot from his window.

"What a tushy!" The Rabbi opined.

Avnar walked into Goram's office, handed him a report, and sat while Goram read.

Goram stared at Avnar for a long time after reading the rabbinic suggestions in the report. Then he pointed at the report.

"He's nuts."

"We need to leave this alone, Sir," Avnar suggested.

"Will any of it work?" Goram asked.

Surprised, Avnar became circumspect.

"With undue force, any of those ideas will work; it just depends on what degree and the amount of effort applied for the value gain."

"Which has the best chance of success?"

Avnar remained reticent.

"Depends on the level of risk tolerance."

"Thank you; we'll leave it there."

Avnar left.

***

The Israeli desert was baking hot, but this had never been a deterrent to shepherds for generations. So, today was no different. An old shepherd and his young son herd sheep a mile away from the shanty village of Erez Ptessagh on the outskirts of Jerusalem.

A stray bleat from yonder, the shepherd found the lamb trapped inside a cave. He shooed away a snake that frightened Yeanling. He pulled out the agneau and inspected the cave opening, noting that it extended deeper.

He carefully sealed the entrance with rocks and returned to the lamb. The shepherd's kid cared for the lamb while returning to the village.

In the dark, they returned to the cave to find an untouched tomb with a staff, a shrunken baby basket, scrolls, and manuscripts arranged around skeletal remains that had harbored a dormant, unearthly entity for centuries.

Upon human contact, the dormant entity embedded itself in the shepherd's body and extended its tentacles into his heart and brain.

An hour later, on the way home, the shepherd experienced violent tremors. An oval welt immediately appeared behind his earlobe.

"You will tell no one of these findings, you hear?" the shepherd emphatically instructed his young son.

"As you wish, father." The son nodded as they hauled the loot back to the village.

***

A month later, Avnar, in his antiquer mode, ended up in the Erez Ptessagh village market talking to a cantankerous popular merchant dealer, who asked him, "Were you weaned on chicken milk?" Shaming the stranger to haggle pretty for an old tapestry.

"No, on Llama piss, you old goat." Avnar scowled and leaned forward long enough for the old merchant to see the Luger under his jacket.

"Now that you put it *that* way, friend, 100 Shekels will make the trade." He wrapped up the merchandise.

"What I want is…" Avnar pointed to a vase.

"Not for sale." The merchant abandoned the tapestry. Avnar walked away.

The merchant yelled after him, "I have something, but not here."

Avnar was suspicious but returned to the old codger.

Later that evening, at the merchant's hut, Avnar, in surprise, saw a gangly youth walk in with a sack over his shoulder. Avnar turned cynical. "Anyone else coming?"

Avnar, hesitant, shook the fidgety kid's hand after dropping the load.

The young shepherd proudly unwrapped items on the table. Unimpressed, Avnar arose.

"What are these?"

The kid looked warily at the old merchant, who interjected, looking and pleading at Avnar, "Let the kid explain, Mister."

"These are scrolls and manifests that belong to…" The kid's voice trailed off dramatically. He looked around furtively. "Moses," he announced gleefully.

Avnar was at the door about to leave, and the kid yelled, "We have skeletal remains too!"

Avnar hesitated. "Four hundred Shekels for the lot," he spoke without turning around, expecting a rejection.

"I accept."

After rescuing the lamb from the desert cave, the kid was desperate to sell it to treat his father's ailment from a snake bite. The wound festered as his father refused hospital treatments, preferring local remedies that did not work.

The merchant spat to the far wall, unimpressed with the kid's quick cave. Avnar, with evil eyes, dropped Shekels on the table to the merchant's disgust and walked out with the kid.

It was now deep into the night when the kid, Avnar, behind him, walked into his family hut where his father, on a sickbed, coughed in pain. His mother rubbed the lower half of his father's swollen arm, the upper half festooned with scabs over the nasty, putrid wound. Avnar wrinkled his nose from the fetid stench of sickness in the room.

The kid disappeared and soon returned with a sack, to his father's displeasure, as he watched in agony.

The kid displayed promised wares, to Avnar's delight. In addition, Avnar threw in an extra fifty Shekels. The kid's father became animated, stared, and pointed feverishly at something only he could see. Then, finally, he sighed, gasped for breath, and slumped dead while all three were still processing the bizarre turn of events.

Chapter 4

Goram towered over board members, all 6'5" of him, in the sizeable NBT conference room where Avnar presented the curious "Moses" discovery and the strange circumstance that befell the shepherd family.

When Avnar returned from Erez Ptessagh, he visited Goram at home, who called in Erman. All three strategized that NBT might be well-positioned to research what the bones and other artifacts could reveal.

After many discussions, JJ was not convinced to utilize his scarce resources on a "chase," as he puts it...

Just before the meeting moved on, Avnar proposed inviting the young shepherd to NBT for further discussions.

"I don't know what value bringing the shepherd kid here will serve. May I please remind the team that our focus is on gerontology in general and dementia specifically? None of these artifacts will be adding value."

"I hear you, JJ…" Goram interrupted, looking at his CEO, and then continued. "It wouldn't hurt to find out what happened to the kid's father's brain that caused him to hallucinate, for instance. It's possible data from his brain could somehow be relevant to gerontology, no?"

"That may be interesting, but we're not set up for human morbid anatomy assessments here."

Goram took a conciliatory tone. "I may be able to influence that if necessary."

Everyone now casts a longing look at JJ, the young scientist who soon caved.

"Okay, let's bring him in, but not for another two weeks. I will not allow him or anyone else not on the team into our proprietary areas," JJ insisted.

"Fair enough, and thank you," Goram graciously stated and quietly requested the latest broad strokes on the dementia trials.

The young CEO rattled off details.

"The latest batch of Sow gestation anomalies has reduced by 20% while lactation data demonstrated full load nucleic similarity amongst same-sex piglets but differed in—" A loud street Siren goes off outside.

Everyone calmly filed out of the conference room to mix with employees, hopping out of cubicles down the staircase into a basement bunker.

The open, well-lit, stocked bunker had an office sitting arrangement where everyone knew where to go. Goram and his managers sat far off from others, outside of earshot.

"Another Palestinian missile threat, I'm sure," Goram spat while adjusting his yarmulke.

"Mossad continues to fail to identify and eradicate the mad zealots." Avnar's intensity only subsided when Goram's non-verbal facial acquiescence was registered.

Goram turned to the CEO, who resumed his project report updates.

"The twenty-four primary test subjects have yet to show anomalies in the frontal, temporal region, though physical disabilities are onsetting from the lethargy they demonstrate when walking and playing outside. The control population is not showing such 'slow down,'" JJ concluded.

A different sound alarm goes off, signaling that the missile danger has passed. Everyone left the safety shelter.

***

Days later, Erman tested all the "Moses" artifacts and authenticated that they were genuine, dating back almost four thousand years.

Avnar returned to the village, encouraged the shepherd kid, and invited him to NBT to clarify the circumstances of his father's demise, dangling possible rewards.

By the end of two weeks, the kid was at NBT, where he lamented his father's untimely demise with Goram, JJ, Avnar, and Erman in a meeting.

"He had a snake bite that went untreated, then festered, poisoning his blood," the kid explained.

"Your father was quite agitated minutes just before he…" Avnar's voice trailed off.

"That's true." The kid was fidgety.

"Did he see something that displeased him?" Avnar asked.

"I don't recall the details, Sir. But he was very sick and weak. I don't know," the kid concluded.

"I was quite sorry about the whole event…" Avnar's voice trailed off again.

"He's dead now. My mother and I have to move on." The kid looked at Goram.

"Young man, I need to ask you for something."

Goram leaned into the kid across the conference table.

"But before I do, I want everyone else out of the room."

Goram instructed Avnar and Erman and then turned to the kid, "I'd like you to donate your father's body to this lab for scientific studies."

The kid screamed in anger. "How dare you, Sir!"

He stormed out of the office and waited at the exit door for security to process him out.

He turned around and watched the scientists in immaculate white lab coats walk past him, up and down the hallway. Impressed, he changed his mind with a proviso for the promised reward and a tour of the facility to better understand what NBT does. Goram agreed.

A week later, a white truck lurched to a stop outside the NBT warehouse facility gates, with the shepherd kid on the passenger side next to Avnar, who was driving. Avnar waved to the security guard, who recognized him. Avnar backed up to the bay.

As the truck moved, the kid stared at three IEC trucks parked end to end by the warehouse.

"What's going on?"

"Expansion. System updates."

The kid frowned. "We never have problems with the Israeli Electrical Corporation in my village."

"That's good." Avnar frowned in reply, unsure what the statement meant. The truck stopped. A forklift unloaded the wooden box.

Avnar, standing next to the kid on the dock, watched the forklift maneuver the box and placated the young man with a worried look. "You're doing a good deed, kid."

"He should be buried with dignity, not ripped apart for…" The kid's voice trailed off as the forklift honked.

"Your science gift will save many lives. You should be proud of that." Avnar placed a genteel hand on the young man's shoulder as they walked further into the warehouse.

As promised, Avnar conducted the kid and his mother through a multi-floor high-rise building outside Neve Tzedek village, Tel Aviv, bought by NBT in the kid's name.

Avnar handed the shepherd kid the real estate purchase contracts as they walked past technicians servicing the elevator.

Behind Avnar, the child and his mother labored up the stairs in an affluent neighborhood. The child's unbridled enthusiasm contrasted with his widowed mother's sour mood. The child's mother struggled to keep up with the climb toward the third floor.

"Cheer up, mother. It's God's will. Father received the call."

"I'm all alone now," she mumbled with the kid's arms around her shoulders.

Avnar chattered away, describing their new home's great amenities to distract the aged matriarch.

"I'm tired," she complained.

"The elevator repairs will be completed later today," Avnar confirmed.

The kid excitedly pointed things out inside the roomy apartment to his less-than-enthusiastic mother.

"When are you getting married, son?" the mother asked.

Staring out the window, the kid turned around, smiling to face his mother. "In God's time, mother."

"I don't want to die without seeing your son, my grandson," she explained.

"It's God's will, Mother," the kid insisted.

Avnar appeared with a tray full of goodies and drinks.

"It's about time. Else we die of hunger and thirst, first." The mother sourly declared.

She glared at Avnar, picked up a chocolate bar, and threw it back into the tray with disgust. "It's not even Kosher."

"It is," Avnar assured her.

She mumbled, picked up the same chocolate bar again, and unwrapped it. Avnar and the kid smiled at each other as she bit on the candy bar.

***

The seventy-year-old NBT Pathologist was outside smoking a thin cigar when his phone rang.

"You're not out there smoking, are you?" his doctor-son asked.

"No, Sonny," he lied.

"Dad, stage 1 lung cancer isn't anything to play with." The son warned his dad, who got him into medicine in the first place.

"No, I'm not smoking," he lied again and hung up abruptly as he walked towards the entrance of the NBT facility.

"Little shit," he murmured as he entered.

Inside the morgue, he hovered atop the old shepherd's body on the autopsy table in the basement. His concentration was definite, leaning into the body, describing his actions captured via an overhead microphone hanging from the ceiling. Goram and Avnar walked in, decked in white lab coats.

"Nose masks, please!" The doctor commanded without looking up. Both entrants approached a sidewall hanging cabinet for supplies.

The doctor soon guided them to an X-ray film illuminator box.

"This unusual depression…" He allows the observers to hone in.

"Like what?"

The doctor looked at him and shrugged. "It's anyone's guess. But damn right, unusual. If I were to describe it in a non-medical way, I'd say it's like a circuit."

"What?" Avnar asked.

"Circuit," the doctor confirmed. Avnar shook his head in disbelief.

Goram wanted the bottom line. "Well, what does it all mean?"

"I only cut them up for science. However, this will require more input from experts. I need to figure out what kind of experts."

Goram became quite adamant. "This stays in-house."

The doctor was lulled into momentary confusion by Goram's attitude. "But we have to know—"

Avnar cuts him off. "I will instruct you on the next steps, Doctor."

Goram was already at the door; Avnar hurried to catch up.

In the conference room, Goram, JJ, Avnar, and Erman discussed the peculiarities of the old shepherd's pathological report.

Goram, in excitement and anger, wondered aloud if the Pathologist could be trusted to keep mum about the autopsy results.

"He will," JJ reiterated.

"I'll have a word with him; he's my hire."

"I suggest not," Erman argued, then continued.

Goram asked a rhetorical question. "What now?"

A month later, after moving into their new apartment, the kid collected on his condition for donating his father's body to science to tour the NBT lab and better understand the sacrifice.

The kid followed behind JJ, who had ensured all safety precautions were in place. Both were properly garbed from head to toe, including safety glasses.

"Please, don't touch anything, even if the place goes up in flames. Just alert me immediately." The kid nodded as he excitedly followed JJ.

As planned, JJ only took him through the farrowing farm. Beaming, the kid made conversation.

"You will make a lot of money in our village with how fat your pigs are."

JJ looked back and cautioned him to stay within the central line in the aisle separating the two sides of the pig pen.

"Don't stray, kid. Sows are possessive."

The kid smiled. "You're telling me. *Kudi* will head butt you if you even sniff her lamb."

JJ relaxed. "I take it. Kudi, is this your favorite ewe?"

"You know it, Sir." The kid strayed outside the line to steal a better look at a multicolored Sow.

"Please, get back on the line, please!" JJ admonished.

"Sorry." The innocent shepherd was having a field day.

JJ looked sternly at the kid. "Do not move from here," JJ pointed to the back wall.

"I'm going over there to check the electrical panel quickly. Don't move." JJ walked away.

JJ was only halfway between himself and the kid when a sudden electronic surge caused massive interference to electrical equipment. Ceiling light fixtures flashed on and off, and electronic doors to all the animal enclosures clicked open.

The kid noticed a pigpen door slightly ajar and saw a tiny piglet underneath the large Sow about to be crushed. He charged into the pen to rescue the piglet. Startled, the protective Sow sank her long, sharp canines into the kid's wrist, severing arteries and cracking bones.

Another electrical surge followed, slamming shut all the pen doors as the kid struggled to extricate himself, bleeding profusely, and then passed out.

JJ rushed back and pulled the wall alarm, which sounded but kept cutting off intermittently. He pulled on the pen door without any luck as the kid's blood gushed out, dying.

JJ screamed for help and dashed away to seek help.

People rushed into the husbandry basement as a loud emergency alarm soon dominated the building.

The kid remained unconscious next to the Sow while six piglets suckled in a macabre, bloody mess.

Goram, John, Erman, and Avnar, now present, watched the emergency medical team's futile attempts to revive the kid.

The Sow was put down before the EMT arrived, and all the piglets were isolated.

Two hours later, the EMT pronounced the kid dead and began to pack up the safety and revival gear.

The next month tested NBT's commitment and determination to stay focused on what was important: cooperating with the authority's investigations and soon returning to the business of dismantling dementia.

NBT worked through the rotation of agencies, inundating the operation with inquiries on the fatality.

The area was roped off by the police and quarantined.

Occupational Safety, OS, analogous to US OSHA, was on site for a protracted period.

The police sent in two detectives to investigate.

An insurance Agent representing the Shepherd family was tenacious and garrulous throughout the month, showing up daily, and other obscure scientific overseer associations almost halted all the research activities except for data gathering.

Goram, Avnar, Erman, and two other directors were not spared from repeatedly sitting in conference rooms to answer the same questions, but it was nothing compared to what JJ withstood.

At a meeting, JJ addressed his colleagues.

"I thought hard about how best to proceed after cycling through many emotions. Regret at first, anger next, and sadness for a young life lost. Thank you for all your participation, and now we move on.

"The first item is to scrub the incident site. By that, I mean to remove all the related..." Avnar puts up a hand, and JJ pauses.

"Do we still need to replace the primary test subjects?"

"Yes, fatality is unequaled in its negatively enduring reputation. Remember that regardless of how pristine our research studies' outcomes are, and they will be stellar, there will always be an asterisk that a life was lost during the exercise."

The mood in the room was solemn and not in unison with the proposed solution, but JJ's adamance left little room for compromise. Goram changed tactics.

"JJ, my business accomplishments thus far have only happened because of my intuitive actions when opportunities beckon. Can we do anything else?" He raised his hand as JJ was about to interrupt.

"...I acknowledge the fatality impact, but can you reconsider?"

"I've asked myself tons of questions about what I could have done differently, but none of those thoughts provided any solace short of the outright removal of the section."

The room went quiet until Goram broke the spell.

"I guess that's that," Goram concluded and began to pack up, signaling an end to the meeting.

Chapter 5

The Pathologist finished his smoke and walked inside NBT to autopsy the shepherd's son.

He presented his report and was directed to perform an autopsy on the Sow. He looked around in surprise. "You're kidding, right?" He asked.

Everyone in the room was stoic and serious.

"I'm not a Vet; besides, it requires a different medical mindset to…" Goram interrupted the old Pathologist.

"I want to keep NBT open and not be re-exposed to OS re-audit for involving anyone else in the aftermath of the fatality."

"This is most unusual, and any of my findings would be amateurish, to say the least," the Pathologist concurred.

"I can live with that," Goram concluded.

Two days later, the Pathologist presented a report on the Sow, confirming that a similar 'circuit' had been found in the carcass.

It's been a week since the autopsies. Goram had yet to decide on a path forward regarding refocusing on the original gerontology research or embarking on the runaway MAD - 'Moses Artifact Digression' as JJ coined.

"How long do we have to trap ourselves in this MAD dash?" JJ asked, sitting opposite Goram in his office.

Goram chuckled. "You named it?"

"It helps me to compartmentalize."

"But MAD? Isn't that a little strong?"

"It has to be, Goram. We need to return to *your* project, " JJ insisted.

Goram thought for a while before responding. "Okay, I agree, but let's include the others. Set up something for tomorrow."

JJ left, relieved.

JJ, Goram, Erman, Anvar, and the Pathologist met the following morning.

"I still believe there's something in the MAD that's keeping me instinctively reluctant to let go," Goram announced, opening the meeting.

"MAD?" Avnar asked, to Goram's chagrin, who turned to face the ever-serious JJ.

"Moses Artifact Digression," he snarked in stoicism.

"So, what happens now?" Erman asked.

JJ heaved a sigh and launched in. "I want to get this MAD thing over with, so I will suggest what we scientists call a 'line of sight' conclusion."

Everyone looked around in confusion, except for the bored Pathologist who chimed in.

"It's a tactic utilized when stuck on a project. It engenders the researcher to trace all occurrences from Onset to Sunset."

Everyone still looked around, dazed, when JJ translated. "Start from the shepherd's son's fatality to what happened to the piglets…Onset to Sunset!"

"Impressive," Goram uttered and turned to face the Pathologist.

"Oh, no, I'm not dissecting piglets. Oh, hell, no."

A week later, the Pathologist presented his findings on the three piglet dissections but didn't mention that halfway through the anatomy, he snagged his glove on the bone shard that pricked his palm sharply, through his glove, resulting in broken skin and drawing blood.

"Shit," he said as he headed to the sink to wash off the now bleeding palm. Pig bones are reputed to be one of the hardest in the animal kingdom.

At the next meeting, Goram, staring at JJ, asked if they were ready to move forward.

"What do you mean?" JJ asked.

"Close out MAD and return to your original work."

"Yes, but I thought more about MAD and noted I missed a step," JJ confessed. Everyone eagerly waited.

"Which?" Goram asked cautiously.

"Remember the Onset to Sunset tactic? The last step would be to analyze all the fluids collected from the fatal scene and retained for OS investigations."

"I never thought of that," Goram said in adoration, to which JJ remained expressionless.

"Okay. Let's get to it," Goram commanded.

The lab went to work, and then many lab analysts began to murmur as they examined their microscopes.

The lead lab analyst called JJ on the phone. "You better come in here, Sir."

He walked into the lab to mild chaos, where all the lab analysts talked simultaneously and were glued to their microscope eyepieces.

"Stop. Please." JJ commanded.

Half an hour later, he returned to his office to compile a report he hoped would end the 'MAD' dash. He called Goram.

"I'll be in your office in a few minutes with the report on MAD Onset to Sunset."

Goram was in a meeting with Avnar and Erman. Goram ended the session and watched them leave as JJ walked in.

"There's a significant twist to this whole MAD thing that threw my lab assistants into a tizzy. They found strange live entities in the Sow/shepherd son's recovered fluid, the mammary gland, and the pig milk. Identical entities."

"Like some kind of bacteria or virus?" Goram asked.

"No, they were like nothing in any medical or biological encyclopedias. I checked thoroughly before coming."

"What is it then?"

"I don't know, Goram, but I think we should inform OS so as not to kickstart another pandemic inadvertently."

"No." Goram left his chair and sat beside JJ, conciliatory, and continued.

"OS is NOT our friend, and I'd like to finish this to identify whatever the hell the entity is."

"It's illegal not to report this, Sir!"

Goram returned to his desk. As he addressed JJ, he was not looking up, which was a sign of dismissal.

"No, I will NOT report this to OS, nor should you."

"Sir?"

"My mind is made up, JJ. Let it go."

JJ remained seated for a long time, not talking until, eventually, JJ walked out, truculent.

Back in his office, JJ paced, talked angrily, and then sat behind his desk to document another infraction in his ever-expanding coded file on his computer.

From then on, Goram permanently bifurcated NBT into gerontology and MAD research. He had no idea what he planned to do with the entity, but events would confirm the real identity of the foreign body.

…The old Pathologist smoker collapsed and died at home. His son's report, who was with him when he passed, detailed his hallucination as if he saw something just before he expired.

But unawares, the son had no way of knowing that once he touched his father's body after death, the entity embedded into him.

The son mentioned the hallucination incident to Goram when he came to settle his father's affairs with NBT…

At home, Goram convened with Avnar and Erman. Collectively, they reexamined the totality of all information, starting from the shepherd's death to the shepherd's son's death and the Pathologist's death. The commonality boiled down to the age of the two people who hallucinated at death's door. Both were seventy.

***

Avnar flew down the highway toward the Daliet El Carmel weekend market, ready to indulge in the most important passion of his life: antiquing...

Two hours later, he returned to the parking lot with an oblong package in a large plastic bag, which he threw into the back seat of his vintage Jeep Wrangler—the item inside the bag shifted, revealing parts of a crossbow.

Goram Naphtali recognized the enormity of the findings and the implications of Rabbi Chosky's ideology.

When Goram had to think, he usually preferred to do it in an open space that was removed from any office environment. So, he went to a café in downtown Tel Aviv. He sat under the angled solar shade, shadows on the buzzing sidewalk café.

He watched patrons across the street glide in and out of El Kapitan, the rumored drinking hole for Mossad, though the establishment vehemently denied it. He chuckled because the rumor had a strong foundation.

As he sipped, his attention was diverted to a four-way traffic intersection where a blonde student in a blue skirt and white blouse held the hand of an elderly Arab with a white Kefiya. The traffic lights at the crossings turned red.

Pedestrians, including the student and the older man, migrated across to flashing green lights. She adjusted the oversized backpack on her back, lumbered along, halted in the middle, and yelled something before she blew up. Chaos immediately ensued.

Goram was flung against the café wall from the blast, but far off enough to sustain limited injury. He scrambled with a nosebleed and noticed people trooping out of El Kapitan and heading for the blast zone.

Goram's cell phone rang; Avnar, returning from an antique flea market, was calling.

Goram walked away from the melee to a quiet corner to answer the call.

"What's that awful noise, Sir?"

"A suicide bomber just blew herself up."

"Are you hurt, Sir?"

"No, minor lacerations, and my ears are ringing."

"I'll return all the same, Sir."

"What?" Goram could hardly hear as his nose started to bleed again.

"I should be back in a couple of hours…" Goram didn't hear the last sentence as he talked over Avnar.

"I have to go…" He hung up as loud Sirens made it impossible to hear anything and ran towards the blast zone to help.

The incident catalyzes Goram's resolve to work with Rabbi Chosky and THE ORDER.

**

THE ORDER members eagerly awaited Goram in the basement at Rabbi Chosky's office.

Goram, all business, walked directly to the podium and plugged in his laptop; the screen came to life and was projected to the back wall. He then left the podium and set up a video recorder focused on him in the back corner.

A recorded film of him talking on-screen about the tomb found in the desert began to play. Fifteen minutes later, Goram returned to the stage as the film concluded.

Goram was circumspect, lecturing the group.

"Our strategies to fulfill THE ORDER objectives have begun." He looked up. The rapt expectations pushed his narrative forward.

"Next, the technology was a happenstance, which could either be a good omen or a foreshadowed disaster.

"The product will begin manufacturing in two weeks, and the first batch will be ready and tested in two months. I will not bore you with technical details, I hardly understand myself."

Murmurs arose in the room; Rabbi Chosky quelled them non-verbally.

"Any concerns?" asked Abulafia.

Chosky turned to face Goram.

"None. We have to wait for when it hits. If it works as anticipated, the news will be globally deafening."

"That potent?" Abulafia seemed doubtful.

"I've learned that there are never guarantees in science. They either radically exceed expectations or fail spectacularly. Both spectrums are real possibilities for us."

Chosky turned to Goram. "What if it worked?"

"Then you get your wish, Rabbi."

"I'm excited." The Rabbi vibrated in delight.

Goram waxed cautious. "I hope your excitement holds, or you may wish that old rocking chair got you first."

"What?" someone asked.

"That you grow old, naturally." Goram translated.

Goram finished up and left as perfunctorily as he'd arrived.

***

A few years back, Avnar Barak, a Major in the Israeli Army uniform with epaulets on his shoulder, left behind a cloud of dust on the dirt road leading to his village homestead outside Tel Aviv.

The property registered to House Speaker Josef Matursky was the only inheritance from Avnar's biological father, who succumbed to colon cancer when Avnar was five. His mother died of labor pains during his birth. Josef Matursky, his maternal uncle, had been his guardian since he became an early orphan.

He pulled up behind the homestead and went directly to the shed. He opened a wooden front door to reveal a sturdy steel door leading to a room.

He turned on the light that showcased a bright, modern room in contrast to the immediate outside.

The room had three shelves on each of the three walls full of an eclectic collection of carefully and clearly labeled antique items: an Edwardian Diamond ring, an Art Deco Chandelier, a Georgian Siver Teapot, a First edition Jane Austin book, a Tiffany studios hanging head dragonfly chandelier, and William
Shakespeare's Comedies, Histories, and tragedies.

A hand-knotted Persian rug was spread at the center of the room, and a Victorian Chaise sofa was to its left, away from the door. Avnar sat on a high chair a few feet away, quietly but slowly concentrating on each item, clockwise and then repeatedly anticlockwise, for hours.

Two years later, Avnar, honorably discharged from the Army, was recruited into Mossad. His second assignment a year later saw him leading a task force in Iran, along with his team, mostly his Army day colleagues, instructed to sabotage the Iranian nuclear ambitions, specifically to identify, corrupt, or assassinate critical scientists.

The secondary objective was to inflict significant unrecoverable damage to any standing physical structures relative to nuclear bomb manufacturing. The Israeli government spared no expense for the operation.

The operation soon ran into funding problems, which hindered effective operational processes and eventually led to its cancellation. Shin Bet's investigations into fund embezzlement went nowhere, and no credible outward signs of ostentatious living by the task force members were found. Avnar was never charged with a crime but was encouraged to leave Mossad.

He soon found an international security company with two friends from his Mossad days and members of the failed Iranian sabotage assignment, Abishak Terrel and Southpaw Frieda Homel.

Throughout his ordeal, Avnar always indulged in his major passion, antiquing. He was forever in village antique markets, crisscrossing the country when not working. Avnar's security business quickly fizzled when Shin Bet mounted a quiet lobby with potential clients against the business.

His uncle then matched him up with Goram Naphtali as a security detail. The relationship quickly expanded to Avnar managing Goram's personal and business security. In effect, he became a Majordomo...

***

Goram Naphtali made Avnar Barak the general manager of Project Negelin, as he named MAD, while the disgruntled JJ continued the gerontology path. Erman Ertergu floated between the two projects.

"Negelin?" Avnar asked.

"The overall objective, utilization, and deployment are still in flux."

"I don't get it," Avnar queried.

"All will become clear as we progress. Now, let's move on, please."

The Negelin dossier spelled out justifications for the steps:

1) We will extract the entities I've named Foreign Objects (FOs) into vials of synthetic

60

compounds with an identical composition to Sow's biochemistry, mixed with the shepherd kid's blood as the growth medium.

2) We will build a plant with minimum personnel under a severely strict security check protocol.

The sections shall function as follows:

Human plasma vessels shall supply the farrowing sows.

Piglets shall suckle as Sows feed on plasma-mixed feed.

FOs shall be extracted from pulverized piglet saliva gland extracts mixed with Sow milk and compounded into a pH-controlled solution to suspend the FOs.

Next, the FOs shall be blistered and Quality Assurance-tested utilizing an iPad to confirm FO presence in solutions before packaging.

Blisters shall be cold-packaged and stored at 32 degrees Fahrenheit.

Now in charge, Avnar Barak decided to surround himself with trusted people.

He shielded his eyes to focus as he entered El Kapitán's bar.

Southpaw Frieda Homel, ex-Mossad, saluted in jest. Then, Abishak Terrel, ex-Mossad, kicked out a chair for their former colleague.

"We almost left."

Avnar waved at the barman.

"We already ordered for you," Frieda confirmed.

The barman approached with a tray. Impatient, Abishak got to it. "What's this all about?"

"Nothing, just some beer drinking and doing nothing."

Both ex-Mossad looked at him funny. "I thought you were joking, knowing you never take time off except to buy some old shit."

Avnar laughed. "Don't knock it. It's therapeutic."

Abishak and Frieda looked at each other and burst out in hearty laughter. "Yeah."

"I need you both to come work for me."

Thinking it was a joke, Frieda banged slightly on the table, making the drinks jump.

"You work in a research company; we play with guns and bad guys."

"Don't knock it; some bookworms can be devilish in their ways," Avnar suggested.

Frieda got up, went to the jukebox, selected Mamas and Papas' "California Dreamin'," and started to dance to it by herself on the small dance floor. Though the bar was half full, no one paid her any attention.

Abishak smiled at her; she ignored him, closed her eyes, and surrendered to the song's mood. He turned to face Avnar.

"Do you know anything about the Universe?"

"What?"

"The cosmos?"

"What are you talking about?"

Abishak paused a little. "Astronomy, dumbass. Spooky at a distance?"

"Spooky what?" Avnar was now totally lost and losing interest fast, as Abishak explained.

"This was from Einstein, probably the highest IQ we ever had. When told that an action applied to something can cause an immediate action to something else billions of miles away, he uttered that statement."

"And your point, Abi?"

"It's an allegory." It went over Avnar's head.

"There you go again," Avnar complained.

"Spooky at a distance, my friend…"

Before Avnar could respond, Abishak got up and started dancing toward Frieda on the dance floor, rocking to the rhythm of the music without touching each other.

Avnar sat back and watched them with one of those blank looks; it was difficult to guess what was behind the eyes.

Chapter 6

As manufacturing began, a supervisor walked Avnar through the process as they watched an operator atop a tank outside.

The tank operator clamped on his facemask, throttled the hissing air vent, opened the pothole, and stared down at the dark-bluish compound in the lit tank, mixing with a large central agitator.

Happy, he closed the port, climbed down the tank, and turned on the iPad, which identified the tank name as "Human Plasma Tank—HPT."

A long outlet below the HPT dumped into four interconnected mid-size rectangular stainless steel (SSV) vessels, flushing into the main building's back walls.

Another pipe gravity-blew grains from a silo into the SSV.

Screw conveyors inside the SSV mixed the content and extruded through a line that disappeared into the Sow farrowing enclosure, advancing on a conveyor belt to feed the animals. Water bottles are hung from the ceiling and are accessible via long, thin plastic hoses with nipple-shaped terminations.

A mixture of forty farrowing and lactating Sows and cavorting piglets grunted around the trough and drink apertures.

The piglets were strictly fed on their mother's mammary teats and not from the perpetual motion conveyor belt feeder.

The FO extraction floor was divided into labeled sections separated by mesh wires.

The saliva was extracted from hung piglet carcasses upside down with mouths agape to drain into buckets.

At the same time, butchers cut out and dump salivary glands hanging down the sides of piglet mouths into the same buckets.

FOs were severed from quartered piglets on several stainless-steel tables and placed in individual glass jar arrangements on a trolley in the abattoir.

The remaining parts went over mesh wires into a pulverizer shoot in the next section.

In the end, a prominent tub collector retained the red mass.

Filtration occurred when the red mass in the tub went to the next section alongside the salivary gland. Buckets emptied into a tall steaming composite vessel containing gallons of Sow milk, all agitated slowly with a side-entry mixer.

The now bluish mix continuously evacuated the container from the base through a large filtering screen port into a large transparent glass container on wheels that resembled a large "milk bottle."

The Quality Control team then lined the milk bottles against the wall and obtained samples from small taps in the vessel's middle. Several chemical testing apparatuses enabled testing in a temperature-controlled room atmosphere of 32 degrees Fahrenheit.

QC managers approve passed milk bottles and advance them to the quarantine side of the room. These now pH-controlled suspension liquids are ready to sustain dormant FOs.

Quality Assurance personnel monitor trolleys with glass jars containing active FOs lining the blistering room's walls. Periodically, the FOs bounce around sporadically in the jars, much like ticks.

Four blister machines arranged end-to-end churn out packs containing six FOs suspended in liquids per pack.

Each blister was a transdermal reservoir system with a clear vinyl bubble top and a three-layer backing with membrane, adhesive, and liner skin.

Operators hand-packed the blisters into white boxes.

Quality Assurance personnel with iPads periodically retrieve samples from the line for random testing.

At the final QA section, personnel carefully pry blisters open with tweezers under lit safety hoods containing iPads turned on to measure FO activities. Seconds after the blister unsealing, the iPad oscilloscope screen graph berserks, emitting a loud chirping alarm noise.

The blisters were cold-packaged and stored at a small temporary construction maintained at 32 degrees Fahrenheit. The construction boasts shrink-wrapped pallets awaiting shipment.

The first batch of Negelin was shipped labeled as Antibiotics, as Goram took to the road to acquire nursing homes worldwide for distribution and controlled points of application. He signed an acquisition contract for Hillcrest Home in Milan, Italy.

* * *

In Switzerland, fresh snow hung off tall alpine trees in the Alps Forest at the Bernese-Oberland Ski Trail.

The eager crowd flew downhill, some on slow-moving ski lifts, ready to pounce. A few ardent faces wore COVID-19 masks.

It was getting dark now. Yves Montego loitered near a tree and lit dope, displeasing his girlfriend beside him. She admonished, "Put that stinky shit out."

He giggled and extended the thin roll joint to her. "Take a hit."

She wrinkled her nose and sped off in anger. "Jerk."

He caught up to her and other patrons migrating from the slopes to the ski lodge restaurant where Contessa, a former Italian beauty pageant winner with perfectly coiffured short gray hair, dined at a corner table with a decorated cake.

The Contessa turned to the floor-to-ceiling glass wall overlooking the ski slope; the Count walked towards the exit. After briefly looking at the skiers, she turned to face her husband, the Count, sitting across from her.

It was his birthday. No one was there. The Contessa lazily scanned the room, only to see the back of The Count's pepper-gray hair about to enter a weird door. The Contessa hurried toward her husband, which drew attention. She arrived to see the Count walk into an edgeless, cloudy, shimmering nothingness. The Contessa screamed, "Don't go into that Whitemelt!"

Based on facial expressions, restaurant patrons who heard the Contessa scream seemed to wonder where or what the "Whitemelt" was, except for Yves Montego, stoned, sitting at a table close to the exit, who saw the Count happily step into the void-Whitemelt.

To his girlfriend's disgust, Yves gobbled more fries, giggled, and chewed openly. Yves cackled and pointed to the portal where the Count had just vanished. "Whitemelt," he joked. His girlfriend turned around to look, saw nothing, and mouthed off with her back to the door. "Dopehead."

People gathered around the hysterical Contessa, unsure of how to help her.

***

The Count's disappearance was prominently featured on the news everywhere in Italy.

At the Vatican, the Pope and a retired Colonel, the Pope's head of security, sat at the refectory. The Papal leaned forward, herbal tea in hand, questioning in a mellow tone, "What's Whitemelt, Colonel?"

"It's the Contessa's word, Your Grace."

"We lead the world ahead of such rumors. Don't you think so, Colonel?"

"Yes, Your Grace."

The Pope stared intently at his security Czar. "This is within Enzo Lupara's expertise. Is it not?"

The Colonel nodded in agreement.

"Is Rabbi Chosky in Israel behind this?" the Papal queried.

"Hard to fathom, Your Grace."

"Religious terrorism, I tell you," the Pope reiterated.

"You may be onto something there, Your Grace."

The Pope sat back in contemplation and sipped with a faraway look. "And the Americans?"

"The New York Cardinal will call tonight, Your Grace."

The Pope sipped and turned his back, signaling dismissal. The Colonel signed the cross as he backed out of the refectory.

***

Enzo was claustrophobic in The Colonel's Vatican basement office, sitting across the desk. The Colonel noticed the discomfort. "Anything wrong, Enzo?"

Enzo fidgeted in response. "I prefer off Vatican premises for our meetings. Just so we, I, don't buckle from the overpowering religiosity."

The Colonel asked in surprise. "Why will you work for the Pope, the most notable religious entity globally?"

"Because you asked me." Enzo's answer floored the Colonel to perplexity, so much so that he changed the subject. "Any new developments on the Whitemelted Count?"

"Yes, but nothing significant. I think the Contessa is troubled. I plan to investigate the radical Israeli Rabbi Chosky to understand why he harbored hatred against the Pope."

"Why him now? I'm unclear about the connection with the Count's disappearance," the Colonel queried.

"The buzz at the Interpol in France suggested possible connections," Enzo argued.

The Colonel pondered. "How long a trip and when?"

"A week or two, starting next week after my session with…" he trailed off.

"How's that going?" the Colonel digressed.

"Tolerable." Enzo was tense, irritable, and unwilling to discuss the forced therapy sessions he endured.

"Make it work, Enzo. Your job depends on it." The Colonel arose from behind the desk to close the meeting.

Enzo, sulking, hurried out of the "tomb."

***

It was late evening when the Colonel entered Bar Delle Grazie, a famous Café near the Vatican.

He adjusted his vision in the dark enclave. He saw Enzo at the bar, absentmindedly massaging an oval scar on the fleshy part of his left palm—a half-full cappuccino mug before him.

...In the war-torn village of Quetta, Helman Province, Afghanistan, Capitano Enzo Lupara, 32, of the Italian Army, rested his back against the wall inside a four-walled mud compound home of orphaned siblings: Hamza Haqqani and his sister, Halimah Haqqani.

A large borehole, aka water-well, rested in the middle of the compound.

Two armed Allievo Ufficiale (young officers) stood guard on either end of the West wall, overlooking the village's access hill.

A loud commotion from inside a hut disturbed the peace in the hot afternoon. Halimah rushed into the compound, holding a tin bucket with a long-wound rope tied to the handle. Hurriedly, she covered her face with a black Burka.

Hamza emerged behind her, akimbo at the door, a long sword around his waist. He yelled at his sister as she dropped the bucket into the well.

"You're a harlot! Cover your face before the heathen sees you."

Fuming, Hamza retreated into the hut. Enzo watched with disinterest.

Halimah slumped and began to thrash on the ground. Enzo rushed to her aid and waved for the guards to stay at their posts.

He pulled off her Burka, looked around briefly, and forced his left palm, the fleshy part below the pinky, between her upper and lower jaws.

She bit down hard and drew blood; Enzo winced in pain and straightened out the violent trembling of her lower torso with his free hand.

Hamza emerged from his hut and saw Halimah under Enzo. He drew his sword, rushed forward, and plunged it into Enzo's back.

Enzo, in pain, yanked out his raw, bleeding hand from Halimah's mouth, rolled off, and watched Hamza stick his sword into Halimah's abdomen.

Enzo struggled, and Hamza turned around and wielded the sword. Enzo pulled out his pistol and shot Hamza dead.

Hamza fell next to his sister.

Enzo collapsed, unconscious, surrounded by colleagues...

"Hey. Snap out of it!" The Colonel tapped Enzo on the shoulder.

Enzo returned to the present and assured the Colonel he was okay before reaching for his cappuccino.

The Colonel pulled up a barstool and placed an order with the barman.

"Has the Pope decided to investigate Whitemelt rumors yet?"

The Colonel bypassed the query from the honorably discharged veteran from the Italian Army he'd recruited into the Vatican Security Services. "You worry me, Enzo. Have you seen the Army Psychologist yet?"

"In the works, boss." Enzo tugged at his scar. "Are we investigating?"

The Colonel studied him briefly. "Yes, the Papal has decided to investigate, but you need sessions with the psychologist first."

Enzo smiled and stopped rubbing the scar on his hand.

***

Enzo walked off the street the next afternoon into a nondescript edifice surrounded by quaint, modernized buildings.

He climbed the stone stairs onto the second floor to his Psychologist's office and knocked on the door.

The door opened into an airy office with bare furnishings.

The Psychologist directed him to a consulting divan facing a lone chair in the middle of the room. "Tough day?"

"Better than most, but Roman traffic, a menace, doc. Sorry, I'm late."

"Would you want to schedule a little later to allow more time for you?"

Enzo was embarrassed and apologetic. "No, Ma'am."

The Psychologist readied her clipboard. "Do you have something that triggers…?" She allowed the unfinished question to linger.

Enzo's right hand unconsciously massaged the scar on his left hand. "We were trapped in a mud hut waiting for rescue when Halimah Haqqani suffered an epileptic seizure while fetching water at the well."

He stopped briefly to collect himself. The Psychologist remained quiet.

"Her twin brother, Hamza Haqqani, plunged a sword into my back while I was on top of Halimah to prevent her from biting off her tongue."

The Psychologist jotted down notes and asked questions. "Why would he stab you?"

"I later learned my colleagues heard Hamza yell at me not to rape her sister before the attack." Enzo paused.

"Then what happened?"

"My left palm was in Halimah's mouth to prevent an epileptic tongue bite at the time. Once stabbed, I yanked out my bloody hand and reeled on the ground in pain, only to see Hamza plunge the sword into his sister's belly as she thrashed about in a fit."

The Psychologist's eyebrows furrowed. "Why didn't your colleagues come to your rescue?"

"Good question. Hamza then turned to me, wielding the sword again. That's when I shot him dead." Enzo became remorseful.

The Psychologist remained quiet, allowing the moment to develop.

"I woke up in a makeshift ICU hours later." Enzo clammed up, closing his eyes. "One minute break, Doc?"

The Psychologist got up. "I'm sorry, soldier. Yes, I could use a break, too. Five minutes? Would you like something to drink?"

"Yes, please."

The Psychologist left the office briefly and returned with a can of Coke and a water bottle.

"I'm not sure which you might prefer."

"Thank you." Tense and mentally exhausted, Enzo took the bottled water, welcomed the break, and stood up slowly while the Psychologist approached her desk. He massaged his scar, pacing.

Both soon returned to the session.

"I noticed you massage your hand frequently, Enzo. Are you in pain?"

Enzo jerked both hands apart. "It's nothing." He obscured them beneath his thighs on the couch.

"May I see them, please?" The Psychologist gently extended her open palms.

Enzo hesitated, then surrendered his hands to hers.

She examined the scar professionally, nothing sensual, and asked, "Does it still hurt?"

"Not anymore," he quietly responded.

The Psychologist released his hands. "I'd like to recommend something that may work." Enzo leaned forward.

"You say these words three times to yourself each time you need to massage your scar, Enzo."

"What words?"

"I was a hero to Halimah; I was a hero to Halimah; I was a hero to Halimah."

She watched his reaction. Enzo remained expressionless.

"It's innocuous. Our brain processes information in a very strange way. Think about how many times you've thought of something happening; voila, it does. It means we all have an element of prescience in us."

"Prescience?" He asked.

"The fact of knowing something before it takes place; foreknowledge." She explained.

"Oh."

"Please, say the words, Enzo. I promise it'd help when you least expect it to."

"It's silly." Enzo showed embarrassment.

"Humor me, soldier."

Enzo reluctantly repeated the words. "I was a hero to Halimah; I was a hero to Halimah; I was a hero to Halimah." He concluded with an expectant look. "I don't feel any different."

"It'll take a while."

They both stared at each other in silence.

"Would you like to continue, although I have the next client due very soon?"

"No doc., I think it's a good place to stop."

Enzo rose from the couch. "Next time, then?"

"Thank you for coming, soldier; I'm sure I can help, and don't forget the mantra," she reminded him.

Enzo, standing, saluted. "Yes, Ma'am."

The Psychologist smiled, and Enzo left the room.

Chapter 7

Enzo drove off Ben Gurion airport in a small rental car, heading to Rabbi Rabin Chosky's office twenty-six kilometers away in Tel Aviv. He navigated to the street location he wanted and pulled into the parking lot.

After thoroughly checking his credentials, the stern security guard at the front desk let him in, drawing a sharp stare for his Vatican affiliation. Enzo was surprised at the high-security level at which the facility operated.

The door opened as Enzo was about to knock on the Rabbi's door at the top of the staircase.

Enzo towered over the diminutive Rabbi but respectfully bowed in deference as he entered the office. He stood until the Rabbi briefly scrutinized the Roman detective's face before making an offer.

"Please, sit down." Enzo's façade was inscrutable throughout the ordeal.

First, Enzo laid copies of the Rabbi's letters to the Pope on the desk and asked, "What exactly do you require of the Papal, Sir?"

Rabbi Chosky checked his anger calmly. "Many of my letters to the Pope…" His thoughts trailed off before he continued, "Attempt to explain to the preeminent global authority on religion the critical path to follow for the human existential continuity."

He sat back with self-satisfaction. Then, he jumped in as Enzo was about to speak.

"The Eminence has to publicly support the three scores and ten initiatives." The Rabbi then waved Enzo to speak. And he did.

"The Pope respects the Jewish people and the great State of Israel and will consider the best avenue to advance religiosity. Is there a particular message you wish to convey to the Pope?"

Despite himself, the Rabbi took a liking to Enzo. He leaned forward conspiratorially.

"Señor Lupara, the age-old divide between Christianity and Judaism is an endless chasm fostered at the beginning of time. The Pope has to side with us to close that time tear, The Order. Humans should not live beyond seventy to leave enough resources for those who follow, yes?"

Enzo listened until the Rabbi had thoroughly vented.

"Sir, as much as I would like to agree or disagree with your position, my function here is only as a messenger. Besides, I'm an atheist."

Rabbi Chosky almost choked in shock and then burst out in hearty laughter.

"I can now openly call to question the Pope's claim to global religious leadership, and I argue he's partly responsible for the Jewish ills in the diaspora. After all, he has you, an atheist, as a messenger."

Enzo maintained stoic composure throughout the Rabbi's vehement digression, then mounted a defense.

"Sir, my belief mechanism is still omnipotent, but less the acknowledgment of a supreme physical entity. Rather, I embrace a psychological non-religious-miasmic existence to maintain my tranquil altitude."

"What?" Confused, the Rabbi looked at his wristwatch. "I'm sorry, Mister Lupara, my next appointment is at hand, but I shall welcome a follow-up meeting if you wish."

"Thank you, Sir, I wish."

Enzo exited the building and hit the highway towards his hotel near the airport.

That evening, the Vatican colonel called Enzo to redirect him to France to assist the Interpol investigation of the Swiss Alps ski lodge Whitemelt.

***

Enzo left Israel and headed to Lyon, France, to consult with Interpol.

The relatively benign Lyon airport traffic gnawed at Lens Kasper's nerves as he idled by the arrivals exit, looking for a colleague he'd never met. He quickly scanned Enzo Lupara's picture on his cell phone. He spotted him with a leather backpack and honked.

"Not horrible like Leonardo da Vinci Airport," Enzo commented, entering the passenger side.

"A hassle still, Mon Ami. We'll shake hands later."

Lens carelessly merged into traffic, to an angry horn blast by a cabbie getting inadvertently cut off.

"Now, that's more like Rome," Enzo quipped at the brief melee.

Minutes later, Enzo made conversation as Lens cruised the nearly empty dual carriageway. "The highway is light. Is that normal?"

"It's a public holiday on Sunday, so everyone has left the city."

"No holidays for you?"

Lens sneaked a look at Enzo. "You'll be riding your ass if I wasn't here."

Enzo laughed, creating a relaxed, cordial atmosphere.

"To the office, yeah?"

"Not yet. A stop first." Lens exits the highway.

The high-rise apartment center of Lyon stuck out as Lens parked.

"A guy claimed he saw something at the resort."

Both exited the car, and Enzo slipped on his backpack. Lens gave him a funny look.

Inside, Yves was glued to a gaming TV console as his blonde girlfriend, Emma, opened the front door, revealing several pieces of ski equipment against the lounge wall.

Emma walked to the kitchen, and Lens and Enzo lolled around. Lens soon hovered above Yves. "What did you see at the Bernese-Oberland Ski Resort?"

Yves ignored him. Emma says, "He's been smoking all morning."

Enzo walked off to inspect the ski equipment lying around. Lens stared at a large bong on the center table next to smoking paraphernalia.

"You listening?" Lens reiterated a little firmer.

"The old guy went into a shimmering, cloudy wall. Melt up." He giggled, still playing his game.

Enzo walked over.

"Stop playing, Yves," Enzo commanded with a steely voice.

Emma sensed tension and pulled the TV plug out of the wall. Yves dropped the gaming handle, lay flat on the couch, snickering, and stared at the two men above him. "I told you the guy walked into some white cloud that was melting up. Tell them," Yves pleaded with Emma.

Returning to the kitchen, Emma offered, "I didn't see anything. I already told you Yves was high."

"Fuck that. I saw what I saw." Yves insisted.

Lens forcibly pulled Yves' legs off the couch and sat beside him. Enzo moved to Yves's other side and sat next to him. Both keep Yves in the middle. Emma looked on with trepidation.

"Did you make it all up?" Enzo asked.

"I didn't," Yves was furious.

"Describe what you saw."

Emma walked over. "He's high; you'll never get anything else out of him now."

Both cops stared at Yves in exasperation. Lens Kasper got up.

"Let's get out of here."

At the door, Lens turned back to Yves. "You'll be hearing from us.

When the door closed behind the detectives, Yves grabbed his half-smoke.

Emma walked over and snatched the weed from him. He began to laugh hysterically and roll another joint.

"You could be in trouble, Yves, and could be arrested."

Now he got angry. "For what? I saw what I saw, babe."

"Yeah, but nobody else did… babe." She walked to the kitchen; he followed her, having trouble properly rolling the joint.

"That fancy woman with the hairstyle—"

"The Contessa," Emma interrupted.

"Yes, her. She saw it, too," Yves confirmed.

Without looking at him, Emma spoke. "It's her husband, probably hysterical."

Yves threw the badly rolled joint on the kitchen counter.

"Shit."

Emma snickered at his struggle. "That's telling you to stop smoking."

He sidled up to her; she allowed him to hold her waist from behind as she stirred the pot.

"You smoke too, Emma." He accused.

She wiggled out of the embrace to face him. "But not all the time, Yves. It's getting old."

He sulked and walked away to flop on the sofa.

"You hungry?" She asked.

He jumped up like a tick. "Hell, yes."

She smiled, and he beamed widely. They were back cuddling.

***

Enzo did not find Lyon Interpol HQ's glassy design impressive. He gazed around as Lens accessed the building with an electronic key card.

"I thought it'd be bigger."

"It's an old building." Lens stared back at Enzo with cynicism. "And it's French." The Frenchman reaffirmed, prideful.

Enzo was staring at a video from the Bernese-Oberland Ski Resort at a desk in the empty office. "I don't see anything shocking or interesting here."

"I know. I watched it several times but found nothing." Lens confirmed.

Enzo opened a binder report of the case.

Yards away on the computer, Lens asked, "Why is the Vatican interested in this?"

"Self-preservation. The Papal wish to rule out religious nuts."

"Maybe it's aliens," Lens suggested.

"We like to believe in miracles, but this is not one." Enzo spun.

"Crazy," Lens sighed.

"Could be a clever hoax, Lens."

"To what end?" The Frenchman was doubtful.

"Money, fame, notoriety- pick one." Enzo continued to read as he defended his investigation.

Lens walked over. "Did I miss anything?"

"No." Enzo closed the report folder and got up. "Any coffee around here?'

"Kitchen." Lens led the way.

"When do we arrive at the ski resort tomorrow?" Enzo inquired as they loitered.

"Long drive. Four hours, at least," Lens confirmed.

It was late afternoon in Switzerland when the Bernese-Oberland Ski Resort manager ushered the two detectives through the crowded dining hall to his stuffy back office.

He jumped in before Lens could speak.

The manager asked, "Who are you?"

Lens pointed. "That's detective Enzo Lupara from Rome. The Vatican."

The manager's left eyebrow arched up.

Lens Kasper continued before the manager could speak. "And I'm Lens Kasper, Interpol."

"You're here about the incident." The manager hardly took a breath as he walked on. "I already spoke to the Swiss authority. Bizarre encounter." He made a disappearing hand gesture in the air. "Poof."

The two investigators removed files from chairs but were unsure where to place them. The manager collected the items and piled them atop others on a steel cabinet.

Enzo turned serious. "What do you know?"

"Nothing. It was just another crowded room until the Contessa screamed. I rushed out of the back room. She was inconsolable."

"The Contessa?" Lens clarified.

"Yes," The manager confirmed.

"The Count, her husband, vanished? Were there witnesses to the episode?" Enzo asked; Lens remained expressionless.

The manager grew impatient.

"We run a great establishment here, in operation for fifty years. Nothing like this has ever happened."

"So, no one saw a thing?" Enzo was irritated.

The manager threw his hands in the air in exasperation. "I can show you where it happened," he volunteered.

Unimpressed, Lens got up.

The manager described how pleasant that day was with fluffy snow, just as patrons liked it. But he added no new or meaningful insight beyond what was already known.

Enzo took many pictures with his cell phone outside the resort's dining facility before leaving.

***

Enzo landed in Milan and drove to a Castle in the blazing afternoon sun to interview the Contessa.

He followed the maid into the sunroom behind the villa to meet the Contessa, sitting inclined on a converted hospital bed.

Enzo was gentle in his approach. "Contessa, I'm Enzo Lupara from the Vatican. I want to discuss your unfortunate experience at the Bernese-Oberland Ski Resort."

The Contessa turned to face him. "Such good weather we're having. Don't you think?" She smiled.

"What did you see at the resort when your husband…vanished?" The Contessa waved at the hovering maid for a drink.

"Your grace." The maid handed her the drink and walked away.

The Contessa sipped from the decorative glass straw and turned to Enzo. "When is the Count returning home?"

Enzo, expressionless, moved even closer. She flinched and then screamed, throwing a tantrum. He froze in horror as the maid calmed the Contessa.

The maid commandingly ushered Enzo toward the parking lot in front of the home.

"She will need her medication now. I'm afraid that's it for the day," the maid stated flatly.

"How long has she been like this?"

The maid stopped walking and turned to face Enzo in anger.

"Like what?" she challenged.

Her stance took Enzo by surprise.

She continued passionately, "Did you know they lost their only child, a son, Peterio, in 2001, almost twenty years ago? She never got over it, so please, be human. It was my first year in the Castle, and every year on his anniversary, they go to the cemetery.

"The Count could never go near the grave, but she always does, cleaning debris and fresh flowers. I was with them during one of those sad trips…"

A Black Bentley had pulled through Cimitero Monumentale di Milano (Milan Cemetery). The Count and the Contessa rested in the backseat as the Corsican driver-cum-Major Domo drove.

The driver had pulled across the path from a modest graveyard and stopped the engine.

Holding hands in the back seat, the Contessa stared at the Count, who refused to look at her.

"Please come with me, honey," she pleaded.

He ignored her.

She gave up and exited the vehicle.

The driver rolled down the window. "Contessa?" He handed her a bouquet from the front passenger seat.

"Thank you."

She crossed the path, wearing a flattering bouffant summer floral gown with black elbow-length velvet hand gloves.

The Contessa stood, looking at the headstone of her son's grave: 1991 – 2001.

She then stooped to clean off dried-up leaf debris on the grave, replaced the old bouquet, stood up, and turned around to see the Count leaning against the car, smoking.

She stared down, daring him to come to his son's grave. He didn't.

She walked back to the car.

The Bentley drove off...

"I apologize. Now I'm sure unstable was not the right word," Enzo confessed. The combative maid didn't let Enzo off.

"No, Sir, it wasn't. She lost her son, and now her husband is missing. The only thing keeping her sane is her volunteer work. But, unfortunately, even that may not be enough."

"I apologize again. Where does the Contessa volunteer?" He asked.

The maid hesitated and stared hard at Enzo for a prolonged time before answering. "Home From Home in the City."

She turned and marched towards the villa; Enzo sadly walked towards his rental.

***

Goram Naphtali next bought Blossom Plaza Home in LA and exported Negelin, which was labeled as antibiotics.

The Blossom Plaza Home facility was located on the outskirts of Los Angeles, adjacent to a sister sanatorium of the same name.

The new facility director, Joel Schummer, removed a pair of new, bright red signposts from his car trunk. The signs read Blossom Plaza Home, the new name for the recently acquired elder home.

Inside the building, Joel walked next to a pretty Spanish traveling nurse. She carried a heavy container down the aisle.

"Heavy?" he asked.

"It's okay, Mr. Soomer. I manage," she replied in broken English.

Inside, residents leisureed in the shared games room, busy with various entertainment activities, such as TV, table card games, and foosball.

Joel walked amongst the residents and supervised the traveling nurse in applying the antibiotic transdermal patches to some residents.

Hari Hapa, a janitor, curiously noticed only a few residents received the patches as he swept the floor.

"I leave now, Señor Soomer." The Spanish nurse announced after the last patch was applied.

***

In DTLA, Lewis and Anna Cantor managed a rare books store on Hollywood Boulevard, the bequest to them by their wealthy uncle, Levi Straus, a staunch benefactor for Jewish causes, and to the Queens, New York, Yom Marantz synagogue where he worshiped, closely associated with Rabbi Chosky before he vanished.

Anna, an accountant, managed the books while Lewis did everything else. But Lewis was always searching for a fast buck to settle several gambling debts sustained through illegal back-alley joints in LA. He was thousands of dollars in the hole to two rough gangsters, Joey Campo and Hondo Kendricks.

Uncle Levi's death a few months earlier hit Anna hard, devolving her into the early stages of dementia, and she eventually succumbed to full memory loss months later.

Years earlier in Tel Aviv, when Lewis and Anna were adolescents, their father, Levi's younger brother, and their mother were killed in a direct missile attack. Levi assumed their guardianship and moved both youngsters to America.

A week after Lewis hadn't heard or seen Anna, Lewis knocked several times at Anna's Koreatown front door, thinking she wasn't home. When the door opened, he was about to call on his cell phone. Anna stared at him, questioning,

"Who are you?"

In shock, Lewis introduced himself. "It's me, Anna. I'm your brother."

After a long pause, she remembered where she was.

"Come on inside, then. Don't dawdle with your phone."

In a daze, he followed her inside.

The living room was chaotic, with clothes strewn over the kitchen sink and dirty plates. Lewis opened the windows to let light and air in.

"I'll make tea," he announced. Anna perked up and hurried to sit at the dining table.

She quietly sipped her tea at the table and burst into tears. "Why didn't Uncle Levi come visit me?"

Lewis placated her. "Can I stay the night with you so we can both wait for him?"

Anna agreed, simmered down, improved her mood, and was full of energy to tidy up.

Lewis pulled out his cell phone and smiled at her as she cleaned while he made a call. "Doctor Atkins?"

"Is Anna okay?" Romeo Atkins was Levi's doctor who introduced him to his niece and nephew.

"She's not, doc. She didn't recognize me when I arrived at her place. She needs help."

"Can you bring her to the clinic?"

Lewis's hesitation caused the doctor to change his mind.

"I'll be right over. Keep Anna calm, meanwhile."

"Okay." Lewis hung up and smiled at Anna, who was still giddy from cleaning up.

Chapter 8

Doctor Romeo Atkins walked into a conference room on the 2nd floor of a Bethesda, Maryland, hotel overlooking the NIA HQ building. Minutes later, a National Institute on Aging (NIA) representative introduced himself to the "Alzheimer's Be Gone" volunteers, all medical doctors.

"Gentlemen and Ladies, you're welcome to this critical symposium. I'll be your Team Leader of the 'Alzheimer's Be Gone' Team."

He paused, scanned eager, erudite faces, and then continued,

Congress authorized the formation of the National Institute on Aging (NIA) in 1974 to provide leadership in aging research, training, health information dissemination, and other programs relevant to the elderly.

"Subsequent amendments to this legislation designated the NIA as the primary Federal agency for Alzheimer's disease research. We have ambitious plans to eradicate mental deterioration amongst our senior citizens."

A team member asked. "How would this work?"

"Around the nation, including California, a series of surveys conducted last year selected nursing homes to participate based on a scale designed by the National

Institute of Health (NIH). So, look in the binder under your chairs for details," the team leader responded.

"I represent the Blossom Plaza facility in Los Angeles. Is it within the study scope to manage multiple homes?" Doctor Romeo Atkins posed the question.

"No. Intense devotion to care demands deep data gathering of residents' health conditions, followed by mandatory weekly report submission, which is enough effort to overwhelm anyone. Hence, each volunteer has responsibilities for only one facility."

"Any implication to the Whitemelt crisis?" came the question from the back of the room.

The Team Leader paused.

"None. The NIH and other government agencies consult with the WhiteHouse to unravel the mystery."

"Are the disappearances age-related?" The questioner followed up.

"Hard to say. At the NIA, I have no detailed knowledge about the victims or circumstances of their disappearances."

More questions followed. The Team Leader continued to steer discussions toward the volunteer program while participants were bent on exploring the Whitemelt crisis.

An hour later, the room splintered into small groups after the speech to discuss the impact of Alzheimer's.

Doctor Romeo Atkins, loitering adjacent to a three-person group, overheard a conversation ruminating about the motivation for volunteering.

A man in his forties lamented.

"My seventy-two-year-old dad was an Olympic Javelin thrower in his days. He won a bronze medal. But when I showed him the medal, he had no idea what it was. It saddens me."

Another group member said, "I'm only fifty-seven and beginning to forget where I put things, especially in the kitchen. I live alone, and I am afraid I will forget to turn off the gas cooker and burn the whole place down."

Others nodded in agreement. The third person, a lady, was quiet while the other two awaited her story. Then, she said, "My mother was a famous Hollywood dancer before rehearsal rigor became impossible to navigate. She was thirty-nine at the time, ten years ago. Now, she sits comatose and stares at nothing all day. I cry each time I visit."

Doctor Atkins walked away towards the window, stared at the NIH building, and recalled the last time he visited his father before the forced admission into a nursing home.

...In the late afternoon, Romeo sat close to his father on the wooden bungalow porch where his father had lived for fifty years. Romeo, an only child, grew up in the house.

"Hey, Dad."

His father swatted flies and watched the neighborhood kids as they rode their bicycles around.

Romeo tried again to engage the old-timer. "Dad, can you fix me something to drink?"

"Ask your mother." The instant rebuke registered as a reference to the ritual they both played during his weekly visit with his father.

"Mama is long gone, Pops," he admonished lovingly.

His father, in the porch recliner, turned to him. "Then, who's that lady always fussing around in there?" He pointed inside the house.

"It's your nurse, Dad."

"Then let her get you something to drink," he commanded.

Romeo gave up and walked into the house...

Then, a tap on the shoulder by the Team Leader snapped Romeo back to the present.

"Do you have a minute to spare?"

After a short discussion with the team leader, Doctor Atkins left and headed for Blossom Plaza.

***

Although the original Muscle Beach was in Santa Monica, "muscle" was added to Venice Beach in Los Angeles, California, in 1987. The world-famous seaside real estate boasts an eclectic art scene, drawing interesting characters.

Tara and Hari Hapa walked through the narrow dune path of a secluded section of the beach.

Hari picked up a stick just as the ocean gently lapped waves ashore. Tara also picked up a stick and called to him,

"Wait up."

He headed straight for the rocky section by the ocean, where several outcrops jutted out of the sea on the beach. Hari poked between rocks at clams stuck to rock surfaces and other shellfish.

Tara walked onto the beach, periodically picking up shells. She saw something bobbing up and down on the water. She yelled,

"Hari?"

No response.

She approached the object to see a box with two blackened skeletal hands with rusty chain-bound wrists held tight on either end of the box. She gently pushed the box ashore with a stick, watched it for a few seconds, then looked for Hari, still poking amongst the rocks afar.

She bent down to move the box further up the shore. Her hand inadvertently brushed against the skeletal hand. The entity, dormant for centuries, embedded into Tara's body upon touch and extended its tentacles to her heart and brain. She fell unconscious.

Minutes later, Hari was hovering over her.

"Wake up, damn it," he repeats until she shows signs of life.

He heaved a sigh of relief.

"You okay?" He anxiously touched her face.

She looked around, unsure of what had happened, pushed off his hand, and pointed to the box.

He was curious as he approached it.

"What is it?" He asked.

Hari kicked off both skeletal hands and successfully opened the sealed box. Inside, he found a leather-bound book.

He was about to angrily throw the book back into the ocean when Tara pulled it from him.

"That's mine."

It was late evening when Hari drove Tara back to the Blossom Plaza Home Sanatorium, where she lived.

On the way, Tara experiences violent tremors. In addition, an oval welt appeared behind her right earlobe. Hari noticed her discomfort.

"Are you sick or something?"

She shook her head, but her face and eyes said otherwise as she fidgeted.

Upon arrival, Tara exited the car and walked towards the facility entrance.

Worriedly, Hari watched the front door close behind his only living relative before departing.

A week later, Hari knocked on her door. Skinny Tara, virtually emaciated overnight since she found the book at Venice Beach, paced the claustrophobic room.

"Tara, it's me. Open the door, please."

"Have you eaten? Remember, Mama always says a good meal a day saves the soul."

He heard scratches coming from inside her room.

From experience, he knew Tara was summoning the courage to open the door.

"I'm here, Sis. I'll always be here."

He heard the final creak of movement towards the door.

The door opened slowly. Expressionless, Tara waited for her brother's customary peck on the cheek, then retreated to her chair facing the window.

She sat with her back straight and stared out the window. Hari sat on the bed, talking.

"I'm having a great morning, Tara. How about you?"

He was not expecting an answer but continued the one-way conversation, knowing how wary Tara was of human contact, even from her brother.

A couple of hours later, he got up and eyed the leather-bound book on the bed as he left. As he opened the door to go, Tara spoke without changing position: "I love you."

"I love you, too," he echoed as he closed the door behind him.

Hari returned to work across the road and changed into his janitor's uniform in the locker room.

He swept the floor in the standard room and greeted all the old-timers who passed by him, stopping briefly to chat with as many residents as possible when his supervisor was elsewhere.

He saw Doctor Romeo Atkins talking to another resident while pushing the broom around.

Hari waved to Anna Cantor, whose younger brother, Lewis Cantor, often visited.

"Are you okay today, Miss Cantor?"

Hari rested on the broom handle as he addressed Anna, sitting beside her walker.

Anna suffered from the early stages of dementia with elevated anatomical levels of Lewy bodies characterized by slow, jerky movements, slurring her words, and visual hallucinations.

"You can call me Anna, young man. What's your name?" She smiled and continued crocheting.

Hari smiled back. "Yes, Miss Cantor, Anna. My name is Hari. Hari Hapa." He tells her that almost daily.

She leaned forward towards Hari conciliatorily.

"My kid brother, Lewis, is visiting me today."

She beamed and then continued.

"Do you know he owns a bookstore and sells old antique books?"

"Really?" Hari encouraged her.

"I'll introduce you when Lewis arrives. Stay close."

She receded into her chair as the supervisor approached from behind Hari.

Hari sensed something off and straightened.

"Goodbye, Miss Cantor," Hari said, then walked away.

Half an hour later, Hari walked into Evans Square's office at the end of his shift.

Hari's supervisor was busy scratching phantom itches.

Hari knew his boss was high on drugs, but kept it to himself.

"I need help for my sister. Boss." Hari requested.

Evans showed disinterest.

"Did you hear me, Sir?" Hari pressed.

Evans, head down, continued to write, scratched briefly, but it occurred often.

"Did you hear me, Sir?" Hari pressed again.

Evans looked up with disdain and slurred.

"This is neither Goodwill nor Salvation Army. You should do your job and not disturb the residents with your goody-two-shoes thingy."

"I need to bring my sister to the facility health center for an MRI," Hari blurted out.

Evans slurred even more with rage. "Have you any idea how much an MRI costs? The answer is no."

"But I have insurance covering my sister, my only living relative," Hari insisted.

"The answer is still no. You can see the manager if you wish, but you'll get the same answer. We just got the cost-cutting memo. I'm busy."

Hari left, and Evans continued scratching.

Hari waited for Evans to leave the premises and bribed a Russian Blossom Plaza health center technician for an MRI scan on Tara.

Hari rushed across the road and guided Tara into the MRI room.

Then, all prepped and about to step onto the MRI bed, Evans showed up with security and threw the siblings out without explanation.

Evans issued Hari a formal warning letter for robbery and company property theft.

Tara Hapa and Hari Hapa had shuffled within the California child services system, specifically Los Angeles County, from one foster home to another for over two decades. Hari dealt with increasing challenges to ensure no separation from his autistic younger sister.

In finding a job to sustain them both, Tara couldn't work; Hari's goal was always to keep her near, even at work. It took ages for him to find Blossom Plaza with an adjacent sanatorium to house Tara.

Tara fared well, albeit with constant monitoring by her brother, who checked on her early in the day and late at night as often as his schedule permitted. But Tara's mental condition and stability took a bad turn when she found a skeletal hand and a journal washed ashore at Venice Beach. Since then, she had engaged in endless doodling at all hours in the found journal to her self-neglect.

At first, Hari attempted to wrest the journal away, which triggered a massive mental breakdown. She wailed and cried until Hari relented and gave her back the journal. Periodically, she allowed Hari to touch the journal but only to move it aside to make room when she was not doodling.

She hardly ate but doodled incessantly. Her meal regimen suffered, leading to gross physical emaciation.

Since the find, Hari has often found an untouched breakfast platter when he checks on her in the evenings.

When not doodling, she usually sat immobile at the window in her room, the journal in her lap, staring at the adjacent wood five hundred yards away, day and night, in the dark.

Several medical diagnoses always concluded that there was nothing wrong physically, but there were loads of psychological dead spots.

Chapter 9

Forty miles away from LAX, at her part-time job in the affluent Encino community, a nurse on a side hustle hummed a Spanish lullaby to an unresponsive, comatose teenage boy in his hospital-like bedroom at the Verano home while massaging his feet.

Rick Verano and Hilda Verano walked in. The nurse who worked full time at the Blossom Plaza elderly home side hustled with the Veranos. She greeted them in English, laden with a Spanish accent, "Good boy today."

Hilda stared lovingly at her son and took over the foot massage.

Rick pulled up a chair next to the bed. The nurse rummaged in her purse and brought out a blister patch of antibiotics. "Señor Verano, I think this will help. No?"

He turned around and inspected the package. "No name?" he questioned.

The nurse turned very serious. "It's from my job, Blossom Plaza Home for old people."

"Does everyone there take it?"

"Yes, all the old people, but Mr. Rick, I am not a doctor, and I'm unsure if I should give you this."

"Does it work?"

"I don't know, Mr. Rick, but it's a chance for him. It cannot be worse than how he is now, no? But I don't know if it works or not. Maybe I should not give it to him?"

Rick Verano was now totally confused, but then looked at his unmoving son.

"I shall try it on him." He looked at his wife, Hilda, who agreed while massaging her son's feet.

"Mr. Rick, maybe you should get a second opinion before you use it."

"Okay." Then he looked at her searchingly. "Have you used it?"

The nurse lit up and demonstrated.

"You pop it out, peel off the plastic, then apply it to your upper arm."

She lifted her uniform to reveal the mark left after the patch removal from her person. "It comes off after two hours, Señor Verano."

Hilda, listening, stopped the massage, turned around, hugged the nurse tightly, and burst into tears.

"Thank you ever so much for caring for our son."

"De nada," the nurse replied.

Their son went into a violent spasm two nights later, leading to a massive heart attack. He passed away from the trauma.

▲ ▲ ▲

Weeks of mourning tore the Veranos apart while Rick continued to find ways to stem the breach. Today, they were heading to the LA Zoo, where he and Hilda had first met a quarter of a century earlier.

Facemask-less and bald Rick Verano, overweight, was in an old truck, accelerating up the ramp, when he stopped at the red light before joining the highway. He turned sideways to Hilda with her oversized face mask fiddling with the air conditioner knobs. He looked closely at her almost full-face mask.

"You plan on robbing a bank with that thing on your face?"

She snapped. "You never take anything seriously."

The light turned green; he eased into highway traffic.

"Our son would have—" She cuts him off, changing the subject.

"I plan to see the crocs again, such ancient creatures."

Restless, she tugged at a cooling knob. "Shit."

He gently placed his palm on hers. Hilda jerked off his hand and sulked.

He took it in stride and tried to appease her. "Remember when he was six years old and poured hot water into the truck's air conditioner vent when he overheard you complaining the air in the vehicle was too cold?"

A faint smile appeared on Hilda's face while listening to her husband, but she remained quiet.

He continued. "He would certainly stuff ice cubes down the truck vent if he were here now."

Her developing smile vanished just as quickly.

Rick patted her on the knee. She shuts him down again.

"Focus, Rick. Our exit is coming up."

He took the Alameda Avenue ramp towards the LA Zoo.

With a Green Bay Packer woolly hat, Rick was delighted as the crowd thronged after the eighteen-month post-COVID-19 pandemic lock-up release. Then, he checked them into the LA Zoo.

Hilda headed to the food vendor kiosk just off the main path to the zoo attractions, and Rick followed closely behind.

"Small Diet Coke, please." She ordered.

"Make mine a large with large syrup butter popcorn." He corrected.

Hilda glared at him in disgust. "With that gunk, you'll see our son sooner than later."

The orders arrived. Rick was already eating before they walked off the kiosk.

"Jesus, Rick?"

"What?" He crammed an impossibly large handful of popcorn into his mouth.

Hilda walked away from him, sulking.

He caught her up at the empty crocodile display.

"Where's everybody?" he asked.

Hilda ignored him and read off a fact sheet posted on the Croc pavilion fence.

"Did you know crocodiles have the strongest bite of any animal?"

He reached for more popcorn. It was all gone. He sucked on the soda straw and loudly drew out only air. She shook her head in disgust.

"I'll be right back," he announced, walking towards the nearby trash bin.

Rick returned and saw Hilda floating inside the crocodile fence toward a cloudy, shimmering portal. He broke into a run and arrived just in time to see her vanish into a gate.

He collapsed from a heart attack.

Still, all over the news in Europe, the Whitemelt disappearance news at the Swiss ski resort slowly gained traction in the Americas due to incessant cable network broadcasts. Then, it happened in the United States.

US President Bender Castle called his cabinet to prepare for a possible fallout after the first Whitemelt hit the LA Zoo.

A rigid Marine guard saluted President Bender Castle at the Oval Office door as the Chief of Staff shoveled papers behind his boss.

The President's Cabinet rose upon his ingress into the conference room.

"Sit, please," he commanded.

The Attorney General, AG, and the Homeland Security Secretary, HSS, were in the room with Barry DaSilva, the CIA Director, wearing an eye patch.

The Chief of Staff walked to the large sidewall screen with the United States emblem and clicked to display the chaos at the LA Zoo, showing EMTs using CPR attempts on Rick Verano.

"Whitemelt reports are pouring into the WhiteHouse and the UN-WHO—" The President interrupted,

"Whitemelt?"

Barry DaSilva spoke. "Coined by the widow of an Italian Count who vanished at a Swiss Alps ski resort. Interpol is investigating."

"I need answers in less than a week on this Whitemelt thing."

The President abruptly headed for the exit door, forcing cabinet members to scramble off their seats in courtesy.

They all started talking simultaneously once the door closed, until the HSS tapped on the table. "C'mon, guys!"

Diminutive Barry spoke. "This thing is about to blow wide open. A week is insufficient to do anything. We need a small, fast task force—" The AG interrupted,

"This is domestic, Barry. FBI does the heavy lifting."

Barry interrupted, "I know, but it's happening globally." The AG replied, "With all due respect, Barry, this is my call. The FBI will initiate and lead a task force."

Barry tugged angrily at his patch.

"Bunch of FBI Yahoos," he muttered, alone in the conference room.

***

Berlin Yords's Swedish parents, blonde and blue-eyed, met at an agricultural college in Wisconsin where both studied in the 70s.

They married, graduated, and soon had Berlin, a pretty blonde and blue-eyed specimen, thoroughly tomboyish with boundless energy. When she turned nine, her father enrolled her in a karate school. She excelled.

Berlin had an athletic college scholarship where she was severely assaulted and almost raped trying to protect a female African student attacked in a religious hate crime for wearing a Hijab.

She suffered major physical trauma and received extensive psychological counseling; Berlin and the female African became lifelong friends.

Berlin took up a counseling job after college to counsel at-risk girls; she was rarely fully taken seriously because of her pretty looks, an asset she'd subconsciously buried deep within her psyche.

The weight of the job exposed her to the ire of jealous partners, settling scores. Once again, Berlin suffered physical abuse and trauma from a home invasion by one such irate boyfriend. During the post-attack counseling and support group sessions, someone casually suggested she join law enforcement, at least, to learn how to protect herself since she seemed so susceptible to attacks.

She applied and was accepted into the FBI. But again, her physical attributes became a drawback and unfairly undermined her progress until a feisty mentor, an FBI Assistant Director In Charge, ADIC, Leeloo Chang, in the Bureau, came to her rescue.

***

Berlin thought she lucked out when she ran into her old African friend from college in downtown New York in her rookie year, her first posting.

The two young women affectionately hugged and walked hand in hand down Times Square.

"So, we meet again after so many years," Berlin spoke amidst happy giggles.

The African smiled widely, displaying a very white set of teeth.

"Inevitable, my friend. I've been eagerly waiting since we talked, and you said you've been assigned to the City."

"I know, I couldn't wait, either." They both entered a small Chinese restaurant.

Seated, Berlin perused the menu thrust at her while her friend placed orders immediately like someone quite familiar and comfortable in her environment.

Minutes later, Berlin's friend chopsticks some meat in a small bowl of soup as Berlin kept cracking open abundant fortune cookies, only to read the fortunes and abandon the cookies to the side.

"How many children in Africa could do with those?" her friend playfully chided.

"I'm sorry." Berlin smiled in embarrassment. Her friend bursts into laughter.

"You're so gullible."

"I'm so not." Berlin changed the subject. "How is the job?"

Her friend sighed. "The City is full of predators, dirty old men just waiting in the wings to pounce. It's often disheartening but rewarding when those perverts are put away for good. Anyway, let's talk about pleasant things. How's Primy?"

Berlin beamed as the food arrived. "Oh, she's a handful, but lucky for me, her babysitter is a Yoga enthusiast, so she was worn out when I got home."

Both friends launched into their meals.

A week later, the African friend was murdered.

***

A man, above average height and well-built in a Transgender outfit, would presumably have been a masculine physical specimen in normal clothing. However, he looked radically transformed as he expertly walked on a fiercely tall pump.

Such was his attire when he turned up at the wake of Berlin's African friend in Queens, New York.

His high-collar pink suit was complemented by a shoulder-length blonde wig garnished with a small daffodil flower on the left side. The blatant, bold look was garish, yet people couldn't look away, just like Berlin couldn't.

After the wake, Berlin sorted him out as he hurriedly walked down the avenue in the pink pumps, still bawling.

"Do you know her?" Berlin asked from behind.

He stopped and turned around, Akimbo.

"Who wants to know? Are you Fed?"

Berlin was stomped. "What makes you think I'm Fed?"

"I've lived in New York all my life. Plus, you're in a black suit with a white shirt underneath and probably packing heat. Are you packing heat?"

Berlin checked herself to see if her gun bulge was showing. It wasn't.

"You never answered my question about her."

He looked across the street at a café.

"I'm buying," Berlin confirmed and crossed the road at a stop sign; he followed.

Now sipping, he was relaxed.

"We called her Shandy-white on account of her very gorgeous white teeth. She was once my counselor."

"Are you okay? Were you…" Berlin began to say.

"Abused," he finished for her, and then continued.

"No, nothing like that. Wait a minute. Who are you?"

Berlin sidestepped the question. "Why were you crying so hard?"

"I cry at the drop of a hat. Talking about that, I gotta go."

He got up.

"I'd like to talk more about her if you have the time." Berlin offered.

Standing, he took a good look at Berlin, still sitting down.

"You're pretty." He stuck his hand out, momentarily confusing Berlin. She soon caught on and brought out one of her business cards.

He read it, smiled knowingly, and headed out. Berlin looked at him expertly, walking on the high pumps with his head held high.

At their next meeting at a bar in the City, Berlin learned he was of Jewish Romanian ancestry whose family attended the Queens Yom Marantz synagogue where Rabin Chosky was once a gabbai, a person whose responsibilities include calling people from the congregation to read from the Torah.

"So, what do you do?" Berlin asked.

He smiled.

"Thanks for not treating me like a freak. I work as a bartender wherever I go, but I'm more interested in computers than anything else. So, are you a top Agent or something? Have you ever shot anybody? Can…f"

Berlin raised a hand to stop him from talking any further.

"My African friend?" She reminded him.

He collapsed into his seat, deflated, and remained quiet for a short while.

"She was kind-hearted and calm to all the poor girls who came to her for legal advice and empathy. My boyfriend slapped me because I slapped him first for ogling another man at the bar where I worked.

"She happened to be there that night. When the bar closed, she asked me if I needed legal help. That was how it started."

"And did you?" Berlin asked.

"Did I what?

"Needed legal help?"

"No. I prefer to suffer in silence. I remember she didn't like that at all."

"Are you still with that boyfriend?"

He became coy; Berlin changed the subject.

"Do you know any of her other clients?

He looked at her funny. "Shouldn't that be your FBI thingy?"

Berlin ignored his sass. "So, who's helping those girls now?"

"What's that to you, Agent?"

It was Berlin's turn to be coy. "There may be some money coming your way."

He perked up. "Like what?"

"You know, helping."

"How?"

"You said you've lived in New York all your life, so you must know lots."

"What don't you know?" He asked.

"Why don't you ask me straight up, New York style, what you wanted?"

Berlin leaned in. "$100 a month for starters as my CI."

"A fink?"

"No, CI."

"Same difference, Agent."

"Think about it." Berlin walked off.

He turned around, looking at her with curiosity.

***

FBI Assistant Director in Charge ADIC Leeloo Chang recently began mentoring Agent Berlin Yords. Chang advised that little wins would shape opinions around her detrimental good looks, causing Berlin to redouble her professional efforts.

Her first case since relocation to New York with a new confidential informant, CI, was to capture a murderous pedophile in the act, killing across the Northeast that the NYPD botched due to politics: the state AG was a Republican. At the same time, the police chief was a Democrat in an election year.

The suspect was about to be arrested, but was a big Republican Political Action Committee (PAC) donor. The New York Republican political machine kicked into high gear, thwarting the NYPD's attempt to obtain a subpoena to engineer the arrest. The police chief fought back by referring the case to the FBI without the AG's knowledge.

The blow-up caused the police chief to lose his job, but the FBI was now engaged. However, the CI's inexperience caused him to disappoint Berlin during the arrest...

"Are you ready?" Berlin whispered into her microphone, talking to her new CI, dressed normally, in a Manhattan hotel lobby.

"He just came in, but she's outside. What should I do?"

"Just relax, stay put, and point your cell phone camera as I showed you so I can see him."

The CI nervously did as instructed. The target, in a suit, checked in and looked back at the entrance door, where a young girl hung out.

"Hurry up, please," the man commanded at the hotel check-in desk.

The CI got up, turned off the camera, walked to the door, and confronted the girl. A commotion ensued at the hotel entrance, causing everyone in the lobby to stare.

The target absconded, blowing up Berlin's stakeout with all the armed personnel in position left out in the cold.

An hour later, Berlin was furious and tongue-lashed the CI at an obscure café far from the City.

"What the hell happened?"

He was downcast. "I don't know what came over me; I just…" He trailed off.

"Several hours of effort down the drain. Are you sure you're up to this CI thing?"

"I can do this, Agent Yords; I just couldn't sit by and watch the girl used."

His reasoning confused Berlin.

"I don't understand, but it's for her good; she needs to grow up normal, plus she could turn up dead and…" He raised his hand in surrender.

"You're right; it won't happen again."

"That, I'm sure of." Berlin walked off.

"Am I still your CI?"

The café door closed.

The CI's 2nd chance came from his familiarity with zealot members of the Yom Marantz synagogue in Queens, where he and his parents worshipped until he stopped attending in his twenties.

Still, the CI couldn't help Berlin with advance information concerning a widely broadcasted kidnapping of a young prostitute later traced to perpetrators from his synagogue.

Immediately after the shootout broadcast of the kidnappers' arrest, he visited Berlin at the hospital after several hours of surgery, but he wasn't allowed past tight security.

A month later, he returned and was allowed in at Berlin's nod to the uniform outside her hospital room door.

Berlin buzzed the bed to raise her head as he cowered in the corner, far away from the Agent.

"Reports are all out there, and you didn't know something about the two idiots from your synagogue that you attended with your parents for years? Look at me; all shot up because my CI didn't CI as expected."

He folded his arms, not looking up. "I'm so sorry, Berlin and..."

Berlin cuts in, "Agent Yords to you. What's the excuse this time?"

The CI moved closer but remained standing. "I knew the first kidnapper but not the second guy. It's being..."

"You should have called me, at least, when all the newspapers and cable channels went at it." Berlin spat.

"Agent. It's been a minute since I saw those guys last, plus I don't read the news."

"You have to do better than that. I'm doing much worse with you as a CI. Why is that?"

"I don't know, Berl... Agent Yords. Maybe I'm just bad at finking..."

"Really? But you keep taking the money that has now gone up to a grand a month."

"It's not the money, Agent; you're the only law enforcement person I know who doesn't judge me and..."

"That has nothing to do with anything. You got my partner killed, and also could have gotten me killed. Your warning could have made the difference."

He sighed, looked up, pulled a chair to the bed, and tried to hold Berlin's hand, who pulled away.

"I don't know how else to apologize. I like you; I dare to say I love you, though you're very different from your African friend. But being near you makes me feel closer to her, if that makes sense."

Berlin remained quiet for a long time. He then got up and headed for the door.

"I'm sorry, so, so sorry."

"Yeah, thanks for almost getting me killed."

The door closed softly behind the CI.

Chapter 10

President Bender Castle charged into the emergency WhiteHouse cabinet meeting room without acknowledging his team's warm welcome. Instead, he laid into them. The chief of staff hovered closely behind him.

"I'm not sure why there are happy faces while some nut job out there has citizens disappearing. I want him found. So, here's what will happen. The AG and the FBI will quell the Whitemelt before it gains further traction. So, we're all not voted out of office."

The chief of staff whispered into his ear. The President glared at him and continued, "I understand the Los Angeles FBI ADIC, Leeloo Chang, is on point. Right?"

Leeloo, sitting behind the AG, stood up. The President waved her down halfway up and glanced across the room.

"Questions?" He didn't wait for a response and walked out.

The AG sauntered to Leeloo and shook her hand. "You have my sympathy, " he said, then walked out.

Barry called him just before he reached the door. "Is that it?"

The AG paused. "Your help is always welcome, Barry. Please let me know how, but I'm pressed for time now. Sorry." He vacated the room.

Leeloo stared at Barry mischievously. "You scared off the little rats again."

Barry gathered his documents and walked out without a word to Leeloo.

Leeloo Chang stared out the window at her top-floor downtown Los Angeles FBI building office. Berlin Yords sat quietly.

"Your legs hurt, Yords?"

"Like a bent Mizuno driver, boss."

Leeloo whipped around.

Berlin stammered, "Golf clubs made in—"

Leeloo interrupted, "I'm a two-handicap. Thank you."

"Sorry, I'm almost fully back," Berlin babbled.

"Primy okay, soldier?"

"Yes, Ma'am. In Sweden with my folks."

Leeloo sat behind her desk. "Now, Whitemelt."

Berlin leaned forward, expectant. "Is it mine?"

Leeloo regarded her briefly. "Don't muck it up."

A hint of a smile on Berlin's face disappeared as quickly as it had appeared. "Not a chance, boss."

"Berlin, this is a mudslide disaster waiting to roll over anyone dumb enough to play in it. Understood?"

Leeloo's stare deliberated intimidation long enough to render Berlin uncomfortable.

"I will not allow it to become an avalanche, boss."

"DNI will test you."

Berlin squirmed but was confident.

"And so will the CIA, Ma'am. I get that." Berlin added.

Leeloo smiled. "One-eyed Jack will pounce when least expected. Watch out."

Berlin stiffened her back. "I'll be ready."

Leeloo snapped off her chair, stared out the window, and fiddled with her cell phone.

Berlin waited for a while and then tried to leave.

Still facing the window, Leeloo spoke, "No press bombshells."

Berlin stopped and then responded, "Won't happen, Ma'am. I promise."

Leeloo turned around and smiled at her protégé.

"Lens Kasper, Interpol, Swiss Alps Whitemelt. Check your text."

A text alert chimed on Berlin's cell phone.

Leeloo turned around again to stare out the window.

Berlin gently closed the door behind her.

She pumped her fist outside the door with an awkward, zero-rhythm dance.

***

Berlin flashed her shield to gain entry into the LA Zoo.

Inside, a brief discussion with a uniform attendant revealed the admin building.

The second-floor manager's office contained books, maps, and zoo items. The office window looked down at the zoo entrance gate.

The manager welcomed her with his down-yonder accent.

"Take the load off. I'm sure we have lots to eschew. A freaky affair, that one, cooped up for months, can drive anyone up the wall." He said.

The manager smiled and walked to sit behind his desk. "How may I help you, Miss?"

"The incident report was sketchy, at best. Is there anything you can add or something related that occurred since the Whitemelt?"

"Whitemelt. What a turn of phrase. Ma'am, the trauma was still palpable. When people walk by, we see patrons on security footage skirt the croc area."

"Got the tape?"

"Follow me."

Two uniformed security guards at the zoo's security control room stared at screens from multiple cameras across the park.

The manager grabbed a chair at a console and expertly navigated the screen until he located dated footage.

"All yours." The manager stood up, and Berlin sat.

They watch a slow-motion playback of Hilda Verano's disappearance.

It showed Rick running towards the croc area, pausing, staring at something, then grabbing his left arm and collapsing.

Berlin pressed the video pause button and turned to the manager.

"I don't see anything strange."

The manager, with arms folded, concurred. "No one does. The rest is the chaos of the patron receiving help from the EMT crew."

Berlin resumed play until the Alhambra Ambulance carts Rick Verano away.

"Can I look around the croc area?"

"Yes, but do not enter the enclosure. Please, stay behind the police tape at all times."

The manager handed Berlin a USB.

Berlin arrived and displayed her shield to ensure the queue saw her sidearm.

"Folks, halt just a moment, and I'll soon let you be."

She beckoned the older female attendant to step out from behind the kiosk.

"I'll talk to you while your partner handles business."

Berlin turned to the queue. "I apologize. I either interview here or at the office, and hear there's no replacement kiosk attendant for at least an hour."

The murmur quieted, and the attendant became eager to help. She spoke animatedly: "It was wild. The guy was fooling with his order while his wife was serious."

"Any other strange thing you remember from that day?"

The attendant paused to think. Berlin remained patient.

Moments later, Berlin walked towards the police tape at the croc pavilion. Nothing unusual was visible.

She left the zoo disappointed, without knowing what had transpired.

In deep concentration at the DTLA FBI office, Berlin searched for clues in the video footage of the EMT crew attending to Rick Verano at the LA Zoo when his wife, Hilda Verano, vanished. No luck, so she headed out to the Alhambra Ambulances office at Griffith Park.

She circled the busy locality unsuccessfully, not finding a parking spot, not even an illegal opening where she could display a law enforcement "park anywhere pass" on the windshield.

Fifteen minutes on, she fought a minivan for a sudden open slot.

Her mood frayed as she eyed men in green uniforms washing ambulances at an open annex enclosure as she charged into the Alhambra Medical Specialty Company building.

The company occupied a medium-sized facility adjacent to the Griffith Park Medical Hospital.

"May I help you?" the receptionist asked without looking up, busy filing her long-painted nails.

Berlin flashed her shield and failed to impress the heavily made-up young receptionist.

Finally, she acknowledged the testy FBI Agent. "Do you have an appointment?"

Berlin stepped in closer and shouted, "Call your boss before I shut this dump down."

The receptionist eyed her down briefly. Then, with pink, brightly painted nails, she dialed a number, staring hard at Berlin.

"I have a FED here threatening to shut us down."

A tall, gray-haired man in a green uniform appeared before the receptionist dropped the call.

"I've warned you several times about your attitude," he admonishes the unyielding receptionist.

"I'm sorry, Dad, I had to take a short, late lunch." She remained petulant.

"Can I help you?"

"Yes, but not out here," Berlin said, already on the move.

He hurried past her. "Please, follow me. My daughter is—" Berlin interrupted, "Are you on contract with Griffith Park Medical Hospital?"

She almost ran into his back when he stopped at the door.

He shut the door behind them.

"Why do you want to know?"

"The Disappearance at the LA Zoo."

He remained blank and quiet.

"Didn't you guys handle it?" Berlin pressed.

"Why?"

His question got a raise from the Agent.

"I'm rapidly losing patience with you. Are you hiding something?"

The accusation took the business owner by surprise.

Agitated, he explained, "My wife normally runs the business while I tend to the vehicles. She's out for minor dental surgery but will be back tomorrow. So I have no idea what you're talking about."

Berlin relaxed a little. "Your team responded to an emergency at the LA Zoo twice within two months. First, I want to talk to the crew."

He picked up the phone. "Bring me the schedule for the last three months, pronto." He hung up and stared dolefully at Berlin.

Minutes later, he rifled through the pages of a ledger, called out a name, and showed Berlin the responder's picture.

"He responded to the last two calls from the LA Zoo." He sits back with self-satisfaction.

"Is he here now? I need to talk to him." Berlin was already up.

"He's washing the vehicles as we speak."

He hurried behind Berlin out of the office.

"I'll handle it from here." Berlin was near the exit door.

The responder stopped washing the ambulance passenger window as Berlin approached.

"You have a minute?" Berlin flashed her shield. He flinched noticeably.

"Yes, why?" His voice and attitude were laden with a thick East European accent.

"We can do this at the FBI office if you prefer."

When he didn't respond, Berlin asked, "What did you see at the LA Zoo at the croc display area?"

Berlin noticed he relaxed instantly after her question.

"Nothing. The guy was in pain, having a heart attack, was sobbing, pointing to the croc area, but couldn't speak. I later read that his wife disappeared. Crazy."

She shoved a business card into his shirt pocket and stared hard at the EMT before speaking. "Call me if you recall anything else."

Berlin got to her car and found a parking violation ticket on the windshield. She had missed a sign that only allowed a ten-minute parking duration.

"Yeah," she said as she snatched off the ticket.

She zoomed off fast, heading for Encino.

A maid welcomed Berlin into a ritzy duplex where Rick Verano dined. The maid returned to dusting plush, brown leather furniture.

"Join me?" Rick pointed to a high island kitchen chair in the bright room. "Coffee?"

Berlin declined. Rick giggled in insanity. "The burial was sinful. Wasn't it?"

Berlin remained expressionless.

"We found no apparent clues to the disappearance at the Zoo, Mr. Verano."

"Bagel?"

Rick pushed a basket full of baked niceties.

Berlin ignored the temptation and asked, "Your account of the incident was—" Berlin stopped talking as Rick stepped off the chair and walked towards the maid.

Then, with his back turned to Berlin, he spoke softly.

"Have you lost two loved ones within weeks of each other?"

"The FBI hopes to find your wife and return her to—"

Rick interrupted Berlin again, his voice rising.

"She's gone, you idiots. You should have seen what I saw."

Finally, Rick returned to the table.

Berlin allowed him to settle in.

"That's what we're trying to ascertain, Sir."

Rick stared at the Agent briefly before speaking.

"I only left briefly to dump the trash. So there Hilda was, floating behind the damn croc enclosure."

"Like, in the air?" Berlin asked, leaning forward.

Rick looked at Berlin like she was stupid.

"I wasn't drunk or high."

"I'm sorry, but I don't understand, Sir."

"Yeah, you and I both." Rick bit hard on a bagel.

"How did she get behind the Vista fence?"

"Wouldn't we all like to know?" he reiterated.

Berlin shifted in the chair, about to take a croissant, but stopped when Rick yelled, "No."

"That will ruin your teeth," he said.

Berlin reared back in confusion. "Sir?"

"What? You think I'm crazy?"

"Sir. Please explain what you saw." She leaned in even more.

Rick got off the chair, almost toppling over. The maid turned around at the commotion. Berlin got up to help.

"Leave me the heck alone! I need you to leave right now," Rick yelled.

They both remained standing, staring each other down.

Rick then began to disrobe. He took off his shirt, pants, and shorts.

Now completely naked, both the maid and Berlin stared at him, unsure of what to do.

The maid ran out of the lounge.

Expressionless, Berlin slowly placed a business card on the kitchen table and walked toward the front door.

Rick watched her close the front door behind her.

Outside, Berlin halted briefly to process what had just transpired to the man who had lost his wife.

"Jesus," she exclaimed.

Chapter 11

Lewis Cantor whistled in his car as he headed toward Blossom Plaza. He turned into the parking lot, still in an excellent mood to visit his sister, Anna.

Anna introduced Hari as he walked by, cleaning.

"Thank you for your patience with my sister."

Lewis turned on the charm to an expressionless Hari resting on a broomstick beside the siblings. Anna possessively held onto Lewis's arm.

"She's easy to love." Hari returned the favor. Anna beamed.

Hari broached the subject of old books that piqued Lewis's interest. Hari needed money to give Tara all the care she needed.

"I hear you have a bookstore. I may have something to show you." Lewis's interest notched up.

"I have some time today after my visit. Is that good?" Lewis asked.

"Yes, yes. But…" Hari said.

"Is there a problem?"

"None." Hari shook his head firmly.

"Okay, then," Lewis retorted and turned to Hari, signaling he wanted to be alone with his sister. Hari glided off, cleaning.

After Lewis visits Anna, he walks with Hari across the Blossom Plaza campus to Tara's sanatorium.

"It's me, Tara." Hari waited at the door. Lewis watched with interest.

The door opened carefully. Tara froze, uncomfortable at Lewis's presence. She began to shake from anxiety.

"It's okay, Sis. He's harmless. He wants to see your book."

"No." She refuses but lets them in reluctantly.

She quickly rescued the book from the bed beside her doll to sit by the window. Lewis followed closely behind Hari into the room. Hari sat on the bed.

Lewis approached Tara with the book on her lap.

"The book looks old," Lewis noted.

She ignored him and stared at the woods demarcating the Plaza property.

"The cover is magnificent. Can I touch it?"

Tara pulled the book closer to her chest. "No. Now, go away."

Lewis's face pleaded for Hari to intervene.

"Lewis wants to see the book, Tara. I will not let him take it away," Hari promised. Then, he hummed her favorite lullaby as he gently pried the book from her and replaced it with the doll. He passed the book behind his back to Lewis.

Lewis, on the bed, quietly flipped pages, unable to disguise his awe at the diagrams, writings, and the hand-drawn doodles made by Tara. By now, she was standing over Lewis suspiciously. Her knuckles were drained, strangling her doll.

"Did you draw all these?" Lewis marveled. Tara stayed taciturn. Hari began to worry, watching Tara start to vibrate, literally.

"Lewis, it's time to leave. The book, please?" Hari demanded, but Lewis was reluctant. Hari forcefully wrested the book away from Lewis and passed it to Tara.

She returned to the window, caressing the book on her lap.

Hari quietly shoved Lewis out of the room and closed the door behind them as they left Tara's room.

It's 2 a.m. in LA. Hondo Kendricks rested against a black Buick at the corner of a dimly lit street in Koreatown, watching the back door in the dark alley of an illegal gambling joint. Lewis Cantor emerged from the door, shit-faced. Hondo flicked off his cigarette, hurried out of the vehicle, and ran down the path after Lewis, heading in the opposite direction.

Joey Campo, driving, sped to cut Lewis off at the other end of the alley.

Lewis stiffened when he heard car tires screeching and turned around, only to face Hondo coming at him. He raised his hands in surrender. "You got me," he said.

Joey drove up to meet them.

Cornered, Lewis emptied his pockets to show he had no money. Hondo slapped him so hard that he buckled as Joey stepped out of the car, grinning maliciously.

On his knees, Lewis rapidly announced a plan to save himself from further pain.

"I have a new rare book that could fetch as much as $500k, and I—" Lewis yelled in pain as Hondo ground his boot on his foot in his open-toe flip-flop.

Joey shouted at Hondo, "Let him explain, goddamnit."

"Listen, guys. You must help me steal the book, but it's not dangerous. The owner is an autistic girl."

Hondo kicked him hard. "You are one disgusting piece of shit suggesting we rob a disabled person. You should be ashamed."

Joey signaled Hondo, who lifted Lewis off the ground only to slug him hard in the face again, drawing blood.

Lewis fell to the ground. Joey and Hondo then stood back to watch Lewis gather himself off the ground, bleeding profusely from the mouth.

Hondo announced, "We steal the book tonight, yeah? You better be ready, or you…" He made a throat-slit gesture at Lewis.

A sheepish, self-loathing grin crossed Lewis's face as he headed down the alley. He hugged the wall to keep from getting crushed as the Buick zoomed by, tires screeching.

"Assholes."

At 9:00 p.m., Lewis's tense, white knuckles gripped the steering wheel hard as he headed towards Blossom Plaza sanatorium, where Anna resided.

He turned five hundred yards short of the nursing home into a dead-end residential road, then hit the trees. He pulled onto the forest dirt road, and a restless Joey sat beside him.

"Are we there yet?" Hondo, in the back seat, giggled knowingly at Lewis's nervousness. Then, finally, Lewis pulled up and turned to face Joey.

"Do you remember the sanatorium layout? The girl must not be hurt. Tell me you understand, Joey."

"Fuck you," Joey smirked and exited the car.

Hondo, behind Joey, navigated through the trees into the open area behind the Blossom Plaza Sanatorium. Crouching, they ran towards the back delivery door.

Joey stopped when he saw a young security guard far away, walking away in the opposite direction.

"Watch it, goddamnit," he admonished Hondo, who ran into his back and almost stabbed him with the toothpick in his mouth.

Joey picked the lock to let them into the facility. They crept silently through the building.

Tara Hapa sat in a chair with the lights off, facing the woods as she had customarily done all evening.

She remained expressionless as she watched Joey and Hondo scurry toward the building. Scratchy noises at her door, which she ignored, also rang out.

Joey and Hondo broke into her room; she remained motionless and fearlessly stared at them. Joey plunged a tranquilizer syringe into her neck without any resistance. She went limp.

He arranged for her to sit on the chair facing the window and removed the leather-bound book from under her pillow, where Lewis said it'd be.

Meanwhile, Hondo carefully replaced the ceiling smoke detector batteries with dead batteries. Then, he sprayed glue into the sprinkler head, rigged her electric space heater in the closet, plugged it into the power outlet, and followed Joey out of the room.

Joey and Hondo crept silently through the building. Hondo almost ran into Joey's back again, who angrily snatched the toothpick from Hondo's mouth as they ran out the same way they came in.

Lewis stood at the woods' edge, looking at the windows, knowing exactly where Tara's window was. He saw smoke thickening in the room as Joey and Hondo ran in his direction. He attempted to run towards the building. Hondo slugs him unconscious. They both carry Lewis back into the car.

***

It's 3:50 a.m., and Hari's phone rings. He turns on the bedside lamp and picks up the cell phone. He looks at the caller ID. It's from the sanatorium. He jumps out of bed.

"What happened?"

"Are you Hari Hapa?" the voice inquired.

"Yes. What's happened to Tara?"

Driving like a madman, Hari arrived at the sanatorium at 4:00 a.m., where there was chaos of activities, with fire engines, ambulances, and patrol cars flashing red and blue as he drove in.

He arrived just in time to see two emergency crews push an odd-shaped white object on a gurney, which looked like a chair under the covering. He instinctively burst through and pulled the cover up to see half of Tara sitting fused onto what remained of the metal chair, and froze in shock.

Someone gently led him away from the dreadful scene.

He sat on the sidewalk, head in his hand, away from everyone, his tears falling onto the asphalt. The ambulance blasted off with a Siren.

Hari walked around Tara's room in a daze, wondering why it burned. Finally, he settled near the window and fixated on the floor's burn mark and the bed, looking for Tara's journal. It was missing.

At the Los Angeles Coroner building, a ramrod police detective pulled the purple vape contraption from his mouth to enter the mentally abysmal edifice alongside Hari Hapa.

"Are you ready to do this?" the cop wondered aloud.

"No,"

Hari bemoaned and waited in the outer office while the detective disappeared behind doors, heading into the autopsy room.

149

Doctor Lilly Chen lifted the white linen covering Tara Hapa's half-burnt body in the autopsy room. She carefully pulled back Tara's fused arm with gloved hands to straighten it when the detective loudly pushed open the door.

Lilly flinched, and her glove snagged on a bone and ripped, causing her bare flesh to make contact with the body, enabling the entity in Tara to embed into the doctor.

"Stop. You're a bull in a China shop; do you know that, detective?" The angry pathologist lamented, unaware that the significant disruption to her DNA had already begun.

The detective froze by the door. "I'm sorry, Lilly, I didn't think anything could ever startle you, considering…" The detective's voice trailed off as he pointed at cadavers on steel slabs against walls.

She glared at him. "You'll be surprised, Joe. What do you want now?"

The detective glided over and pecked her on the cheek. She relaxed. He then looked at her with bemusement.

"China shop? Really?"

Lilly smiled. "What? I can't use that idiom because I'm Chinese. Is this the Dark Ages? Anyway, what the hell do you want, detective?"

"You done with the crispy chair girl from the Sanatorium?"

She pointed to the table in front of her. "Are you blind?"

"How much longer, doc? Her brother is outside. Sad!"

"Half an hour, tops. But you have to wait outside."

Hari walked into the pathology room alongside the detective with trepidation all over his face.

Doctor Lilly Chen slowly walked them to the steel slab with a white linen covering Tara's body.

Hari turned to the pathologist. "I'm ready."

She lifted the linen to reveal the charred body, whose size now resembled a child. Hari's eyes misted over.

He asked, "How did she die?"

Doctor Chen looked at the detective for assistance. The detective answered,

"Once declared a crime, nothing can be divulged just yet, Mister Hapa."

Hari's back stiffened. "Meaning her death was not an accident?"

"I'm sorry, Hari. I can only conclude that, after my investigations."

Hari moved away from them and began to sob quietly in a corner.

"What do I do now? Tara was my only living relative."

Doctor Chen approached Hari but was confused about whether to hug him. So, instead, she patted him on the shoulder, signaling the detective to take him out of the dreary arena.

The detective led Hari out of the room and then doubled back.

"Where are her personal effects?"

Lilly pointed to a corner table envelope.

Back in the waiting room, Hari took the envelope from the detective.

Hari Hapa stood between Lewis Cantor and Doctor Romeo Atkins at the Reseda Cemetery to bury Tara in a black suit. As they walked off, it began to drizzle. Lewis leaned over.

"Would you like to go somewhere to relax a little?" Red-eyed Hari shook his head.

Doctor Atkins signaled Lewis to let Hari grieve in peace. But Lewis won't let go.

"Let me know if I can help in any way," Lewis insisted.

Hari nodded, and then the rain increased in intensity, forcing them to flee, but Hari stopped and waved Lewis and Doctor Atkins to go ahead.

For days after Tara's internment, Hari hibernated on bereavement leave from work, sitting on the bed with Tara's autopsy and the police report strewn around him as he haphazardly jumped from reading one report page to the next.

He finally sat back, head on the bed's headboard in exhaustion, staring into space to think. He heard a knock on the door.

Doctor Romeo Atkins walked in, loaded with groceries.

"The nursing home told me you took some time off, but no one has heard from you. They're worried. Are you okay?"

"It's been tough, doc."

"I'm sure, Hari. Can I use your bathroom, please?"

Hari nodded.

Romeo glanced at the papers scattered on the floor in Hari's room as he went to the bathroom.

Upon his return, he saw Hari unbagging groceries in the kitchen, and then the doctor pulled back the window shades to let in the light.

"It's always been such a thin line between grief and depression. What both have in common is the remedy for escape. I want some tea if you would, Hari."

"Will coffee do? I'm out of teabags," Hari confessed.

"We're in luck, then. Check the second grocery bag." Romeo pointed.

"Your next best move to break the doldrums is to channel."

Hari halted and turned to face the physician. "How's that?"

"Tara must have some interest that you can assume to feel closer to her and lessen the loss temporarily. No?"

The kettle whistled, and Hari returned to the kitchen.

Both sipped their tea in quietness. Hari's demeanor improved, but he remained in the kitchen long after Romeo's departure.

At work in Blossom Plaza Home, Hari received word that Lewis Cantor and another man, Hondo Kendricks, had asked about Tara's incident.

The Russian whispered into Hari's ear in the corridor.

"I think the guy with Anna's brother was a thug. He had a gun." Hari stared strangely at the Russian, processing the information.

"What were they saying? Wait, how do you know the guy had a gun?"

"I'm Russkie. I know a jacket bulge when I see one. Anyway, I didn't hear anything specific. But he scared me."

They split up when they saw Supervisor Evans walking up the aisle.

Lewis Cantor, who had puffy eyes and lips from a beating the night before for not selling the book quickly enough, stared at himself in the bathroom mirror.

His call around the infamous rare book forgery community yielded zilch. So, now desperate, he called upon a benefactor he abhorred.

"My uncle was your supporter for as long as stars are in the sky. So, it's payback time, Rabbi."

Rabbi Chosky switched the phone call to the loudspeaker when Lewis's rising voice grated on his nerves at his Tel Aviv office.

"How can I be of help? Rabbi Levi was truly one of a kind."

"You received the sample copy of the documents I sent you. Right? Can you find me an interpreter? To use your words, Rabbi, the book is truly a one-of-a-kind item."

"Yes, I did. But the artifact trade in Israel and the whole Middle East is face-to-face. You do understand, don't you, my child?"

Lewis becomes irate. "I'm not your child. I was only asked to interpret drawings and doodling in a rare book, I think, that belongs to the old Latin era. Is that so hard to do?"

"I must confess, Lewis, I cannot interpret as you requested, but I may know people who can. But they need to see the original document. If I may ask, why are you doing this?"

Lewis rolled his eyes in exasperation. "I have a rich, Jewish-friendly client who needed to donate this to the Smithsonian but was eager to understand the tax implications, if you know what I mean," Lewis lied.

"Mail the original book, and I'll see what I can do."

Lewis stiffened.

Hari Hapa, across the street, had been tailing Lewis since the Russian revealed his possible involvement with Tara's demise.

A week later, in exasperation at the bookstore's back office, Lewis yelled at Rabbi Chosky on the phone.

"Where the hell are we, Rabbi? It's been over a week already."

Rabbi Chosky immediately dropped the phone call. Lewis redialed.

"Listen, Rabbi. I admit I was out of line earlier. Any progress?"

"Still working on it, Lewis. Be patient."

Lewis lost control again and started to yell.

"I want my leather-bound book back, Rabbi *Chokey*. You're useless to me."

Rabbi Chosky had already hung up. Lewis yelled at the dead phone.

Hari Hapa charged into the bookstore and found Lewis yelling in the back office. Hari looked around but saw no one.

"You, spineless worm, killed my sister. Why?" Hari yelled above Lewis's voice.

Lewis fidgeted, wary of Hari's right hand hidden behind his back, afraid Hari held a weapon.

Lewis arose slowly and waved his hands in surrender.

"Where is her leather-bound book? You're the only soul to see the book outside Tara and me."

Lewis stepped out from behind the desk. Hari motioned for him to sit down behind the desk.

"Who are those goons who assaulted you in the parking lot the other night, and why?"

Lewis's face betrayed nothing, and he instead pleaded,

"Don't throw away your life, Hari, hurting the likes of me. I'm not worth it."

"Why did you kill Tara?"

"So, what happens now?" Lewis asked.

"You confess, Lewis. That's what's next."

"I did nothing."

At an impasse, they stared at each other.

Unsure of what to do next, Hari backed up towards the door.

Lewis lunged at Hari, who easily sidestepped him.

Lewis crashed into boxes lined against the wall.

Hari then revealed the hand behind his back, holding a cell phone and recording.

"I got your confession on tape, bastard."

"You got nothing."

Hari hurried out of the bookstore.

Chapter 12

It was early morning in Tel Aviv's Goram Naphtali's majestic home on Rothschild Street.

Goram, though sitting at the head of a long dining table in his lounge, still towered over Avnar Barak and Paleography professor Erman Erturgu, who were perched on opposite ends of each other. They all rose as Rabbi Chosky walked in ahead of the maid.

The maid returned with a platter of steaming tea kettles and traditional Jewish tea mugs. The professor in a bow tie waved her off as she poured for everyone else.

The Rabbi placed Tara's book in the center of the table and pushed it to Goram, who sent it carelessly to the professor.

Professor Erturgu caressed the old leather covering lovingly, almost as if unwilling to open it. He eventually opened the book with everyone in suspended animation, awaiting his response. His facial emotion betrayed nothing as he immediately closed the book.

"I need overnight to decipher what might be a significant outcome."

The following evening, the gang was back in Goram's home except for the Rabbi.

Goram Naphtali, in surprise, regarded the normally stoic professor Erman Erturgu's excitement as he projected his mobile phone onto a wall. Avnar Barak found himself also expectant as the bowtied paleontologist flicked a green pointer onto the screen.

"The analyses you're about to see concentrated on recent hand doodles and drawings, not the ancient writings in the ledger. The study, though quicker than normal, revealed the old writings in the book were daily records of the ship voyage provision depletion and days left to reach their destination. I consider this section of the book routine and mundane."

"What was the ship's destination?"

Erman flatly chastised him, "That's immaterial to the broader significance of this immense discovery, Goram."

Erman, unapologetic, paused, looked around to gauge Goram's reaction, and then continued.

"The doodles represent when the writer was unsure how to extend drawings in one direction or another, literally doodling thoughts before they merged in the mind. The drawings were another matter in that they were not drawn sequentially on pages but after several permutations. I realized that was a long shot, but the sequence was logical."

Avnar forcefully interrupted, "Says who?"

Under the cover of darkness, Frieda and Abishak were back curbside at Doctor Lilly Chen's place, unaware of the company.

Joey and Hondo stood yards away as Avnar, Abishak, and Frieda, all in black suits carrying briefcases, walked to Doctor Lilly Chen's door.

Frieda knocked and displayed a fake FBI ID. Lilly lets them in.

Frieda closed the door behind the doctor and plunged a tranquilizer syringe into the doctor's neck. Avnar and Abishak caught her before she could hit the floor hard. Frieda left through the front door.

She returned, driving the stakeout car into the doctor's garage. Abishak and Avnar ensured the doctor fit in the boot and closed the lid.

Joey and Hondo tailed Frieda on Route 101. Abishak and Avnar, with a kidnapped Doctor Lilly Chen in the trunk, headed back to Lewis's apartment, where they were staying.

It was midnight. Lewis, Avnar, Abishak, and Frieda were deep into their drinking session in Lewis's apartment.

Doctor Lilly Chen remained unconscious in the car boot parked inside Lewis's gated apartment parking lot.

Outside, Joey and Hondo, on a stakeout in the early morning, watched Lewis's apartment. Joey became restless after he ran out of vape canisters.

"We should see what's happening with the body stashed in that car."

Hondo snapped at him. "To do what with her?"

"I don't know."

"No, Joey, you don't. We take them when the time is right."

At dawn, the sun began to color the sky a golden yolk, promising a gorgeous morning. Avnar tapped Frieda and Abishak awake while Lewis snored on the sofa.

The Israelis quietly gathered their belongings and snuck out of Lewis's apartment.

Abishak checked that Doctor Lilly Chen was still alive in the garage. She was.

He removed the doctor from the trunk and lumped her in the back seat next to Frieda.

The car drove off the premises, and Joey and Hondo were tailing it.

Goram defused the situation, preempting the professor. "I do."

"Thank you, Goram. My presentation is a guess, but a damn good professional guess." Erman returned to sit.

Goram and Avnar stared at the doodles and drawings on the screen.

"Do you think there's another entity out there, Avnar?"

Goram's giant leap of faith angered Erman. "You both ignored the broader implication of an alien presence on Earth. This book should not be a profit vehicle. If it is, you've missed the opportunity!"

The room went silent. Goram and Avnar looked scolded. Erman continued in a milder tone.

"I'm worried, Goram. Hence, we should keep the lid on this book until we understand its implications better; otherwise, we'll all end up in a nuthouse."

Avnar then made a quiet, conciliatory comment, surprising Goram and Erman.

"I think the professor's mumbo jumbo might be…"

Goram completed Avnar's thoughts. "Plausible?"

All three then sat back, digesting the enormous information just dispersed.

Erman realized something and faced off with Goram and Avnar.

"You're not thinking of going after another entity in the United States, right?"

Both men remained expressionless as the professor protested.

"No, we already have our hands full here with MAD and…" He trailed off.

***

LAX traffic was as congested as ever.

Lewis Cantor was restless and languished on the curb at arrivals. Minutes later, Avnar Barak, bookended by Abishak Terrel and Frieda Homel, walked out of the airport.

Yards behind, curbside, tailing Lewis, Joey Campo, in the passenger seat in a black Buick, watched a man hand off a brown paper bag to Avnar in stride. Hondo Kendricks in the backseat sneered as Lewis and the Avnar group took off—the black Buick tailing. Avnar noticed.

After a 22-mile drag on Route 405 South, Avnar head-tilted toward Lewis to exit the highway. He pulled into a Freight Company near the LA Port and parked beside a container-converted office at the company parking lot.

Avnar waved at Lewis to stay in the car as he, Abishak, and Frieda exited.

All three disappeared into the office for hours.

162

Lewis cursed at Avnar. "Fucking Bedouin."

Forty minutes later, Avnar, Abishak, and Frieda exited the container office behind a man in a hard hat, pointing at a distant ship in the harbor.

Soon, they walked towards Lewis.

Avnar commanded, "Let's go."

Lewis screeched his tires deliberately. Avnar ignored the tantrum.

Five hundred yards into the drive, Avnar forced Lewis to park yards away from the LA Port entrance and told him nothing.

Avnar walked into the port container depot area, unlocked container VJUT 876234-7, clicked a light switch, and inspected the hospital-converted bed next to a drip stand and a Johnny-on-spot near the door.

He turned off the light and walked out.

It was dusk outside Doctor Lilly Chen's cul-de-sac home, the pathologist who autopsied Tara, and it was getting even darker, just as the two ex-Mossads on stakeout preferred.

"Perfect," Frieda Homel gleefully uttered, chewing on colored candies, to her bored partner, Abishak Terrel.

The southpaw spook, Frieda, slurped aloud as she threw more jellybeans into her mouth, sitting on the passenger side to Abishak, watching Doctor Lilly Chen walk her small Terrier down the street, away from her home.

Frieda dropped the jellybean bag onto the dashboard and snickered at Abishak's evil eye before exiting the car.

Frieda jumped the fence into Doctor Chen's bungalow compound from the back.

She easily broke into the house.

She pulled her weapon, mounted with torchlight, and checked each room inside. The house was empty.

Frieda returned to the stakeout car as the doctor inserted keys into her front door lock.

Abishak looked at Frieda, questioning.

She smirks. "What? The place was empty, and she lives alone."

She reached for the jellybean bag on the dashboard. It was gone.

"What the hell?" she muttered and turned to face Abishak, who refused to look at her.

The jellybean bag lay under the car, below Abishak, whose back tire crushed the little sweets as he pulled away from the stakeout.

Under the cover of darkness, Frieda and Abishak were back curbside at Doctor Lilly Chen's place, unaware of the company.

Joey and Hondo stood yards away as Avnar, Abishak, and Frieda, all in black suits carrying briefcases, walked to Doctor Lilly Chen's door.

Frieda knocked and displayed a fake FBI ID. Lilly lets them in.

Frieda closed the door behind the doctor and plunged a tranquilizer syringe into the doctor's neck. Avnar and Abishak caught her before she could hit the floor hard. Frieda left through the front door.

She returned, driving the stakeout car into the doctor's garage. Abishak and Avnar ensured the doctor fit in the boot and closed the lid.

Joey and Hondo tailed Frieda on Route 101. Abishak and Avnar, with a kidnapped Doctor Lilly Chen in the trunk, headed back to Lewis's apartment, where they were staying.

It was midnight. Lewis, Avnar, Abishak, and Frieda were deep into their drinking session in Lewis's apartment.

Doctor Lilly Chen remained unconscious in the car boot parked inside Lewis's gated apartment parking lot.

Outside, Joey and Hondo, on a stakeout in the early morning, watched Lewis's apartment. Joey became restless after he ran out of vape canisters.

"We should see what's happening with the body stashed in that car."

Hondo snapped at him. "To do what with her?"

"I don't know."

"No, Joey, you don't. We take them when the time is right."

At dawn, the sun began to color the sky a golden yolk, promising a gorgeous morning. Avnar tapped Frieda and Abishak awake while Lewis snored on the sofa.

The Israelis quietly gathered their belongings and snuck out of Lewis's apartment.

Abishak checked that Doctor Lilly Chen was still alive in the garage. She was.

He removed the doctor from the trunk and lumped her in the back seat next to Frieda.

The car drove off the premises, and Joey and Hondo were tailing it.

Avnar parked at the isolated Los Angeles Port container shipyard storage area, and the Israelis headed towards container VJUT 876234-7, Frieda dragging along the semi-conscious doctor, Lilly Chen.

Avnar and Abishak, ahead, unlocked the container door. Joey and Hondo ran up behind them, guns blazing.

Avnar and Abishak returned fire and provided cover for Frieda, guiding dazed Doctor Lilly Chen toward the open container door.

A bullet grazed Frieda in the calf. She fell, dragging the doctor down, and returned fire as everyone ducked between containers, shooting.

Abishak snuck around and cut Joey and Hondo off while Avnar and Frieda kept them busy.

Abishak, from behind, took out Joey and Hondo.

Avnar and Abishak loaded Hondo and Joey's bodies into the container, heading back to Israel.

Chapter 13

Anna Cantor and other residents at Blossom Plaza Home regained lost physical abilities and cognitive impairments once depleted by dementia.

In addition, they demonstrated higher concentration levels when playing card games, showed significant appetite improvements, and had better physical agility, enough to play ping-pong.

Doctor Romeo Atkins, the NIA volunteer, made routine medical checkup rounds.

"Guess what the girls and I did today, doc?" Anna Cantor asked.

Imbued with excitement for no longer walking with a walker, Doctor Atkins had difficulty settling Anna down for the knee reflex check in his Blossom Plaza Home office, which Hari Hapa once termed his "closet office."

"You went jogging," the doctor joked.

"No, silly. We planted Geraniums, got our hands, knees, and clothes dirty..." She trailed off, leaned conciliatorily, and whispered, "The matron didn't like that."

Doctor Atkins played along. "Bad girl." She lapped it up.

Doctor Atkins cycled through her other reflexes, breathing, and observed a rectangular soft spot in her upper arm, to which she smiled.

"It's from a patch the matron gave us the other day. Didn't you get one?"

"Does it hurt?"

She shook her head.

With improved cognitive awareness, Anna then launched into stories of her youth and Lewis, her younger brother, recalling the excitement of arriving at LAX years ago.

Finally, Doctor Atkins cleverly concluded the examination and headed to the resident's R&R lounge.

His father smiled inside the playroom when he saw his son, Doctor Romeo Atkins, approach. Romeo patted the older man lovingly on the shoulder, then led him back to his office for a routine examination.

"Why do you have to do this, Sonny?"

"Mama said so, Pops."

"Where is she? Should I go fetch her?"

Romeo gently restrained his dementia-ridden father from leaving the examination room.

"I hear her coming, Dad."

"Okay," the senior Atkins concurred.

The older man settled down and submitted to the medical prodding.

Romeo checked his upper arm to see if he had patch markings similar to Anna's, but he didn't.

After his father had left, the doctor reviewed each test subject's record. Bells keep ringing in his head, his countenance changing with each revelation of miraculous medical improvement.

Finally, alarmed, he paused, hurriedly gathered his stuff and the documents, and rushed out of the nursing home.

Doctor Romeo Atkins cuts off a female driver, taking too long to fit perfectly into a parking slot. She yelled at him.

"Sorry," he mouthed as he rushed towards the NIA HQ building entrance.

Romeo knocked incessantly on a door.

"You've got only minutes, Romeo; I'm expecting a call from the NIH Secretary. What can't wait for later, Doctor Atkins?" the team leader inquired.

Romeo poked his finger at a tabulated section in a report. He hastily flipped it open on the desk to show unexpected improvements in the resident's mental, physical, and other ailments.

"I think we've got a problem at Blossom Plaza. The results are—" The team leader's phone rings.

"It'll have to wait." He shooed Romeo out, but not before Romeo peeled off a handful of Post-it notes. The team leader waited for the door to close before picking up.

Romeo quickly scratched the Post-it outside the door: *Strange, unexpected improvements in resident physicality. I'm worried.*

Romeo attached the note atop a copy of his latest report. He stuck his head in and left the item on the nearest table. The team leader, on the phone, eyed him something nasty.

Only a week after Doctor Romeo Atkins's visit, the alarm sounded about some people's sudden, unexplainable vigor. Residents in the shared space gawked at Anna Cantor's madness, banging endlessly on the glass wall that looked into the yard.

An elderly lady in a wheelchair, yards away, wondered, "What the hell is she doing?"

Other residents gathered around Anna's apparent meltdown, leaving ample space between them.

Anna, in turn, only saw a portal and wanted to get inside it. The residents then screamed and hollered when her banging increased, fearing she would hurt herself.

Supervisor Evans Square was full of opioids, evident from his dilated pupils. He staggered into the shared space, saw the same Whitemelt apparition as Anna, and rushed towards her, to everyone's chagrin.

A resident shouted, "Now we have two of them, two crazy people!"

Evans lunged to grab Anna's legs to prevent her from walking into the portal.

"Hold on, Anna, I've got you."

Evans yelled in pain and released Anna, who vanished into the portal.

He collapses on the floor, both arms burned and smoking.

Residents, aghast, backed off, afraid to touch him.

Doctor Atkins arrived at the Blossom Plaza for a routine visit and saw ambulances and police patrol cars in the parking lot, unaware of the melee inside.

Security refused to allow him entry at the gate.

He stepped aside and called the facility director, Joel Schummer. Moments later, Joel, still in shock, was at the entrance. He lets Romeo into the facility.

EMTs attended to Evans on the floor in the chaotic entertainment room shared space.

Romeo, in exasperation, looked for answers.

"Will someone please tell me what's happening? Where's my dad?"

He looked around and soon spotted his father, who showed disinterest amongst others, far from the chaos.

Romeo then saw Lewis and asked for Anna in confusion.

Lewis burst into tears and pointed to Joel Schummer to explain.

"She just vanished, doc!"

"People don't just disappear… I take that back. Did anyone see what happened?"

Joel pointed to the gathered residents around Evans and the EMTs. "They all saw it, Doctor Atkins."

"Saw what?"

A resident explained how Anna continuously banged on the glass wall and how Evans hurt himself trying to save her. "…and poof. Anna was gone, and the supervisor was writhing in pain. Weird."

"Gone where?"

The resident shrugged.

President Bender Castle listened to the NIH Secretary's summary of Anna Cantor's surreal disappearance at the Blossom Plaza nursing home. Bender signaled a question.

"Any sign of foul play?"

"None detected thus far, Sir."

Homeland Security Secretary, HSS, agreed.

"We have a subject in our care who suffered mysterious burns at the crime scene."

He then turned to his assistant sitting directly behind him and whispered into her ear. She left the Cabinet conference room immediately.

"Mister President, the intelligence community has all the information to investigate," he concluded.

"Burns to both arms, I heard. From what and where?" Someone asked.

"As we speak, my team is extracting information from the witness. So, we should have something soon."

The President sat back and glared intently at the HSS.

"No rough stuff. The citizen is a witness, not a criminal. From my briefing, he's a victim and a hero at best. As the hammer, you always see everything as a nail…"

The HSS shifted in discomfort, with an inconclusive facial expression of either glee or aversion. The President then turned to the NIH secretary for affirmation.

"I concur, Mr. President. The person is a victim."

"Where is he now?" the President pressed.

"Walter Reed, Mister President."

"Get to it then, fellas," the President commanded.

Once the door closed behind the President, all the Cabinet members were on their cell phones.

HSS called his assistant to confirm adherence to his earlier whispered order to evacuate Evans Square from the local LA hospital to Walter Reed National Military Medical Center, Bethesda, MD.

Leeloo dispatched Berlin to Walter Reed National Military Medical Center, Bethesda, MD.

HSS's assistant and two fierce secret service Agents alight from the helipad atop the Military Medical Center.

The hospital emergency crew rushed to remove the Evans Square gurney from the chopper.

Inside the hospital, the elevator arrived at the Walter Reed Hospital's twelfth floor.

A burly Secret Service Agent confronted Berlin, who was about to exit the elevator.

"Wrong floor," he announced.

Berlin pointed to the FBI Shield dangling on her chest. The fierce Agent didn't look.

"This floor doesn't exist to you, Miss."

He attempted to press the button to close the elevator door. Berlin grabbed his hand and assumed a combat stance. The HSS assistant, yards away, watching the confrontation, yelled a command.

"Soldier, escort the Agent to the office." She pointed to a location opposite Evans's room.

"Yes, Ma'am."

Berlin laid into the HSS assistant when she entered the room.

"Where are we? Bogota? I demand immediate access to Evans Square. He's our best shot to dismantle the frigging Whitemelt dumpster fire."

The assistant allowed the FBI Agent to vent, sitting a yard from Berlin.

"Feel better?"

Berlin sighed and sat back. "Yes."

The assistant extended her hand. Berlin ignored it.

"Now, Agent Berlin, why don't we let our bosses iron this access thing out? I gotta make a call." The assistant left the room. The door locked behind her.

Fuming, Berlin paced the room and then turned the doorknob. It was locked. Her face clouded over in abject fury. She stepped to the window to look at the vast hospital parking lot below, her back stiff as an ironing board. Moments later, the door opened. The assistant walked in and began to talk.

"You have access for half an hour only."

Berlin did not turn around. The assistant kept talking.

"The AG negotiated with the HSS—"

Berlin turned around, interrupting, "Blah, blah, blah."

She walked out of the room. The HSS assistant followed behind in bemusement.

The burly secret service Agent grudgingly stepped aside to allow Berlin to enter Evans Square's room, where the Blossom Plaza nursing home supervisor lied.

Both heavily bandaged arms rested on a string support hanging from the ceiling. Berlin pulled up a chair.

"That looks awful."

Evans wiggled fingers from both arms, sticking out of the bandages. "Not fun. Who are you?"

Berlin pointed to the shield on her chest.

"Same question, the same answer I'll give you too, Agent…" Evans leaned in closer. "…Yords?"

"Yeah, Yords. Just humor me, Mister Evans."

Evans wiggled around in discomfort. He lowered his right arm feverishly, scratching an itch on his face, neck, and other body parts. Berlin watched with horror.

"Are you okay?"

"No. These damn bandages. What do you want again?"

"Your story, Mister Evans. What exactly did you see?"

"I saw a horizontal, upward melting, waxy shimmer within a rectangular silvery panel that everyone called Whitemelt. I grabbed her legs. Anna was trying to climb into the thing," the discomfited patient nonchalantly stated, then thrusts out his arms towards Berlin.

"This is what I get for trying to help, although she was eager to go inside the milky thing."

"Then, why did you try to save her?"

"I don't know. I just…"

"Was there a fire that burned you?"

Evans glared at Berlin. "Lady, there was no fire. I burned when I touched her legs."

"Just like that?" Berlin sounded incredulous.

"Yes, just like that, Agent. Now, please, leave me alone."

Berlin sat back, contemplating where to take the interrogation next. The door opened, and the HSS assistant walked in with a crew of hospital personnel who filed into the room.

"Time's up, Agent."

A doctor injected Evans with a hypodermic needle. He slumped unconscious. Other personnel proceeded to dismantle wall equipment from the bed and the patient.

"Where are you taking him?" Berlin protested.

"Doctor is waiting for you," the HSS assistant announced to Berlin, pointing down the aisle to an office.

The doctor handed over Evans' medical records to Berlin. "Miss Prescott wants you to have this."

Berlin sat back and read the file, flipping through pages of Evans' battery of medical analyses, MRI, X-rays, and blood work that failed to uncover anomalies. His urine, however, showed elevated opioid metabolites.

Berlin looked up. "Is he a drug addict?"

The doctor was evasive. "His blood wasn't clean."

"So, he could have made up all the stuff. Right?" Berlin suggested.

"How, then, do you explain the burns?" the doctor challenged.

"There's that." Berlin concurred and then continued, "So, what happens now?"

"My involvement ends here, Agent. Have a good day." The doctor left the room.

Berlin remains seated, bamboozled.

It was baking hot in the Nevada desert, and heavy dust clouds swirled behind a black SUV speeding down the middle of the unpaved road. A sizeable rectangular metal slab whirred slowly open in the distance.

The vehicle lined up with the gaping hole, which soon swallowed the van containing Evans Square. The hole closed, leaving the terrain as if nothing had happened at the black site minutes earlier.

Evans was subjected to active interrogation techniques and tortured at the Homeland Security black site facility three levels below the surface.

He endured medical probes, lie detector tests, and other legally illicit measures behind a thick glass wall, all of which he continued to pass. As a result, the line blurred regarding his status as either a prisoner or a witness.

Chapter 14

Another bombshell Whitemelt dropped in Lansing, Michigan, two months after Goram Naphtali bought a Home Away From Home boarding house and dispatched antibiotics. Berlin rushed out to the Midwest.

It was late afternoon when FBI Agent Berlin Yords pulled into an abandoned trailer park outside Lansing, Michigan, with six trailers.

She walked up to Hunter Kist's trailer, about to knock, when a large man from behind rushed at her on her blind side. She felt his presence and flipped him hard in a Judo move as the trailer door opened.

An eight-year-old girl looked nonplussed at the man, now with a broken arm, groaning on the ground. The girl pointed. "That's crazy, Uncle Tyler."

Berlin massaged her aching legs, an old injury from the kidnap ordeal. Hunter appeared behind the girl, shooed her inside, and accused Berlin, "You don't look like an FBI Agent dressed like that."

Berlin straightened up in her dark jumpsuit and displayed her shield.

"Are you here about Grandpa?"

Berlin nodded.

Hunter headed inside the trailer. He returned with a tackle box and a fishing rod and drove to Rose Lake, Berlin, behind, where Grandpa Brody Kist disappeared.

"So, what happened?" Berlin asked at the Lake.

She wrinkled her nose, watching Hunter cast a line into the brackish river. Fishing was not her thing.

"No idea. Grandpa just showed up one day and requested to go fishing. We ain't done that in ages."

Hunter jiggled the line.

"What do you mean just showed?" she pressed.

Hunter turned to look at her as if she were stupid. "He's old and immobile for months, then called that week to go fishing."

"How was he when he showed up?"

Hunter stopped, held down the fishing rod with his foot, and turned to face her.

"Come to think of it. Grandpa was more agile than he'd been for a long time. Hm." He returned to fishing.

"So, he wasn't living with you?"

"Lady, are you…" Hunter's voice trailed off as he caught the *don't fuck with me* expression on Berlin's face.

"No, he lived at a nursing home," he quietly stated.

Berlin waited for him to continue. He didn't.

"Well?"

"Well, what?" he asked in surprise.

"The name." She gritted her teeth.

"Oh. Home Away From Home. It isn't far from here. Do you want me to take you?"

Berlin was already walking off.

Berlin winced in pain and caressed her right knee as she exited the rental car in the parking lot of the Home Away From Home facility in Lansing.

The security guard watched her stop for a few seconds through the tinted entrance doors to flick her legs as if shaking off bugs. She was stretching.

Then, after checking an appointment book, the bored sentry lets her into the waiting area. Minutes later, the director, Adele Tallas, led Berlin to her office.

"Did Brody Kist display any unusual behavior before his disappearance?" Berlin asked even before she sat.

"I don't know, Agent Berlin. Brody and some residents showed health improvements before the news of the disappearance hit."

"A copy of Brody's medical records will greatly help the Bureau, ma'am."

"It could, but unfortunately, the policy at this facility prohibits sharing our residents' biographical details."

"Not even if it helps solve this monumental global mystery, Miss Tallas?"

"That's Mrs., uh, Agent. Unfortunately, legal liability prevents me from helping you further," Adele proclaimed smoothly and continued, "I will let you interview residents, particularly Brody's friends, if that helps."

Berlin walked beside Adele to the shared space where residents relaxed, watched TV, and played games. Some did nothing.

Adele pointed out an old Spaniard friend of Brody's, playing cards with three other men.

Berlin interrupted the game to their delight. "Fellas, I need to talk briefly with him."

She guided the Spaniard to a corner wall where Adele waited out of earshot of others.

"Did anything unusual happen to Brody?" Berlin questions the old Spaniard.

"I don't think so, but I'm happy with the physical improvements since the new ownership. Who are you?"

"I'm Berlin Yords, FBI. Were you very close with Brody?"

"Close enough to play cards and watch TV. He could be nasty sometimes, though, especially since the new owners took over the nursing home."

Berlin looked quizzically at Adele. "What changes was he referencing?" the Agent challenged.

"The new owners, Silbert Correal Partners, hired me as the director of this facility a week after they took possession and changed the name to Home Away From Home."

Berlin called the FBI Forensic Accounting Analyst from her car, returning to LA after leaving the old folks' facility. "I need Forensic research on a company."

"Shoot! Hey, Berlin, how's…" His voice trailed off.

Berlin completed the sentence. "Primrose? My daughter?"

"Yeah, yeah, yeah. What a cutie!"

"She's with my parents in Sweden. But, listen, I don't have much time. The company is Silbert Correal Partners, which recently bought a nursing home named 'The Home.' They immediately changed the facility name to 'Home Away From Home.' How soon can I get this?"

"Couple of days tops. Say hi to Primrose."

"Will do." Berlin ended the call.

At the LA Times newspaper bullpen, a busboy trawling the internet caught a back story on The Owl, a local Michigan newspaper. It showed a picture of trailer park resident Tyler Kist, in an arm cast, claiming unprovoked assault by a female FBI Agent. On a hunch, the young reporter made a call.

"Is this Tyler Kist?"

"Who the fuck are you?"

"LA Times. Did an FBI Agent assault you?"

"What's it to you?"

"Citizenry abuse is counter-productive—"

Tyler interrupted, "Am I getting paid for this?"

The line went quiet. Tyler hung up. The phone rang back immediately.

"A couple of bucks, depending on how much detail you provide that I can publish."

"She fucking broke my arm, unprovoked. She was trespassing, so I tried to stop her and—"

"Hold on, Tyler; I have to record this... Go on."

The busboy located Carmine Bartel at the bullpen and dropped a printed copy of The Owl on his desk with 'Berlin Yords' written across Tyler's picture in a red marker.

Carmine scanned through old footage on his computer and found Berlin Yords as the young FBI Agent who solved a brutal kidnapping case, almost losing both legs and fatally losing her partner in the ordeal.

He called the FBI desk.

"Agent Berlin Yords, please."

"Why?"

"I'm Carmine Bartel of the LA Times. Is she available?"

"Please state your case, Sir."

"Can I speak with Agent…" The line went dead. Carmine called back immediately.

"This is the FBI LA office. How may I direct your call?"

Carmine recognized the voice. "Don't hang up. I want to confirm a story about Agent Berlin Yords' brutality of citizens."

The desk clerk puts Carmine on hold to call Berlin, only to get Berlin's voicemail. She patched Carmine through.

"Agent Berlin Yords, I'm Carmine Bartel of the LA Times. What happened in Michigan? My number is…"

Hunter Kist repeated the same story told to Carmine about his grandfather's disappearance in Lansing, Michigan.

Brody Kist's physical rejuvenation to fish caught Carmine's attention. He dug further.

"As I told the FBI lady, I had no idea why Grandpa showed up that day to go fishing. We ain't done that in ages." Hunter was adamant in front of the trailer.

"What do you mean just showed up?"

"What are you? Stupid or hard of hearing? He just showed up, Newspaperman!"

"How was he when he showed up, Hunter?"

"Come to think of it, Grandpa was moving more freely than before. Now, leave me alone."

"How do you think he miraculously regained his physical mobility?"

Hunter stared blankly at Carmine. "I got no idea what you just said."

"Perhaps if you let me inside, we can be more comfortable."

"No, can't do that, mister reporter. You all have that fake news thing going. I'm not falling for it. Trump don' told us!" Hunter turned to return to the trailer.

"Wait, wait." Carmine signaled to the cameraman, who took out a wad of dollar bills and extended the money to Hunter.

Hunter pushed his daughter beside him by the trailer door to get the money.

"What were you jabbering about before, mister?"

Carmine signaled the cameraman to resume shooting.

"How was your father able to walk without pain?"

"I don't know. Maybe there was some experiment thing at the Home."

"What home?"

"Haven't I already told you? Home Away From Home." Hunter turned to his daughter. "We're going inside, baby."

Carmine's protest for more time for questions was in vain.

Carmine instigated chaos at the Home Away From Home security entrance and instructed the cameraman to film when denied entry without an appointment.

"Don't stop filming. These fascists don't know who they're dealing with."

The security guard wielding a threatening baton yelled back at Carmine in front of the nursing home.

"Scream and yell all you want, California scum, just do it elsewhere."

"This is a free country, damn ignoramus," Carmine yelled back, looking to ensure the cameraman continued to film.

The guard, equally recalcitrant, didn't back off. "Damn right. Free country, Trump country, faggot."

A lady in a severe black suit opened the nursing home door, walked towards Carmine, and pretended that the commotion wasn't happening.

"How can I help you? I'm Adele Tallas, facility director."

"Really? That's all you have to say after all the abuse?"

"What abuse? I only see you and your crew attempt to trespass. Now, how can I help you?"

Carmine calmed down and instructed the cameraman to continue filming.

Adele waved a no-finger at the cameraman.

"I will only grant you access to the facility, but no camera or talking to residents."

She waited briefly and then turned around to march inside. Carmine hesitated. "Okay, okay. I accept."

Inside, Adele told Carmine the same story to Berlin, observing residents in the shared area. Carmine secretly signaled the cameraman to film without Adele's knowledge.

"What was Brody Kist like before his disappearance?"

"Normal, though, rumors swirled around that some residents showed health improvements before his disappearance."

"Is it true, Adele? Can I call you that?"

"No, call me Mrs. Tallas. I don't know why the residents' physical dispositions didn't improve. We cater well to our children."

"Your children?"

"Yes, our children. Are we done here, California?"

A resident on a walker intercepted Adele and Carmine. She shouted a question about the patch.

Carmine turned a questioning look at Adele. "What patch?"

Adele shrugged. "Some residents received an antibiotic patch. It's nothing special."

"Not everyone got one?"

"It was on an as-needed basis. Now, I have to ask you to leave."

Adele led the way out of the resident's standard room. The cameraman continued to film discreetly.

Carmine called the FBI office. He got Berlin.

"Thanks for taking my call, Agent. Can you confirm you broke Tyler Kist's arms for no reason?"

"Pardon me?"

"Tyler Kist, Brody Kist's eldest son, at a trailer park in…"

"Can we meet?"

"Can you just confirm the story, please?"

"No. We should meet. There's more to the story…"

"I'm pressed for time and must get my piece in…"

"Does the truth matter?" The line went quiet.

"Ten a.m. tomorrow, Circle Park." He hung up.

"Shit."

Once at the park, Berlin walked up from behind Carmine, who was smoking; he jumped.

"Carmine?"

He pointed them to a park bench. Both remained standing in front of the bench.

"Can I record?"

"No. Not until I hear the version you heard."

"Tyler's arm was in a cast, claiming you assaulted him for no reason other than he walked up to you to ask you not to trespass..."

"Did he happen to tell you that he snuck up from behind me and laid his hand on my shoulder?"

"Was there any witness?"

"What's that to you?"

"He plans to press charges."

"There was that eight-year-old kid. Hunter's daughter."

"That's stretching it, Agent."

"I don't know what to tell you."

"Meaning what?"

"It's still news."

"Yes, if it's told truthfully without any negative slant towards me."

"It's your word against his, Agent."

"The truth still matters. So?"

Carmine became cagey.

"I gotta go; my deadline looms." He walked away.

"Oh, I also saw Adele Tallas…"

That got Berlin's attention, who hurried after the reporter.

"And?"

"It didn't go so well…" Carmine began to jog away from Berlin, who thought about running after him again for a second but didn't.

The White House Press Secretary and a male official walked into a packed briefing room. She took the podium, but a voice from the press corps rang out before she could speak.

LA Times Ace reporter Carmine Bartel squeezed the Secretary.

"What Presidential action has occurred to combat the growing Whitemelt disappearances?"

Then, without looking up, the Press Secretary read a prepared statement.

"The immense intelligence apparatus of the United States has been busy at work, globally, gathering information to uncover the mystery. So, I will leave it there for now."

She looked up to face a hostile audience, multiple hands in the air, ready to grill her. Instead, she avoided Carmine's follow-up question by pointing to a foreign correspondent.

"Thank you, but what my colleague just asked has not been answered directly. What specific actions?"

The official behind the Press Secretary took over the podium.

"Current activities classified, but the President plans to address the nation in a few days. Meanwhile, Switzerland and the United States are struggling with this challenge. The UN has also undertaken measures to gather global data." He stepped off the podium.

"The immigration policy of this administration has been heralded not only by our friends but also by adversaries, including China and—"

Carmine Bartel of the LA Times interrupted,

"I think China should address the Uyghur incarceration before any immigration comments, but that's not even the present issue confronting us all. I repeat the question: What's President Castle done about American citizens' spurious and mysterious disappearances?"

A groundswell of agreeable murmurs courses through the press briefing room. The Press Secretary waved them to quiet.

"President Bender Castle's strong leadership is digging into those unexplained vanishings in Los Angeles,

California, and Lansing, Michigan. Other global reports have forced all arms of the United States intelligence community on deck."

She stopped and pointed to a reporter amongst many with their hands raised to ask questions.

"You practically said nothing. What has the President done to contain people fearing they might be next to poof, disappear into thin air?"

The female reporter challenged the secretary, but before she could answer, Carmine interrupted again, "If the President cannot prevent disappearances, he could at least prevent a decorated FBI Agent, Berlin Yords, from beating up a defenseless citizen into an arm cast whose grandfather recently vanished."

A collective gasp emanated from the room, which then quieted as the Press Secretary gathered her thoughts, only to deny the knowledge.

"This is news, a grave accusation, and injustice that this administration will not tolerate. Besides, it's unfair to ambush, grandstand, and interrupt incessantly, as Mr. Bartel has done today. It's quite disturbing."

The room erupted with follow-up questions. Carmine Bartel, undeterred, ramped up the discussion. "Miss Yords claimed she was attacked from behind, and the only witness is an eight-year-old child. My report will be published tomorrow morning."

The briefing dispersed with loud murmurs amongst reporters as the Press Secretary walked off the stage.

Leeloo Chang and Berlin Yords, remorseful for being called in, listened to the angry AG in a borrowed conference room. He flew in from DC the previous night.

"We have now become the laughing stock of the clandestine apparatus, maiming citizens we swore to protect and prevent from vanishing. I'll never live this down."

"I'm so…" Berlin began to say. Leeloo glared at her to be quiet, but the AG wanted to know.

"Let her tell her side of the story, Loo." He led them to a central conference table.

"Tyler Kist came up behind me as I approached the trailer where Hunter Kist, his younger brother…" she completes her recall. The AG looked at Loo.

"I don't think she's at fault." Loo seemed surprised, pleased, and angry simultaneously.

She said, "I agree, but now we have to get a retraction from the LA Times."

"That'd be a bear, Loo,"

Berlin interjected. "I'll talk to him…"

Loo interrupted her. "I thought you already did."

"Yes, boss, but I think our lines got crossed..." The AG raised his hands for them to stop. He got up.

"Loo, solve it. I have another meeting coming up."

Both ladies vacated the conference room for the Attorney General.

Back in Leeloo's office, a floor below, the ADIC was still furious for being hauled in to defend herself in front of her mentor and boss.

"I was advised to be careful in my choice for this case. But what did the great Chang do? I chose the one Scandinavian petit pois to muddy the waters. I bet that one-eyed, patch-wearing, short CIA dildo, Barry DaSilva, is gloating. Fuck me!"

Leeloo stopped pacing and planted herself, hovering over the cowering Berlin.

"You pulled the wrong tooth this time, Berlin."

The ADIC seemingly calmed down, pulled up a chair, and sat before Berlin.

"What happened?"

"Tyler Kist jumped out of..." Berlin stopped and then continued. "Boss, give me a chance to fix this..."

"No, get that dickhead reporter in here in the next two days by any means necessary. I need to understand why he outed you."

Leeloo returned to sit behind her desk, calm as a pissed-off cobra.

Leeloo immediately started to work on documents on her desk. Contrite, Berlin remained with a blank face.

Minutes later, Berlin gathered herself and headed out. Leeloo spoke as Berlin pulled the door handle to exit, "Two days."

Berlin's spine stiffened. She stood up straighter and returned to the desk with a determined stance.

"Ma'am, Carmine Bartel will be in your office two days or earlier."

Their eyes locked for several seconds, and then Leeloo spoke.

"What are you waiting for, then?"

Berlin hauled ass out of the office.

Berlin walked into the LA Times bullpen and stood directly behind Carmine, giving him a start again.

"You've got to stop doing that."

"What?"

"Sneaking up on people."

"Let's talk outside." She didn't wait for an answer.

Carmine, smoking, explained that he had a deadline and had to do something provocative for his editor.

"Like throwing me under the bus?"

"I'm sorry, but it's done."

"No, Carmine. I had my ass chewed off a day ago by the AG. LA Times will write a retraction."

"That's how you got into this mess in the first place, Agent Yords. You're too pretty for that."

The poor reporter just hit a raw nerve. Berlin, already walking away, swung back.

"Asshole. Without retraction by tomorrow, I will re-dedicate my life to making your existence unbearable."

"Is that a threat?"

"Yes, and a promise. I guaranteed my boss you'll sit in front of her in two days or less to explain why you outed me, so…" Her words trailed off because of how angry she was.

She crossed the busy street, walking rapidly.

A block later, a young man tried to grab her attention from behind by tapping her shoulder. She swung around fast, twisting his wrist into submission. When she saw him cringing in pain, she released her grip.

"I'm sorry. You shouldn't touch people you don't know."

"Shit, that hurts. You FED or something?" She ignored him.

"Who are you? And step back, please."

He moved back out of her personal space.

"I'm a busboy."

She drew a blank.

"LA Times, I saw you talking with Carmine." He brought out his ID. Berlin perused it quickly and professionally, returning it while saying nothing.

"Do you have a problem with Carmine?"

Berlin sized him up. "What's it to you?"

"He stiffed me on a job. He was supposed to share a byline credit for my original story find, but he didn't, and it wasn't the first time, not just me…"

"What? You want payback?" Berlin started walking off, and he followed her. She turned around.

"Whatever you want, I want no part of it." Berlin quickened her pace.

"He gambles too much and misses deadlines…"

Berlin stopped. "I'll buy you coffee."

"Yes, Ma'am."

The following morning, Berlin waited early in front of the LA Times office door for Carmine to show up. She called him to the side and showed him two IOUs totaling ten grand.

"Now, I can ask those guys to quash these or act upon them by the end of today because it's my deadline for you to meet my boss and write a retraction to your story."

Carmine paled. Berlin stuck her business card in his pocket.

"Her address is written behind my card." She walked off.

The retraction of the FBI Agent Berlin Yords' brutal encounter with Tyler Kist was at the bottom of the first page of the LA Times the following morning.

Chapter 15

Christ, the Redeemer, is an art deco statue that looms large over Rio de Janeiro, Brazil. At night, its spectral arms give way to the infamous, terraced Favela homestead.

The great artwork would have been amazing during this period if not for Goram's latest boarding home acquisition in the populous country that recently recorded the first case of Whitemelt in Latin America.

A pimply youth janitor loitered at the Restful Boarding Home dimly-lit aisle holding a broom and spying on a nurse who let herself into the secure pharmaceutical storage room. He hurried to watch her through a glass door and open a cabinet full of medications. She spun around, feeling eyes on her. He ducked just in time.

He brushed against the nurse to steal her keys as she passed him in the aisle.

The next afternoon, he handed Eugenio Machado a brown paper bag in front of his Favela home and gave the kid 100 Real. The kid grumbled in Portuguese, "Is that it, old man?"

"Fuck off," Eugenio barked at the young man.

He backed off and cussed at the older man, "I hope your old dick falls off."

Eugenio pulled off a shoe and threw it at the fleeing youth.

Eugenio's wife, Silvia, cooked in the kitchen, yakking away on a cell phone.

The tiny kitchen jutted off a lounge, where a shabby divan lay against the wall directly adjacent to an old black-and-white TV set.

The four walls lay bare but for a hand-drawn picture of the Christ the Redeemer statue.

She dropped the phone into her apron pocket and yelled as steam bubbled off a tall aluminum pot on the stove.

"You okay, honey?" she called out to him.

"What was that?" The voice floated in from an unseen body.

She screamed louder and cocked her ear for an answer. Then, she hurried toward the bathroom when there was no response. She poked her head inside.

On a break, Eugenio sat on the toilet bowl, removed the vial and hypodermic needle from the brown paper bag, filled the syringe, and injected it into his arm. He then removed an antibiotic transdermal patch from the blister and stuck it to his upper arm as the door opened.

"What the hell is that blue patch?"

"Shut the fuck up, woman." He returned to his chores in the bathroom.

Silvia glared at him and suggested, "Why not use the electric saw?"

He leaned over a half-full, bloody bath with a hacksaw, lazily sawing at a headless human torso.

He paused, got up roughly, pushed her aside, and left the bathroom.

She followed, cursing under her breath, "You are a stubborn, stubborn man," before he pushed her out of the way en route to the corridor.

He felt and rubbed a curious welt behind his earlobe as he walked.

"Why don't you tell your people to send someone younger for the job?" she nagged.

"Eugenio?" she called out loudly for attention. He ignored her.

She seethed with anger and watched him open the basement door.

He flipped the wall light switch to a staircase that led to the basement, and she stared at him as he descended the steps. Just as he reached the landing, a shimmering, cloudy portal appeared before him, into which he disappeared.

Silvia saw the portal; her face contorted in fear. She lost her balance, toppled down the steps, and landed heavily, snapping her femurs before fainting.

Minutes later, she woke up in abject pain, retrieved her cell phone, hesitated briefly, and dialed the emergency call.

Police and ambulance activities descended upon the poor community, where eager onlookers disrupted law enforcement work. Police led Silvia outside, handcuffed her to the gurney, and carted her into an ambulance.

The police officers and CSI personnel sorted out the dreadful scene inside the home as they inspected and collected evidence.

Silvia remained defiant in the hospital recovery room, where a senior detective questioned the disagreeable patient.

"You're going to jail for a long time for butchering a human body. Why?"

"I don't know what you mean. Where's my Eugenio?" Silvia struggled to lift herself off the worn hospital bed with one hand, handcuffed to the railing.

"Whose body was it?" The detective leaned closer, and Silvia reared back, agitated.

"Eugenio went into a white cloud in the basement. Has he come back?"

The detective explained, "You were the only one home when the ambulance arrived to attend to your call. The EMT alerted the police when they saw what you did."

"You're crazy. Why wouldn't you believe me?" Silvia said, lying back, face away from the cop.

The detective got up and checked the handcuffs.

"I'll be back in the morning for more questions. I cannot believe a woman like you can hack up a human being," the detective surmised as he left the room.

Silvia, with her eyes shut, pretended to be asleep.

The detective was back again at the hospital the following morning.

"Let's say I believe you had a husband. Did he use drugs?"

Silvia became remorseful. "Not more than anyone else. You know, the blue pills."

"Viagra?"

"Yes. Eugenio attached the thing to his arm," she told the confused cop.

"Madam, Viagra only comes in pills, not transdermal," the detective clarified.

"What?"

In utter confusion, Silvia waved her free hand in the air.

"Whatever you say, policeman."

The detective read off his little notebook.

"These are what we found in your home, specifically the bathroom. Syringes, an empty blister package labeled 'antibiotics,' a crumpled brown sandwich bag, an empty fentanyl package, etc. Nothing there about Viagra."

"Where is my Eugenio?" Silvia wailed.

The detective walked to the window, returned, and spoke without turning around, "Who is your husband's drug dealer?"

Silvia stopped crying but said nothing.

The detective walked back to her bedside. "Your jail term can be reduced drastically, or you may not even have to serve time, depending on your cooperation. So, I ask again. Who supplied your husband with his illicit drugs?"

"The janitor," she whimpered.

"Who?" He leaned in.

"The janitor. He worked at the old people's place."

She heaves a sigh of relief.

"What old people place?"

She paused in regret before answering, "Restful Boarding Home. That's all I know."

***

UN-WHO Director-General Tambo Gilu watched Eugenio Machado's disappearance reenactment video in his New York office. The footage showed body parts bobbing as the Brazilian CSI poked around the bloody bath. The camera then tilted to the top of the basement staircase, from which Eugenio vanished into the Whitemelt, and Silvia fell, sustaining multiple leg fractures.

Police interrogation video showed Silvia confirming her husband, Eugenio, got his drug supplies from a janitor at the Restful Boarding Home in Rio De Janeiro. Pictures of items pulled out of the bathroom trash bin showed discarded hypodermic needles, empty vials, and a blister pack containing one remaining antibiotic patch.

The blister pack has no printed name. Queried about what happened to her husband, Silvia burst into tears, explaining how she fell down the stairs when Eugenio entered a Whitemelt that appeared at the basement staircase landing.

Tambo folded the report, inserted it into a brown envelope and CD, and then stared into space, still holding the incredible diplomatic dossier. He soon snapped out of it and got on the phone with an Interpol Lieutenant. He demanded updates on the Swiss Alps Whitemelt.

"The CIA has been unpleasant, my friend. Anything?" Tambo confided.

"Good to hear your voice, Mon Ami. Unfortunately, nothing. But we got a visit from the Vatican."

"Vatican, Vatican? Like in Rome?" Tambo was incredulous.

"Self-preservation, I'm told." The Interpol Lieutenant fails to hide a snicker.

The phone remained quiet for longer than usual. "Monsieur Gilu, are you still there?"

"Yes, just thinking. Who's on the case?" the Director-General asked.

The Interpol Lieutenant's smile was pleasant at the question. "My best man, Lens Kasper."

"We must have something soon or face crucifixion," Tambo lamented.

"No one is nailing anybody, my friend." The French lieutenant responded.

"By the way, why was the Pope interested in this?" Tambo pressed.

"I don't know, but when people disappear, we all start to believe." The Frenchman suggested.

"Really? I'm a Muslim."

"What?" The Frenchman asked in confusion.

"Au Revoir Lieutenant." Tambo hung up.

Since Switzerland Whitemelt happened, he's attempted to quietly lobby his international spook contacts to follow the Whitemelt story; today, he'd summoned the UN DG.

Barry knew Tambo was always abegging for funds to prop up perhaps the most toothless international body Barry knew, the UN, an opinion he shared freely.

The CIA Director's office door clicked open, and Tambo Gilu leaned in. "Director?"

"Sit down," Barry DaSilva commanded the Ethiopian UN-WHO Director-General.

Tambo, still standing, started to talk, "Now, Barry—"

Barry interrupted, tugged at his eye patch, and pointed the other finger at the chair opposite his desk. "Sit down, Gilu, before I throw you out."

Tambo fidgeted with brief indecision and then cowered into a chair.

Barry leaned across, conciliatory. "I understand chaos begets cowardice, but grit is a call. No?"

Gilu did not know what Barry said, but acquiesced in confusion. "Right?"

"How many of these Whitemelt reports are on the WHO global record, Tambo?"

"The great, almighty CIA is clueless, Mr. Director?"

"How many, you little ingrate?" Barry yelled.

Tambo squirmed. "Statistics require manpower, that in turn—"

"Why, you beggar thief!" Barry angrily arose from his massive desk and stormed towards Tambo. "I dare you to panhandle me again, Gilu!"

"Four," Tambo stammered.

"What?"

"Four global Whitemelts suspected to date," Tambo clarified.

"UN conducting any investigation?" the chief spook probed.

"Barry, we don't have the United States' promised funds."

Barry yelled, "Get out."

"Barry, this is highly unprofessional." Tambo scrambled off the chair.

Barry discreetly clicked the door open, his head already down to write a memo.

Tambo halted briefly at the door. "INR will benefit from what's coming globally, but your attitude, Barry?"

"You can suck INR all you want, Tambo, but that section can't blow themselves even if they had multiple ten-foot cocks," Barry spat without looking up.

"We'll see about that," Tambo mumbled.

Barry looked up in anger and clicked the door shut.

"Moron."

Knowing Barry would secretly plot ways to undermine him in the global court of public opinion, the UN DG took preemptive action days later.

Tambo Gilu walked onto the green marble background podium of the UN Communication Center Hall, buzzing with noise.

"Gentlemen," he spoke without looking up.

The noise persisted. Tambo Gilu's voice rose commandingly, "Gentlemen."

The din began to soften. Tambo rifled through pages on the podium. He looked up with an endearing smile, exposing the gap in his top front teeth.

"The increasingly loud noise of reported global disappearances has shaken the world. I'm here to address all of your concerns. I will start by saying the disappearance known as Whitemelt threatened our democracy."

Tambo stopped talking as the distracted audience watched the large conference room door close behind a group of protesters led out of the podium. The room returned to calmness.

Tambo looked at the packed audience, including many high-level United States government officials.

CIA director Barry DaSilva and FBI Agent Berlin Yords bookended Leeloo Chang, ADIC FBI.

Tambo continued, "Thus far, there have been four reported global Whitemelt cases."

Behind him, a large digital screen showed abbreviated snippets of reported disappearances at the Bernese-Oberland ski resort in Switzerland and the LA Zoo.

"For now, the Interpol and other global law enforcement agencies are geared up and investigating, but specific details will not be part of this update. I shall keep the various global governments informed as news comes in."

He stopped briefly and tugged at his earpiece. Then, guarded by his security details, he walked off the podium without asking questions.

The confounded audience arose, and the room's noise level increased. Finally, people gathered in groups to talk.

Leeloo stayed in New York for a couple of days, visiting her family in Chinatown, then drove to DC to have dinner with his least favorite person to renew her "shmoose" superpower with the politicos. One such cringeworthy person was Barry DaSilva, whom she considered a perv.

The lighting was mellow in the fine upscale Washington DC restaurant amidst the quiet, gilded crowd. Leeloo Chang and Barry DaSilva, almost hidden from view, sat at a corner table away from windows and doors.

She smirked. "Cone of silence dropping soon?"

Barry tugged at his eye patch. "If necessary, Loo."

She squirmed at the nickname "Loo" and then looked around. "Spooky, even for you, Barry."

Barry smiled. "You never disappoint, Loo."

She hardened. "Don't call me Loo." If surprised, Barry didn't let it show.

"We eating or pussy dipping, Barry?"

Barry giggled. "My wife calls me the two inches of terror." Leeloo ignored the levity.

A waiter appeared. Barry turned to the waiter.

"The usual for me, same for the lady, Gomez."

"House salad for me, *Go...mez,*" she retorted.

"Five minutes, Gomez?" Barry suggested; the waiter nodded and walked away.

Barry devoured his large steak, and Leeloo played absent-mindedly with the salad.

"Let Berlin work unhindered, Barry."

"If it remains domestic, your wish, Loo, is my command." Barry chomped at the bloody carcass. Leeloo was irate.

"Rubbish. It's already global but remains domestic for the United States. So, stay off of her, Barry. And don't call me Loo again."

Barry stopped eating and tugged at the eye patch. "I'm Rabon Solo."

She looked lost. "Who?"

"Why don't we let it all play out, Loo?"

Leeloo, slow and deliberate, walked off without another word.

Leeloo fumed on the phone while speeding toward the Washington, D.C., airport car rental return. She punched Berlin's name into the dashboard cell phone.

"Hello," Berlin answered.

Leeloo jumped right in. "CIA plans to encroach on Whitemelt investigations; be wary." Leeloo hung up.

"Hello, boss. Hello?" Berlin, irate, resets at the gun range and fires off rapid shots in exasperation.

"Shit," she cussed, burning her hand with the hot gun muzzle.

Chapter 16

Goram Naphtali walked off Gimhae International Airport. Ten hours later, he legally owned Gracefully Eternal Home in Busan, South Korea.

The city of Busan, South Korea, began the return to a certain semblance of normalcy post-COVID-19 Pandemic. Tourists shopping buoyed the happiness meter around town.

But for Park Yu Soon, it might be winter as he shuffled down the aisle inside Gracefully Eternal Home on Cheongsapo-ro, Haeundae-gu, to visit his wife of fifty years, Chae-Won, suffering from uterine cancer complicated with dementia.

Sung Tu Sang, the facility director, walked up to Park Yu Soon, caressing his unconscious wife's arm on her sickbed.

"Sir, residents are poised to receive transdermal antibiotics, which are also available to spouses if you're interested."

An hour later, Park Yu Soon was experiencing violent willies as he walked on the street. An oval welt appeared behind his right ear.

It's been two weeks since Chae-Won succumbed to her illness.

Park Yu Soon, yards away, atop a sandy mound at the Busan beach, watched tourists and detested the luxurious homes hanging off the cliffs.

"The wind gods will topple you all to the never, never land soon," he prayed aloud as he zipped up his summer jacket.

Then, a sporadic autumn wind gust blew by. He cursed at the wind god, Yeongdeung, as he removed lunch from a plastic bag.

"Make up your mind, you silly deity," he admonished.

He bit off a Kimchijeon chunk loaded with meat and seaweed fried in butter and smiled pleasantly, praising the same wind god.

"About time, Mister Deity. Thank you."

After three hours, Park Yu Soon struggled to get up, his bones creaking awake from the prolonged inactivity. He talked to his wife as he trekked down the dune.

"The sandwich wasn't as good as you used to make it, Chae-Won, but decent enough."

He had a recall. "Oh, oh, Chae-Won, remember today? Of course, you do. It's the anniversary of our first kiss on this beach."

He giggled, careful to navigate the narrow path away from the beach.

Back in town, Park Yu Soon walked through Gukje Street, the old downtown Busan market, and acknowledged familiar vendors with endless bows. Then, he crossed into the residential zone, where tiny homes began to intrude.

He stopped at his wooden gate, which had a signpost that read, "Gudu Suseongong, cobbler, his home." The small garden was overgrown with weeds.

His neighbor across the street saw him, hurried over, and helped open the gate.

"They don't build them like you anymore. And thank you for your kindness over the years," Park Yu Soon said.

"I'm duty-bound." The neighbor walked back across the street to his home.

Park Yu Soon's living room was full of shoes arranged in stacks around a central table crammed with shoe repair tools.

Pictures of all types of shoes from across the world adorned three walls.

The fourth wall displayed a single pair of shoes encased in a glass box below an old black-and-white picture of Chae-Won, his wife at 20 years of age, in traditional Korean garb. Below the image was a small shrine with burning candles and unlit incense.

He stopped in the middle of the room, stood slightly more erect, took a 360-degree view, and settled on the box shoe above his wife's picture.

Finally, he knelt at the shrine, lit the incense, and talked to the image of his wife as the floor underneath him dissolved into Whitemelt, swallowing him.

It was now dark outside. The neighbor across noticed Park Yu Soon's home remained unusually dark at night. He went over to check and called the police when, after repeated knocks on the door, there was no response.

In a stunning, peaceful ambiance inside, the cops inspected the house thoroughly, failing to locate Park Yu Soon, nor did they observe any sign of disturbance.

***

The crowd began to gather early on this fateful Monday morning in front of the White House, carrying placards protesting the Bender Castle administration's weak immigration strategies.

By noon, the crowd had swelled to include a non-diverse group, mostly middle-aged white folks carrying more extreme placards. The cards called for all Mexicans to return home to their Tortillas and Black bastards to return to the African jungle and reunite with their Chimpanzee ancestors.

The 3:00 p.m. afternoon news began to capture the very incendiary placards. A famous TV news anchor showed a clip of their reporter talking to a protester who claimed to be from Kentucky and carrying a placard showing President Bender Castle's caricature offering bananas to his black cabinet members.

"I thought this protest was for the missing Whitemelt victims. At least, that's what the distributed leaflets claimed." The reporter asked.

"I ain't here for that. Those people are already free from this Guacamole-loving President." The protester walked away.

The reporter found another protester carrying a placard.

"Sir, are you deliberately trying to incite a race riot?" she asked a Kentucky protester.

"You Liberal do-gooders will soon realize race-blending will never stick. So, I ain't starting nothin' that ain't already here."

"What will you do if BLM and Antifa start to counter-protest?"

The Kentucky protester boasted. "I got somethin' for them, black bastards."

The interview went from bad to worse when other protesters threw water bottles at the reporter and her cameraperson. Both backed away.

On the evening TV news, a notable anchor wondered aloud about the FOX network's take on the protest at the CNN studio.

The FOX network showed old footage of President Trump's rallies in Mississippi, but there was no word about the burgeoning protest.

It was now 5:00 p.m., and the WhiteHouse had become a war zone with thick, heavy smoke of tear gas in the air, massive police presence, and loud wailing ambulance Sirens arriving and departing.

Several protesters, old, young, black, white, and Hispanic, were bloodied as EMT groups struggled to contain the mayhem.

Network TV stations blanketed the airwaves with news of civil disobedience's massive breakdown and the chaos of law and order. FOX networks continued to rebroadcast old Trump rallies.

Back at the WhiteHouse, the protest chaos deteriorated into a higher gear when the Black Lives Matter, BLM, Antifa, and other counter-protesters violently engaged the White Supremacist hooligans, ripping the harsh placards from each other's hands, resulting in fistfights. It was only extraordinary that gunshots didn't permeate the melee.

Not seen since the race riots of the 60s, police dogs now began to tear through the crowd for the first time. The primarily female police dog handlers formed a circle separating the two groups, with berserk dogs barking in an atmosphere full of white tear gas to witness the most extensive law breakdown in half a century.

A deep rumble began to bellow everywhere, causing protesters from both sides to halt and slowly look around for the sound source.

Above, a large slant tear began forming in the clear blue sky and expanded by the minute. Everyone began to look at the sky when a large white package fell from the sky and tore through the police circle. The crash was so loud it drowned out the entire melee.

For a precious few seconds, the only audible noises were the dogs barking and whimpering. After that, everybody took off in all directions, further agitating the already manic dogs, dragging most female handlers.

Protesters became spectators and stayed away from the package dropped from the sky.

Finally, a circle formed around the box, one hundred yards away from the object.

Additional massive police arrival dissolved the most intriguing protest ever.

Half an hour later, a five-person CSI crew in complete white hazardous material handling suits approached the object.

Another half-hour later, the package revealed the body of an elderly Asian male whom the FBI later identified as the disappeared body of Park Yu Soon of Busan, South Korea, a reported Whitemelt victim months earlier.

It was already late evening when Leeloo called the AG, her mentor.

"Sir, the Vatican is now investigating Whitemelt in Europe and coming here to—" The AG interrupted,

"Calm down, Loo, and it's all happening towards the same goal."

Leeloo snapped, "Whose idea was this?"

"Not mine, Loo, but that's immaterial."

"But that's—"

The AG cuts her off, "Loo, deal with it. Let me make some calls. Don't do anything stupid while I'm gone."

It was now very late in the evening when AG called the WhiteHouse Chief of Staff.

"Why is the Vatican sticking its religious hands under my Whitemelt investigation's skirt?"

The consummate politician, the chief of staff, smoothed the news over, this being the first time he'd learned of Rome's intervention.

"We cannot police the whole world, but I'll reply soon. Meanwhile, no rash actions, you hear me? The President is in a fucking foul mood." he hung up before the AG could respond.

The AG cursed, looking at his dead phone. "Son of a bitch."

He dialed Leeloo.

"This situation is developing fast in the wee hours of the morning, blindsiding the WhiteHouse, too. So, proceed cautiously with the Vatican. The White House would feed you to the press if things went south because the powerful religious PAC's hand is all over this. So, come to dinner next week. My wife misses you."

Leeloo hung up and paced her office in contemplation.

The Papal, engrossed with the global religious protest of random disappearances, sent the lone Vatican Detective, Enzo Lupara, an Italian Army veteran, to the United States for information sharing.

Enzo was instructed to limit his assignment to only his job: to gather enough information to appease the Pope's angst about the unexplained global events.

But his FBI liaison, ADIC Leeloo Chang, was not a fan. She considered the Roman presence an intrusion into her investigation already assigned to her Agent and mentee, SAIC Berlin Yords, who picked up the visitor at LAX.

"Bongiorno Señorita."

She responded, "Hello, welcome."

Berlin, inside immigration, walked Enzo through easily with her FBI credentials. Both hardly exchanged words.

On the drive to the DTLA FBI office, Enzo tried to engage Berlin, whose terse responses signaled to the Roman to be quiet.

"Was your trip pleasant?" Leeloo asked as soon as both detectives settled into her office.

In his perfect but accented English, he said, "Ladies, I don't necessarily wish to be here, but when one of our citizens vanished in Switzerland and others across the globe, including here in America, the Pope was forced to act because many are worried and scared. So, as soon as I'm done, a few days at most, I shall leave."

Leeloo smiled. "We need all the help we can get, and you're welcome…" She pointed to Berlin, who nodded.

"Anything to add?"

"Not at the moment; we just need to find him an office and…."

Leeloo cuts in, "He'll share your office."

Berlin remained perfectly expressionless. "Of course."

Leeloo got off her chair to stare out the window, which Berlin had come to understand meant the end of the meeting.

Leeloo spoke without turning around when the door knob was twisted.

"I'll introduce Enzo to the AG tomorrow. Seven, sharp."

The first few days were normal, with Berlin updating Enzo on her Whitemelt investigations. And then, another global shoe dropped in Milan.

***

Despite the sun's effort to break through, a light gray and opaque mist hung above the Milan Cimitero Monumentale di Milano in Italy.

Sweaty from work carrying a broom and ready for home, an old cemetery maintenance man, wrapping up for his day, squinted at a figure face up atop a grave from afar.

He wondered aloud to himself, "What is that?"

Now closer, he opined in disgust. "Drunkard, no less."

His grip tightened on the broom handle as he encircled the body, nudged at the drunk, and fled once a realization of death registered.

Then, finally, he exclaimed, running away from the body, "Santa Maria!"

He fumbled, dropping his cell phone several times before getting steady enough to call the Carabinieri.

"There's a dead body at the cemetery!"

The desk officer beckoned a colleague to listen to the cemetery call again, not believing his ears.

The desk sergeant goaded him. "You want the police at the cemetery to see a dead body?"

They laugh at the old cemetery worker.

Their laughter irritated the old-timer, who covered the mouthpiece before letting loose a stream of profanity and returning to the call.

"Yes, a dead body, you dolt."

The now-angry cop did not take kindly to being called an idiot. "Your name, Sir?"

"Ask your mother."

The cop still did not take it seriously. They hung up.

He took a picture of the corpse lying on the gravestone and called the police again. The same cop answered.

"It's you again, it's too early to be drunk and—" He interrupted,

"Why don't I send you a picture?"

The cop, in jest, gave the older man his cell phone number.

"Merda Santa!" the cop yelled once the picture dropped in his cell phone.

Heavy police presence dominated an hour later, surrounding the Count's son's grave.

Carabinieri cleared the path for an old black Bentley.

The driver glided out to open the back door for the Contessa.

She fainted once the Count's body came into view, lying perfectly still atop their son's grave, dead twenty years earlier.

The Count's reappearance dropped another global bombshell to reshape the Whitemelt disappearance episodes.

Leeloo immediately dispatched Berlin to investigate, Enzo in tow, as do many global governmental teams, eager to solve the baffling mystery troupe through the Fiumicino International Airport "Leonardo Da Vinci" in Rome.

Berlin was ready to call it a night, wary of the grim assignment ahead. But then, the very tall Colonel, Enzo's boss, who had a pure British accent, shocked her when he approached them upon their arrival.

"I understand you'll want to prepare for tomorrow, but please, let me entertain you briefly for tonight, and don't be too hard on Enzo for snitching your arrival."

Berlin took a coy look at Enzo.

They exited the airport building into a waiting black limo curbside. The Colonel pointed them to the stretched car. Enzo regarded his boss strangely.

"The Papal is not going to like this."

The Colonel opened the back door for the gracious Berlin as he responded to Enzo.

"At least it's not bullet-proofed."

Enzo and his boss bookended Agent Berlin Yords in the limo backseat.

"I may grow to enjoy this," she commented as the vehicle eased into traffic.

Enzo sat at a table between his boss, the Colonel, and Berlin in the middle of Bar Delle Grazie Café near the Vatican. He sipped a Cappuccino while the Colonel explained the Vatican's protective details. Enzo excused himself.

The giant, 6'7" Supercop, the Colonel, surprised Berlin as he eased into conversation with her.

"Enzo told me you have a daughter."

"I didn't know Enzo talked about me to anyone."

The Colonel became seriously conciliatory.

"He's enigmatic that way, but please don't tell him I told you. He's a very private man."

Berlin made a sign of zipping her mouth shut and then spoke, surprising the Vatican policeman.

"My daughter, Primrose, has lived with my parents in Sweden since the Whitemelt chaos began. I hardly had time for her, plus she'd always wanted to visit her grandparents."

The Colonel remained quiet and thoughtful for a long while before speaking.

"Your life, in a very small way, somehow paralleled Enzo's."

Berlin, puzzled, asked. "How's that?"

The Colonel hesitated.

"His wife and son died at childbirth just before he returned home, wounded from the Afghanistan war."

"That's terrible."

"Yeah, a real sad story, Agent. But don't divulge it came from me."

"Colonel, Enzo will know you told me."

"I suppose you're right. Lessen the blow as much as you can. My nephew is still in a delicate state, even if he doesn't think so. I bet he hasn't told you I'm his uncle."

"No, he hasn't. Enzo preferred to keep stuff locked inside, I've realized."

The Colonel leaned closer to Berlin to dampen the noise.

"Then, he certainly hasn't told you about Afghanistan."

Berlin was all ears. The Colonel continued.

"He, along with his unit, was trapped in a small village in Afghanistan alongside a devastated family with only two survivors, a set of 18-year-old twins, a boy and a girl."

The Colonel paid the barman and continued, "The girl had an epileptic fit fetching water from a well. Enzo watched. He reacted immediately to save the girl by holding her down.

"But unfortunately, her brother appeared at that moment, misconstrued the scenario, plunged a sword into Enzo's back, thrust his sister to death, and returned to finish off Enzo when Enzo shot and killed him…" The Colonel changed the subject as Enzo returned.

On the West side of Tiber Island in Rome, Fatebenefratelli Hospital resembles another old medical building, but it is not. The hospital sheltered Jews during the holocaust by diagnosing them with "Syndrome-K," a fictitious disease.

Today, the "American Team" walked down the long, dark corridor to witness an extraordinary, macabre event.

Vatican detective Enzo Lupara was fidgety alongside the eager-beaver FBI Agent Berlin Yords.

"Creepy in here," Enzo announced.

"I'd have thought you'd feel right at home, Enzo?"

He rubbed his scar, began to mouth his mantra, and ensured Berlin did not see his lips move.

"No. Since my discharge, I hated hospitals."

Berlin pushed open a black-painted door, expecting a dank autopsy room. Instead, a bright, white, stainless-steel-clad space emerged. "Wow."

"Yeah. Wow," Enzo agreed.

They were both in quarantine attire and listened to the Coroner explain findings from the dissected corpse lying on the table.

"Nothing special except that the body seemed to have died within the last twenty-four hours…"

"Wait a minute, the Count went missing months ago and was presumed dead…"

The doctor pushed back.

"Yes, yes, yes, Agent Yords. But the Science told me otherwise." He paused and continued, "I was about to say, despite missing more than eight months and presumed dead, he was remarkably well-preserved."

The doctor paused again and glared at Berlin, daring her to ask a question. She didn't. Enzo discreetly smiled.

"Then there were traces of empty canals from the shoulder to both the heart and the brain—"

Berlin, unable to help herself, interrupted, "Okay, that's it. What canals? Like a gutter?"

"If you let me finish, Agent, you might learn something." The doctor admonished Berlin. Enzo tugged at Berlin's hand to calm her down.

"I'm sorry, doctor. Please continue," Enzo urged.

The doctor offered a terse explanation.

"Analogically, the canal is akin to spaces left behind from the electrical wiring removal from a wall."

It was Enzo's turn to be astonished.

236

"Like in a home electrical wiring conduit? Come on, doc!"

"I bet someone tampered with the corpse," Berlin assumed aloud.

The doctor shrugged concomitantly but couldn't explain the time of death.

"My report goes to the health commissioner in the morning." He turned to Enzo.

"If I were you, I would take as many pictures as possible. You may never see this cadaver again. Arrivederci."

He left the room. Berlin was in shock.

"What just happened?"

Enzo explained, "He was done. Now we take pictures."

Unbeknownst to Enzo, the conversation with the Colonel profoundly affected Berlin. She revised her and Enzo's return itinerary to include a stopover in Sweden to visit her daughter, Primrose.

Enzo, behind Berlin, smiled at her childlike enthusiasm as she exited the Stockholm Arlanda airport, where Berlin's father waited for them outside upon their arrival.

At dinner that night, all spoke English for Enzo's benefit, with Primrose perched between her mother and the Italian detective.

Enzo heard a gentle knock at midnight just before Berlin snuck into his room.

She slid next to him, held him, and pulled the sheet over them. If surprised, Enzo didn't show it.

After a while, she spoke quietly.

"I heard about you and the twins in Afghanistan."

He flinched, and she caressed him.

"It's not your fault, Enzo." She repeated the phrase as he snuggled closer and leaned into her hug.

Soon, Enzo started to whimper, tears flowing. Then, he lets go of his emotions as he speaks for the first time.

"I only wanted to keep her from biting her tongue off. Then her brother attacked me. I had no choice, Berlin. I had no choice."

She held him tighter, consoling him. "I know, I know."

They remain in the embrace until the morning light begins to filter through, when Berlin traces the large scar on his back, waking Enzo up.

Enzo pointed to the wounds on both her legs and then maneuvered to caress the scars with his hands.

She blushed, eased off the bed gently, and snuck out, not realizing her father saw her leave.

In the early morning at the family pig farm, Berlin's father hinted at vast anatomical similarities between pigs and humans as Enzo followed behind in the large pig pen.

Enzo sniffed the air.

"I'm surprised there's no awful smell typical of a pigsty."

Berlin's father explained, without missing a beat, "Our pigs take showers every night."

It was surprising that Enzo believed it until Berlin's father burst into laughter and added, "The pigpen floors are lined with plastic sheets daily while the animals forage outside. We then remove the linings every evening. Experience dictated such necessary rigor significantly limited the extent of typical odors."

Primrose joined them, fully garbed, to work in the pig pen.

Enzo, more curious, pressed for those pig-human similarities. Berlin's father, in his comfort zone, lets loose.

"Pigs are mammals with similar musculature, thoracic and abdominal organs, though differences exist in the liver, intestines, and adrenal glands."

Berlin's father turned around to gauge Enzo's interest. "Should I continue?"

Enzo nodded.

"The thymus, lungs, and skin are very similar..."

Berlin's mother yelled through the farm door for them to return home for brunch.

Primrose ran out.

Chapter 17

Berlin and Enzo, just back from Italy, were in Leeloo's office, watching CNN and FOX's brutal castigation of President Bender Castle's weak governance of disappearances.

Leeloo turned to Berlin. "I need your Italy trip report to explain a concrete resolution action list to the President within a week."

CNN's breaking news jingle caused Berlin, about to leave, to stall, only to witness a bombshell report of another Whitemelt reappearance in Los Angeles.

They rushed off.

Heavy police and ambulance presence clogged the dead Verano's kid's burial place at the Poseidon Cemetery entrance in Thousand Oaks.

Berlin and Leeloo abandoned their cars and walked briskly through the crowd, displaying Shields to advance to the graveside.

Like the Count, Hilda Verano lay perfectly still, face up as if sleeping, atop her son's grave.

Next to Leeloo, Berlin was constantly jostled by intruding onlookers and news camera people searching for optimal shot angles.

"This is creepy. Just like in Rome. Right, Enz..."

Berlin didn't finish the sentence, realizing Leeloo was next to her, not Enzo.

Leeloo turns to Berlin. "Where's Enzo?"

"With an FBI forensic accounting analyst. They think they may have traced the money man funding the takeover of the boarding Homes."

Leeloo, expressionless, pointed to how perfect the body lay on the gravestone.

"This is no coincidence. I think we have a copycat simulating your Rome thing."

"I sure hope so because if not, we have a real diabolic cluster here, boss."

"Now what, Agent?"

"Autopsy. I'll also be curious to see if any conduit is in this one."

ADIC Leeloo Chang was confused.

"It'd be in the report. The Count had like a conduit wiring hole in his body."

Leeloo looked at Berlin as if she were crazy. "Like in-home wiring?"

The coroner finally arrived and examined the body before the CSI crew could go to work.

Leeloo flashed her shield at the Coroner. "How long dead?"

"Hard to say, but I'll know better when we get her situated."

The older pathologist slowly stooped beside the body, explaining without looking up.

Leeloo became impatient. "Hazard a damn guess, Sir."

The pathologist stood up slowly, leaning on both knees to become fully erect. He faced Leeloo.

"That was rude," and then walked off.

Berlin hurried after him. "I apologize on behalf of my boss. We're all kinda…" she trailed off.

The pathologist stopped. "Yeah. Aren't we all? But that was no excuse."

"I agree, Sir. Can you hazard a guess?"

He looked at her like a child. "No more than 24 hours, at the most. Good day, Agent."

"Your name, Sir?"

"My name is immaterial," he spat, walking away.

The autopsy report at the DTLA FBI office revealed Hilda had similar evacuated channels from her shoulder to her heart and brain, like the Count.

"Check out the fucking Poseidon Cemetery report, Enzo. Unreal!"

He did.

"Just like electrical wiring ripped out. Not good!" He commented.

The immense pressure mounted for answers from everywhere tested the two investigators, and then, Berlin received a surprise call from Rick Verano inviting her back to his house.

Wary of her last visit when Rick went commando, Berlin decided to leave Enzo behind to avoid the possibility of Rick fricking out in the presence of an unknown person.

Rick Verano, contrite, welcomed Berlin back into his home.

As he led her inside, he rubbed behind his right ear at a red welt.

- . .

"There's no excuse for my behavior when you last visited. I'm ashamed of who I became that day, Agent Yords. Please accept my unequivocal apologies."

"Accepted. Stress is a killer. It often gets the better of us. Now, how can you help?"

"I called you with information that emanated around my family just before Hilda…" he trailed off.

Berlin allowed a few seconds to elapse.

"Please, go on."

"Before my son succumbed to Leukemia, he had a great Spanish nurse who brought an antibiotic transdermal patch for the whole family. Then I saw the latest disappearance and knew I had to call you."

Rick allowed the cliffhanger to fester, again rubbing behind his right ear. He then leaned forward, conciliatory.

"She worked at Blossom Plaza Home, the same location in the news." Rick leaned back, self-satisfied. Berlin was expressionless.

"Do you still have the antibiotic, Sir?"

Rick deflated. "No."

"Does the nurse still work at Blossom Plaza Home?"

"I don't know."

Rick got up and walked towards the front door, again rubbing behind his right ear.

"That's all I have, Agent."

"Thank you."

Berlin scrambled out of the chair, hurried to follow, and spied behind Rick's right ear more closely than usual. She noticed the welt.

The maid appeared, and both ladies locked eyes. Berlin exited the home.

The tense atmosphere in Joel Schummer's office boiled over when an uninvited employee stuck his head through the door amidst a heated argument.

Both Berlin and Joel yelled simultaneously, "Get out."

Joel then turned to Berlin. "Yes, Agent Yords, I have a nurse on my staff. And no, I cannot divulge where she lives without a court order. It's the law. Why the sudden interest?"

Berlin stonewalled. "It's confidential."

Joel arose and walked towards the door, concluding the meeting. Berlin, still seated, remained quiet. Joel returned to sit.

Berlin leaned towards him across the desk and stared down at the arrogant director.

"Mister Schummer, if I leave this office without contact information for the nurse, you will have violated a national security investigation. Furthermore, an arrest warrant will be issued against you for aiding and abetting a terrorist, causing people to disappear."

In shock and disbelief, Joel blabbed out to Berlin... "Agent Yords, your recklessness is unbecoming of a law enforcement officer. I plan to report you to the authorities. I'm sure your recent assault problems in Michigan will resurface publicly again. So, bring it on."

Berlin slowly reached her ankle, brought out a gun, reached into her bag, retrieved a silencer barrel, and affixed it to the weapon while not looking directly at Joel. By now, he was squirming.

Berlin looked up and fired a suppressed shot at a desk lamp behind him. He flew off his chair and ducked under the desk.

"Get the fuck out from under there, Joel."

"You're crazy," he yelled.

Berlin walked out with the nurse's contact details, carrying the shattered lamp and the bullet casing.

The Blossom Plaza Home nurse wore a one-piece pink bikini with dark sunshades on her off-day lounges. She was alone around the pool at her modest White Oaks apartment complex, sipping a tall umbrella drink.

When Agent Berlin Yords and Vatican detective Enzo Lupara arrived, she removed the sunshades. To Berlin's disgust, her eyes lingered on Enzo.

Berlin got to work quickly. "Do you know the Veranos?"

The nurse's Latina-laden words crawl out of her mouth after inspecting the IDs thrust at her.

"You seem legit... The Verano kid was dying from Leukemia."

She deliberately slurped her drink, sexily ogling Enzo and coming on to the Italian hunk. "Como esta, el Guapo!"

Berlin turned to Enzo, her eyes inquiring about what the nurse said. Enzo shrugged a lie with a glint in his eyes, and both pulled up chairs next to the nurse. Berlin continued to question the Latina.

"Do you still work at Blossom Plaza?"

"My contract…" Her voice trailed off, hands waving as she pointed at Enzo, asking for non-verbal help to complete her sentence.

"Expired." He completed.

"Si," she confirmed and then continued.

"In four weeks, I return to Spain."

"You gave the Veranos the antibiotic patches, yes?" Berlin accused the nurse.

"Yes, I took it from the nursing home. I had a key to the locked cabinet."

"Do you have any left?"

She smiled, puffing her chest out, and addressed Enzo. Berlin rolled her eyes.

"No, Chico, they threw everything away after a while. But the new owners brought the patches. That, I know."

She slurped her drinks again deliberately to irk Berlin. Enzo couldn't hide his smile at the play between the two ladies. The nurse then volunteered more information.

"I had more energy with the patch. Uh, uh, it was like the energy, conejita." Enzo smiled.

Berlin's stoicism has had enough. She arose and eyed Enzo to follow.

As they walked away, the nurse said, "Señor Lupara, I have something for you."

Enzo walked back to the nurse as she rifled through her small purse next to the umbrella drink.

She handed Enzo an empty antibiotic patch and smiled at Berlin, who glared back at her.

In the car returning to the office, Berlin declared she would interview Dr. Romeo Atkins on the medication list from the two boarding homes affected. At the same time,

Enzo researches the potential name of the company that bought the Homes.

Remorseful in his office, Doctor Romeo Atkins lamented to Agent Berlin Yords to learn about the Pharmacology of medications used on residents at Blossom Plaza.

"I wish I'd challenged the NIA Alzheimer study project team leader to act sooner upon my last Blossom Plaza report showing sudden medical rejuvenation across residents, including Anna."

"Rejuvenation?" Berlin sought clarification.

"Yes. Residents showed significant improvement in dementia cognitive impairments and gains in physical agility, unsubstantiated with medical explanations, Agent."

"What stopped you from returning to fight then, doc?"

"Bureaucracy, Miss Yords. At that first crucial meeting, I'd crashed an important team leader's call from the NIH Secretary. So, he threw me out of his office."

Berlin refused to let him off the hook quickly as she stretched her legs and walked around the large office.

"You could have gone back. Right, doc?"

"Perhaps, but by then, Anna had melted down."

Both worked in silence for a brief period.

"Do you think there's a connection between facility ownership change and Anna's disappearance?" Berlin goaded.

Doctor Atkins paused and reflected briefly, "That would be diabolical."

"Interesting." Berlin surmised.

Doctor Atkins then returned to analyze the medication list Berlin had brought.

"Agent, I can confirm heroin and hallucinogenic opioids can cause profound perceptive distortions with short-term effects of euphoria, dry mouth, itching, nausea, vomiting, analgesia, slowed breathing, and heart rate.

"Long-term use implications include collapsed veins; abscesses (swollen tissue with pus); infection of the lining and valves in the heart; constipation and stomach cramps; liver or kidney disease; or pneumonia."

"Why would anyone ingest such things into their bodies?" Berlin wondered aloud.

"They're not all bad, Agent Yords. Their medicinal application can be therapeutic in measured quantities by qualified prescribers.

"Cannabis has short-term effects of enhanced sensory perception and euphoria followed by drowsiness/relaxation, slowed reaction time, problems with balance and coordination, increased heart rate and appetite, problems with learning and memory, and anxiety. Chronic users suffer from long-term mental health problems, coughs, and frequent respiratory infections."

"But that's still a lot of dangerous medications to have in a nursing home, isn't it, doc?"

"Healthcare practitioners manage elderly facilities utilizing such medications on residents, most with age-related debilitating ailments."

"You are… were Anna Cantor's GP. Right?"

"And Lewis, her brother. I also treated their recently deceased uncle, Rabbi Levi Straus. Anna spiraled downward and then fell into full dementia, no longer able to live alone, so we moved her to Blossom Plaza."

"What about Lewis?"

The doctor stopped, staring weirdly at Berlin, which caused her discomfort. Then, she spun around to look at the base of her pants.

"Did I split my pants?"

"No, Agent. Lewis is a different can of worms, but he doted on his sister. Now that she's gone, I question his sanity."

"Is he dangerous?"

"He's unpredictable, Agent."

Both reflected in silence for a few seconds.

"Okay, doc. Anna's medical records?"

"Oh yes, that. Just so you know, I pressed Lewis to enlist Anna for the NIA study, the one candidate selection in LA County, since I was, am, a volunteer for the NIA Alzheimer study project."

Doctor Romeo handed Anna Cantor's medical records to Berlin, including pictures garnered over 20 years as the family GP.

"Doc, let me ask you something… How can a five-foot-nothing woman jump a seven-foot fence at the LA Zoo?"

Doctor Atkins drew a blank and was baffled at the tangential line of questioning. "What are you talking about, Agent?"

"Never mind. It's time I left. Thank you, doc."

"You may want to talk to Lewis; perhaps he knows something I don't know about Anna," the doctor suggested.

It was now past midnight. The Downtown LA FBI office was a ghost town.

Enzo scrolled down the computer screen and reached for the printer, whirring quietly to his right.

He stopped short of picking up the printed paper, leaned towards the computer screen, and enlarged the view of the barely legible document to examine the fine print on the bottom page more closely.

Finally, a hand-written name came into view–Tanakh Enterprises.

"Tanakh Enterprises," he mouthed, sitting back.

While the wheel turned, he dialed an FBI Forensic Accounting and Business Analyst.

So much loud noise in the background caused Enzo to yell into the mouthpiece.

"I can't hear anything!" the analyst yelled.

The line went dead. Enzo threw the phone on the desk.

"Merda," he cursed.

His phone rang, and he snatched it up.

"How can I help you, Mr. Lupara?"

"I'm sorry to call so late—" Enzo began to say.

"Never mind. What do you need?"

"I think I've identified the entity financing the Home Away From Home facility."

The analyst tried to cover the other ear while listening to the street jackhammer working late under brightly lit floodlights.

"What was that, Enzo?"

"Tanakh Enterprises," Enzo repeated.

The analyst drew a blank. "What about whatever that name you mentioned?"

Enzo started to explain, but he realized the noise level was too high for listening and comprehension, so he changed his mind.

"I will call you tomorrow."

It was barely noon when Enzo called the analyst, who was groggy from too little sleep.

"Tanakh Enterprises may also have issued the certified check drawn on Bank of the West, and..."

The analyst interrupted, "Mr. Lupara! The judge denied the Subpoena to allow the FBI to vet Bank of the West's books."

"What? How did you know that?"

"It came late yesterday. I had no time to inform you guys."

"But we spoke last night."

"Yeah, I was caught up in a midnight floodlit one-lane open DPW repair shitstorm. I didn't catch everything."

"Alright, I'm sorry. I plan to revisit the People's First employment agency, which hired the director of the Home

Away From Home facility, which is paid through the Bank of the West. Let's find another judge to help us."

"Mr. Lupara, please don't get worse than Berlin!"

"Thank you." Enzo hung up.

Berlin and Enzo gathered in Leeloo's conference room to summarize Whitemelt activities.

"The AG called last night for me to prepare a report to update the President tomorrow. What do we have?"

Berlin launched.

"The LA Zoo had nothing to offer but led to the Alhambra EMT who carted off Rick Verano, Hilda Verano's husband, the Whitemelt victim."

"What happened to him?" Leeloo asked.

"He survived the heart attack and led us to a Spanish nurse who worked at Blossom Plaza, also off-booked with the Veranos treating their terminal son, who eventually died. But she had an empty sample of an antibiotic sachet."

Berlin brought out the sample. Leeloo looked at it.

"Doesn't look that dangerous," she said.

"I know," Enzo added, and Berlin continued.

"Evans Square, the supervisor at Blossom Plaza, couldn't explain how he got burned but claimed to have seen Anna climbing into a portal. He tried to grab her legs and had to let go, burning. I think he's addicted to something."

"Where is Evans now?" Leeloo asked.

"He disappeared from Walter Reed."

"Fucking Homeland Security," Leeloo commented, confusing Enzo.

"The Home Away From Home disappearance of Brody Kist while fishing was a black hole, except for the financial part," Berlin said, and looked at Enzo, who took over.

"We identified Tanakh Enterprises as the new Home Away From Home boarding house owner who hired the director after acquisition through People's First employment agency and paid through Bank of the West.

"I strongly suspect the same company is behind the Blossom Plaza acquisition, and I just started that inquiry."

"That's great news," Leeloo commented.

Enzo looked at Berlin.

"The reappearances are a different kettle of fish with a single commonality…" Leeloo interjected.

"Let me guess…the electrical wall wiring conduit analogy…"

"Yes," Berlin answered and continued.

"Those are the major clues thus far," Berlin concluded.

"It seems light," Leeloo challenged.

"Oh, one more thing. The medication list analyses did not turn up anything substantial except that all the homes harbored some rather heavy drugs." Berlin added.

Leeloo went to sit behind her desk as she spoke.

"The AG invited me to his next cabinet meeting at the Whitehouse. He also greenlit access to the research team working on the Busan, South Korea reappearance of Park Yu Soon Whitemelt."

"Great news," Berlin said; Leeloo didn't seem all that enthusiastic as she jumped off her seat again.

She paced the room and suggested Berlin and Enzo make fresh rounds of the Homes, including stopping by the UN to investigate if anything came of the international Whitemelt investigations.

"Let's get to it, people," She said as Berlin and Enzo waited after her last comments.

Both detectives jumped up.

Berlin and Enzo were in deep concentration in the basement media room inside the UN-WHO, New York office, invited by the DG, Tambo Gilu, after talking with ADIC Leeloo Chang.

They both watched the videos that captured Park Yu Soon, the South Korean man who vanished in Busan, and Eugenio Machado in Brazil.

Enzo leaned in to discern the fuzzy scene as the older South Korean knelt before an altar and disappeared the next second. He rewound for the umpteenth time, mesmerized each time.

"The floor just disintegrated beneath him," he observed.

"That's weird," she said, tinkering with electronic equipment.

Tambo Gilu, the WHO Secretary-General, walked in amidst Berlin struggling to change CDs in the player.

"When will the WHO join the 21st century technologically?" she joked. Tambo turned serious.

"Agent, do you know why I invited you here?" Berlin stopped tinkering.

"To gather information and possibly locate a clue to nab the Whitemelt perpetrators," she offered.

"Yes, yes… but why you and not the CIA, for instance?"

"I don't know."

"Well, I need your help to intervene with President Castle to fulfill funding the promised UN-WHO charter dues and…"

Berlin gently interrupted, "I would love to help, but that's political and beyond my pay grade."

"I know that, Agent, but I was hopeful you'd lobby on my behalf with your boss, ADIC Chang, to that effect."

Berlin sighed.

"I will, but I can't promise she'd agree to something like that. You know she's an acting director, not the FBI director, right?"

"I do, but ADIC Chang is popular and does right. Great, now I need to get back to work."

Tambo walked towards the basement staircase, heading back upstairs, humming. Enzo looked at him weirdly.

Enzo popped in the last CD from Rio De Janeiro to watch the gory bone sticking out of Silvia Machado's broken leg at the step landing, crumpled up in pain.

Next, the view panned to the bathroom where human body parts bobbed in a half-full, bloody bath. He fast-forwarded, searching for the disappearance scene, but none came into view. Finally, the video concluded with a placard held by a Brazilian cop in uniform, printed with Eugenio Machado's name.

Berlin and Enzo trudged up the staircase toward Tambo's office in emotional exhaustion.

They plumped themselves across the desk from Tambo in the African-themed office, acknowledging the décor for its beauty.

"Did you find the videos useful?" Tambo enquired.

"Yes," Berlin confirmed, looking at Enzo, who agreed.

Minutes later, the detectives left the UN building.

***

FBI ADIC Leeloo Chang walked into the vast, roped-off demarcation quarantine areas in front of the WhiteHouse, where protesters had demonstrated.

Five smaller tents surrounded the giant central tent at the drop zone.

She ducked under the rope and talked to an armed policeman on guard duty.

"Who's in charge here?"

The cop pointed. "In that big 'ring of dogs' tent over there."

Leeloo, already walking away, stopped and turned around. "Ring of dogs?"

"That's what they call where the thing fell from the sky into the circle created by the dog handlers to separate the demonstrating factions."

"Thank you. Good to know." Leeloo walked towards the large white tent, cynical. A white-suited assistant conducted and overwhelmed Leeloo at the prep section to garb up, complete with a face mask and breathing apparatus.

"Is this necessary?" Leeloo complained.

"Yes, and no touching anything in here." The assistant admonished the FBI boss and explained, "Doctor Inshan Goddard insisted no one crosses into the drop zone without being fully equipped as you are now."

Leeloo labored with difficulty, lugging herself towards the zone, and whined, "Jesus!"

Inside, several electronic equipment stations whirred and blinked, hooked up to a central enclosed glass display of an elderly Korean man, Park Yu Soon, a Whitemelt victim.

Leeloo walked over to Doctor Inshan Goddard, who unfortunately turned around just as Leeloo arrived.

"Oh shit."

Leeloo remarked as she recognized the pathologist, she had a run-in at the Poseidon Cemetery when Hilda Verano reappeared.

"Oh shit, indeed, Agent Chang. So, we meet again."

Leeloo awkwardly but instinctively extended her hand, withdrawing it immediately, recalling the protocol.

"FBI Assistant Director In-Charge, Leeloo Chang," Leeloo announced.

The Pathologist had already turned around, expecting Leeloo to follow him.

Leeloo said, "Listen, doc, I'd like to apologize."

"Cut the crap, Agent. We're here to do a job. That's all. I'm not your confessor."

He conducted her around the glass enclosure, showing a thoroughly dissected cadaver. Leeloo gasped when she saw the exposed channel leading to the subject's heart and brain in the upper arm area.

"So, it's true there's something in there—"

Inshan interrupted, "Wait till you see the pay dirt."

He led her to a smaller section with a NO ENTRY sign on the door, boldly marked in red letters.

A long, oval glass jar hung down from the ceiling with tubes and wires connected to electronic equipment. Inside lay an entity with long tentacle extensions from both oval ends.

"What the hell is that?" Leeloo asked in shock as she moved closer to inspect.

"I wouldn't do that…" Doctor Goddard began to say when the entity jerked frantically in the suspended enclosure. Leeloo, scared half to death, reared back and crashed into the doctor. Both ended up on the floor, their quarantine clothing ripped.

The pathologist yelled at her, "We must get out now."

They both ran out of the room.

With jangled nerves, Leeloo was smoking and listening to Doctor Goddard on the grass before the WhiteHouse.

"I have no idea what that thing in there is. But, by tonight, I'm sure 'men in black' will show up, and the thing will probably end up in Area 51."

"You're joking, right?" Leeloo interjected.

"Not exactly. I've done my part. Now, I stay out of the politics of it. I suggest you do the same."

Inshan walked off toward the large tent. Leeloo crushed her half-smoked cigarette and hurried after the elderly physician.

"Wait a minute..."

Chapter 18

The chief of staff at the Oval Office and the President watched a news broadcast about all the Whitemelts.

The topic weighs heavily on President Bender Castle as the public criticized his lackluster resolution to Whitemelt.

"Turn that damn thing off. The end of the world is upon us, and why during my Presidency?" the President commanded.

"Your second term will be perfect, Sir."

Behind the Oval desk, writing, Bender looked up at his chief of staff like a child.

"I suppose, immediately after the Capitol building, Whitemelted. Right?"

"I'll fetch the CIA director. He's been waiting for ages."

President Bender stepped out from behind the desk.

Barry DaSilva waited quietly for the President to hang up the phone.

"Sir, we intercepted communication that pointed to the strange goings-on at a Tel Aviv venture start-up funded by a former Knesset member. I need the authorization to dive deep."

The President walked over and sat on the opposite sofa, gazing challengingly at the diminutive but dangerous spook.

"Why come to me? Seems routine?"

"Not quite, Sir. Knesset members are often hands-off, hence—"

Bender raised his hand in surrender. "How strong a connection to Whitemelt?"

"That's what my team will uncover."

Barry extended a copy of the intel to the President, who sat back to read it.

ILLEGAL EXPERIMENTATION, POSSIBLE ETHICAL COMPROMISE - By JOHN JACOBS, Ph.D.

Abridged summary of a foreign entity splicing with human biochemistry. I have witnessed the operation. I am highly suspicious of its existence behind a literal wall of secrecy.

It's imperative to affirm that the events enumerated below are NOT cloning, where cells harvested grow externally to the donor. I believe a dormant foreign entity is mixed with human body fluid for sinister purposes, but I cannot go beyond this supposition.

The President looks up strangely at the CIA Director. "Is this some joke, Barry? This is very thin and weak, and that's giving it too much credit."

"Sir, our experts think they're doing something spooky, and since no other solid leads to these disappearances, maybe it's time we go weird, too."

The President got up to fetch a drink. He did not offer one to Barry.

"Tread carefully, Barry. No blowbacks."

Barry rubbed his eye patch and suppressed a snide smile as he arose. "Yes, Sir."

The Chief of Staff closed the door behind the CIA Director and walked towards the President, nursing a drink.

"That short shit of a spook gives me the heebie-jeebies, and that's why I'm glad he's on our side."

Barry DaSilva knew he was generally despised but reveled in that as a strength and a free ad for anyone not to fuck with him, a reputation that had permeated the global spy network.

The often whispered moniker about him goes like this… "Fuck with Barry; then you must always look to the sky when you drive because you'll never know when a missile will descend upon you…"

**

Jueves Abramov was playing chess with Moshe when his phone rang. Jueves got up, and Moshe noticed a surprise flash across the older man's face as he said hello. The younger man has no way of knowing Barry DaSilva, the CIA Director, was on the other end and his uncle's old friend.

Back inside the house for privacy, Jueves argued with his old friend.

"Off the books is always tricky. You know that, Barry."

The CIA director applied subtle pressure on his former war colleague. "And yet, here we are, old friend."

Jueves pushed back. "This will be with a light touch, nothing explosive, right?"

"Juvy, his pet name, you're more than capable of anything, and you know it."

"Be that as it may, Barry, I'm now just a simple records keeper with the Israeli agency."

Barry chuckled at the word "simple" before he hung up. "Simple? Of course you are, Juvy."

Jueves returned to the balcony. "Keep tabs on Goram and his people, Moshe, and report back to me."

Moshe sneaked a stare at the prominent scar across his uncle's throat as he accepted the assignment.

Jueves mumbled as he walked away. "I'll tell you about the scar one day, kid."

...In Egypt in 1973, Barry DaSilva, dressed in a dark layered Jellabiya with a black turban, had blended into the crowds of Cairo's lively Fustat street market late in the evening.

Trumpery merchants had plied their trade to eager tourists while food vendors fried, grilled, and sautéed delicacies whose delicious smoky aroma had wafted delightfully.

Minutes later, Barry had left the buoyant savory market din for the solemn embassy row, from where the young CIA operative had sneaked into a waiting car behind Cairo's United States embassy.

Another Mossad, Aminata Gottschalk (Jueves's future boss), is at the wheel, Jueves Abramov, Mossad, passenger side. It had been mid-September 1973, weeks before the Yom Kippur War.

Atop an ancient rooftop, Jueves, next to Barry, had trained a rifle on General Taofik Almuerzan, the Egyptian Acting Defense Minister, who was leaving the mosque after prayers, surrounded by security details. The bullet had smashed into the Minister's head. Death was instant.

Amidst the chaos, a security detail had caught the sun's reflection as Jueves had dismantled the gun. Then, the security detail shot at them as an armed protective truck with two bodyguards took off to look for the shooter. Jueves and Barry scrambled off the building. Aminata was at the wheel, idling, and drove out of the city with Jueves and Barry. When she thought they were clear, the armed truck with two bodyguards appeared from behind.

Now outside Cairo city limits, the passenger side bodyguard fired a bazooka at the fleeing car. The car toppled over, throwing Jueves and Barry and pinning Aminata's right leg.

On the ground, Jueves saw the bazooka bodyguard walk towards Aminat; he hustled towards her but was grabbed from behind by the second bodyguard, who started to slit Jueve's throat. Bleeding from the right eye, Barry hazily saw Jueves in trouble and shot the second bodyguard dead before collapsing.

Almost atop Aminata, the bazooka bodyguard aimed his pistol at her when Jueves jumped him. The bodyguard lost the gun as they both struggled on the ground. Aminata grabbed the gun and shot the bodyguard.

Barry struggled to walk with his bleeding right eye. He drove the bodyguard's truck to Jueves and Aminata, loaded them into the backseat, and sped off...

Chapter 19

Lewis was groggy at the bookstore's back office and chugged black coffee while opening mail. He opened an unstamped and unaddressed envelope. A USB dropped on the desk.

"What the hell?"

He stared at the computer screen, watching the USB, and slid off the chair to the floor in a faint spell, pulling the table's contents with him; luckily, the coffee mug was empty.

He jerked up minutes later and picked up the picture to see Hondo and Joey inside his apartment.

"Sleep with one eye open tonight. The explosives under your bed, kitchen, bathroom, or lounge are ready to ..."

Lewis grabbed the phone and dialed El AL.

Across the road from Lewis Cantor's bookstore, Hari Hapa stood curbside and watched patrons go in and out. Soon, Lewis emerged, and Hari followed.

Next, Lewis ran errands and stopped at the Walgreens Pharmacy. Once Lewis drove off, Hari went into the Walgreens Pharmacy.

He window-shopped, grabbed a small bag of Doritos, and walked to the empty checkout counter.

"Was my uncle just in here? Where did he go?"

The young store attendant was suspicious. Hari babbled on like a dolt.

"Oh no, no. My uncle forgot his painkiller tabs in the car and with the crutches…" Hari rifled in his pocket for money. The attendant softened.

"Your uncle was at the pharmacy but asked me to re-test for COVID-19 first. He's flying out somewhere, he said."

"Duh!" Hari imitated a clueless person and paid for the snack bag.

"Thank you." Hari walked out of the store.

Hari, back home, slammed the Doritos bag on the kitchen table, busting the pack. Chips flew all over the place. "Shit!"

***

Miles into the heavens, airborne, bored to bits on a flight to Israel, Lewis Cantor stared out the aircraft window as it descended over the brown, ancient city at dawn.

He passed through immigration at Ben Gurion.

At the airport, Moshe complained to his uncle about nothing happening since he'd been tasked by the Vatican Colonel to watch Rabbi Chosky, who suspected the Rabbi of involvement with Whitemelt.

The Rabbi had driven to the airport minutes earlier, briefly went inside, emerged seconds later, and stood outside doing nothing.

"Dohd, nothing is happening here; when do I stop?"

"Do you have another job, Goyim?" Jueves spat.

"No."

"Is the money the Vatican Colonel paying you bad?"

"No." The line went dead; Moshe sulked.

Then, a man, Lewis Cantor, exited the arrival door to the outside, followed by another, Hari Hapa. Moshe quickly picked up on the non-professional tailing by the man behind.

Lewis got into a rental by the curb, and so did Hari.

Chosky was now driving behind them, talking animatedly on the phone, until three black SUVs appeared behind him on the highway.

Chosky took the next exit off the highway.

Moshe, watching, got on the phone and followed the SUVs at a safe distance.

"Oh shit," he exclaimed to his uncle.

"Some people are harassing two men who just arrived at the airport and were fingered by Chosky."

"Why?" Moshe, in exasperation, almost lost control.

"I have to go, Dohd." He hung up before a response.

The three black SUVs hemmed in Lewis and Hari's cars and forcibly halted them to a standstill on the highway, oncoming vehicles blasting horns at the chaos.

They extracted Lewis and Hari from their vehicles, dragged them into the last SUV, and took them away.

Avnar, on the phone, instructed Abishak in another SUV to get rid of Moshe as soon as he caught on to Moshe following them.

Minutes later, Abishak and Frieda's SUVs surprised Moshe from behind.

They stay on either side of Moshe, menacingly forcing him to slow down, enabling Avnar's SUV to disappear from view.

Moshe locked eyes with Abishak and then Frieda, but did not know them, and recognized the Mossad-driving technique as they continued their harassment.

Moshe, in peril, maneuvered to exit the highway just as Abishak and Frieda wanted.

Frieda's southpaw flipped him off just before disappearing.

Jueves Abramov, an old spy now marking time with Mossad in Tel Aviv, had a prominent scar across his throat; he sipped tea on his apartment balcony, across from his nephew, Moshe Shula, a former Mossad agent forced out of the espionage agency due to his uncle's political fallout. He snuck a quick look at his uncle's scar. He's caught.

"For an ex-Mossad, you should be brave enough to ask me about the scar. How many years have you been staring at that thing?"

"I, I…"

"You didn't mean to stare?"

"No, Sir."

Jueves laughed.

"I will tell you about it when you ask me directly." Jueves waited, but nothing—then his cell phone rang.

"I just made a sign of the cross as I saw your name." A Colonel, the Vatican head of security, and Enzo Lupara's boss are on the line.

"It's been ages, my friend." Jueves smiled. Moshe got up to leave and give his uncle privacy, but Jueves waved him to sit.

"It must be serious for you to call out of the blue."

"Well, yes and no. I'm not sure there's anything to call about, but this clue in me keeps tugging. You know the old saying… there's no smoke without fire." Jueves chuckled.

"Is your inkling the smoke or the fire?"

"It's the smoke, and I hope it doesn't burst into flames."

"What is it?"

"There's a rumor going around the Vatican that Israel is the source of the Whitemelt." The line went quiet.

"Jueves?"

"Yes. I'm just in shock. I would have thought the Russians or even the Chinese would be cooking something like this up, but us?"

"It's a rumor, my friend… but can you check it out?" Jueves snickered.

"Where do you start a thing like that?"

"You're the spook; it should be right up your alley. Does your Nephew still do his thing with Mossad? Such a promise." Jueves looked at Moshe, to the younger man's discomfort.

"Is it urgent?"

"I don't know. We're waiting for the next Whitemelt shoe to drop, and it did."

"Switzerland is ours, that started this whole inquiry." That jogged Jueves' memory.

"That's right, a Roman Count skiing in the Alps… Yes, I'll have Moshe sniff around."

"Thank you. Hello, and thank you to Moshe when you see him."

"Will do." He hung up.

"We have work to do. Rather, you have work to do."

Moshe leaned forward in anticipation.

…It was 2015, and the Pope (the current Pope), whose Motorcade protection detail had left many TV watchers reminiscent of the 1970s American Secret Service Agents hustling after the American President's limousine entourage on State visits. This time, however, in 2015, Israeli secret service Agents had done the hustling.

At a Jerusalem street corner, an Arab Israeli youngster playing cards had broken away from his friends a mile from the papal motorcade detail.

Sweaty but fit, Moshe Shula, a Mossad agent amongst the twelve protecting the pope, jogged alongside the transparent motorcade "bubble" vehicle. He was behind the Vatican's lead security personnel, a Colonel.

The Colonel looked behind to instruct the young Mossad. "Stay close, don't breathe through your mouth."

Filled with confidence, Moshe flashed a cocky smile as the cacophony paraded through downtown in the procession of the global religious leader.

The Arab Israeli youngster had climbed the long spiral staircase to the top of the Jalil mosque, where he had a panoramic view of the old city. He had taken out powerful binoculars from his backpack.

The Roman Cop and retired Army Colonel had continued to banter with the young Mossad Agent, Moshe.

"How's your uncle?"

Moshe smiled knowingly. "I know you're trying to calm me down, but there's nothing to worry about, Colonel."

The Colonel ignored the savvy young man.

The Arab Israeli youngster, now in a replica Secret Service suit, had watched the papal motorcade through the binoculars.

He then carefully removed an explosive-laden harness from a backpack, strapping it beneath his jacket before he sprayed water on his face to simulate sweat. Descending the mosque and the spiral staircase, he entered the street wearing a white Djellaba.

Sweaty but not lagging behind the mostly younger Agents, the Colonel galloped along, surrounding the motorcade.

"Is Mr. Abramov in town as we speak?"

"Uncle Jueves still had his scar. Do you know how he got it, Colonel?"

The Colonel ignores the inquisitive young Mossad. "He normally organizes these things. Why is he not here today?" The Colonel pointed at the Motorcade.

Enraged for not getting a straight answer, Moshe slowed down to increase the distance between them. The Colonel kept talking, unaware of Moshe's distance.

"Keep your eyes peeled, Moshe. These are troubled times."

The motorcade arrived at its destination, the Western Wall, Hebrew Ha-Kotel Ha-Ma'aravi, also called the Wailing Wall, in the Old City of Jerusalem.

The pope had been praying at the Wailing Wall when a "secret service Agent" rushed at him, yelling something unintelligible.

Moshe instinctively tackled the "Agent" as a small explosion detonated in a puff plume of white smoke.

There had been minimal casualties due to tight security and the failure of the enormous explosive to ignite.

Moshe Shula was in an ambulance receiving treatment. Majid Al-Humtal was in handcuffs.

It had been a month since the assassination attempt on the Pope at the Wailing Wall in Jerusalem.

Jueves Abramov, Mossad's Western Ops Head in Tel Aviv, sat in front of Josef Matursky, who headed Shin Bet (Internal Security) in Jerusalem at the time.

"Your nephew, Moshe Shula, will be dismissed from the—"

Jueves attempted to interrupt, and Josef silenced him with a hard, mean look.

"Moshe will accept heroic early retirement from injuries sustained protecting a visiting foreign dignitary. His records will show an honorable discharge, but you and I know otherwise. So now, you may talk."

"Sir, Moshe is more than qualified as an Agent, and the exposure to Motorcade detail was just an aside—"

Josef interrupted. "That almost killed the global religious leader on Israeli soil. Imagine the calamity if the attempt had been successful. Your detractors are claiming gross nepotism."

"But, Sir, the suicide attempt was successfully thwarted by my nephew. He did his job, and I..."

The Shin Bet leader steps from behind his desk to stand over Jueves.

"This is the hardest part that gives me no pleasure, Jueves Abramov. The Prime Minister has authorized your immediate removal from your current position. You have a choice: fight it, which you will lose, or accept my proposal."

Jueves jumped off the chair. Josef moved just in time to prevent a collision.

"What are you saying? Am I fired?"

Josef returned to his desk and pulled a black dossier bound with a red ribbon from a drawer. He opened it, scanned it briefly, and then closed it.

"Knesset House speaker at the time, Aram Marzheim, insisted upon your termination but for the intervention of several retired high-ranking veterans who recognized your past military contribution."

Jueves sat down, deeply saddened.

"Now what? Forty years of service down the drain?"

Josef became conciliatory. "With your experience, Corporations will compete for your services—"

Jueves interrupted and pleaded, "Is there anything I can do to remain in the government?"

Josef shook his head in disbelief. "Why won't you take the opportunity to live a quieter life? You will leave with your full military ranking, pension, and a military passport to enable you to travel the world more freely. So why remain inside Mossad?"

Jueves, remorseful, walked around the small office. "It's all I know and all I am, Josef. I'd be dead within months if I left. What can you do to keep me in?"

An uncomfortable silence between the two government officials was abruptly broken when the desk telephone rang. Josef answered, listened silently, and then hung up.

"If I were you, I would leave now to enjoy the rest of my life in peace. However, I will look for a position that will not ruffle feathers, but you may not like it."

Jueves collected his briefcase to leave. "I understand, Josef. Let me know."...

Chapter 20

Leeloo and her team visit the CIA director's office to strategize before a big meeting with the President.

Barry DaSilva, CIA Director, sat behind the desk in his large office, lecturing Berlin, Enzo, and a discomfited Leeloo Chang.

"The current passive strategic trajectory is inconsequential in identifying culprits behind various disappearances," Leeloo interrupted to cut through his self-flagellation.

"Sitting back to cast procedural judgment for a never-before-seen occurrence is disingenuous and professionally rude at worst. Positive, actionable suggestions are welcome, not pontification."

The CIA Director interrupted a defense. "I agree to some extent, Loo, but you insisted my team butted out earlier."

Leeloo erupted, "Barry, I shall no longer verbally warn you to reference me as Loo. Rather, I will file an official complaint against you and your cohorts for sexual harassment," Barry interrupted.

"It's time we allow cooler heads to prevail, ADIC Chang. I harbor no ill feelings or derogation in addressing you. If misconstrued, I apologize on my behalf…" Leeloo jumped in.

"No. Despite several of my complaints, you will never stop referring to me as 'Loo', and President Bender Castle was obvious in responsibility assignments...."

Enzo Lupara was quietly expressionless at the high-level bureaucratic fracas.

Leeloo looked at Berlin, signaling to her that it was time to leave the pot-boiler meeting.

She walked off and turned mid-step to gloat. "We have new knowledge of potential perpetrators. We plan to communicate when appropriate."

Barry spoke aloud as Leeloo, Berlin, and Enzo neared the door.

"You meant Tanakh Enterprises, the Israeli outfit involved in recent senior home acquisitions, right?"

Leeloo halted with her hand on the doorknob. Berlin nearly ran into Leeloo from behind, but Enzo gently held her back.

"Whitemelt investigation is mine. Back off," Leeloo yelled.

Both female FBI Agents stormed out of the CIA director's office, and Enzo was in tow.

Behind the Oval desk, President Bender Castle watched silently as his Cabinet members bickered on the sofa.

Barry DaSilva, the CIA Director, laid into FBI ADIC Leeloo Chang.

"The AG shouldn't have included you in this meeting for…" His voice trailed off.

The WhiteHouse Chief of Staff interjected,

"This is the most powerful office globally. Food-fighting and name-calling should be beneath us."

He looked around for support, but none came.

The brief silence was shattered when Leeloo began to speak,

"Tanakh Enterprises, the FBI diligently found, and we intend to—" Barry interrupted, "Thanks to my Israeli..." as the President coughed, and the room went silent.

Then, finally, he left the desk, walked to the window, turned his back to the room, stared outside, and his back stiffened.

"I made a grave error of judgment allowing you lot on my ticket to solve American problems after the Conservative political scorch Earth Tinder called Trumpism befell us all!"

He stopped talking briefly to glare and then continued.

"Well?" he asked, angry.

Barry began to talk, "Well, mister—"

"Shut the hell up, Barry, and immediately discontinue your concerted, habitual, and useless macho efforts to undermine any member of my capable Cabinet."

The President's furious repudiation took by surprise even Barry DaSilva, the calm professional.

Bender Castle then turned around to face the audience. He softened his tone and walked over to the sitting, shell-shocked politicians.

"We have a large sticky mud pile of shit rolling down the hill. I will not have Americans continue to disappear under my watch." He turned to face Barry DaSilva squarely.

"Get with that slimy Aram Marzheim in Israel. Tell him the United States' annual $40 billion aid hangs in the balance. I will aim mighty USA big guns at him if he continues to slow-walk this thing."

The President returned to sit behind the Oval Desk to continue working, reviewing, and signing documents. The stupefied Cabinet members were unsure what would happen next. Finally, the chief of staff broke the awkward silence.

"That's all, folks. The President thanks you."

The Cabinet members filed out of the Oval Office.

Israeli PM Aram Marzheim was on the line talking to the President. The chief of Staff had again gathered Barry DaSilva, the CIA director, and ADIC Leeloo Chang at the Oval Office.

The President, behind his desk, answered the call on the speakerphone.

"President Castle, we know how to handle our business as promised. My emissary should have arrived with potential Whitemelt evidence you'll find useful, but you should not act upon it. Israel plans to do that."

"Thank you, PM, you're a man of your word; I think this Whitemelt is about to end…"

The PM interrupted, "I beg your pardon, Sir, but I must say this for clarity."

"What is that?"

"I am completely wary of Director DaSilva and would encourage your oversight so no unfortunate interference on our sovereignty accidentally occurs."

"Like what?" President Castle Goaded.

"No missile shooting out of the sky or soldiers on foot in my country."

President Castle sidestepped.

"I shall review all the evidence forwarded and count on your precise capabilities to arrest the situation. Now, I must sign off." The line went dead; the President faced Barry and Leeloo.

"Are you all set to stick it to these Yahoos?"

Barry deferred to Leeloo, surprising the embattled ADIC.

"Thank you for that, Barry. And, Mr. President, as you know, we're already on the ground, and thanks again to Barry for activating one of his old assets?"

She looked at Barry. "Old friend." He confirmed. Leeloo continued.

"We're light and nimble, aside from a slight complication of two American civilians caught up in the mess, but we're on top of it."

"Civilians?"

"We're still sorting out why and whom, Sir."

The President looked at the chief of staff, who ushered the spies out of the Oval Office and handed copies of all the presented Israeli evidence in a diplomatic pouch that had arrived.

A week later…

On the phone with Israeli Prime Minister Aram Marzheim, President Bender Castle sought cooperation to investigate Tanakh Enterprises, a business interested in the global fight against Whitemelt disappearances.

"Mr. President, the full force of the Israeli intelligence apparatus agreed to support this important global effort."

President Castle looked cynical and suspicious as he listened to the Middle East leader's glowing surrender. He waved his chief of staff over as he challenged the Israeli leader.

"So, we can count on your quick access to this group or groups for 'talks'?"

"Within reason, Mister President."

As the Jewish leader hedged, Bender Castle immediately latched onto the tough Middle-Eastern double talk.

"What would those reasons entail, Aram?"

"The company mentioned, though unknown to me, may be important to the Jewish people. So, I caution my optimism, Bender, old friend."

"Do we have a free hand or not, Aram?"

"Yes, Sir, you do. But, please, be cautious. Israel is not America, where…" the Israeli Prime Minister's voice trailed off.

"Enough said, Aram; Barry will do what Barry does."

The top CIA name immediately raised defensive flags to the Prime Minister.

"That's what I'm afraid of, Mister President. Please let me reiterate the need to recognize that Israel is a small nation that cannot withstand the large footprint of certain activities. Mister DaSilva has a rather large foot that..." Aram trailed off again.

President Castle was having none of it.

"My CIA Director is a delicate curmudgeon, experienced in such circumstances. I have to end this call, Prime Minister Marzheim. Thank you."

President Castle hung up unceremoniously.

The chief of staff arrived ready with a glass of some liquor to refresh the puffy-eyed leader of the free world.

"Thank you."

Bender Castle collapsed on the sofa.

"What's next?"

***

The grounds of the opulent, well-lit, hilltop official residence of the Israeli Prime Minister, Aram Marzheim, do not please him this evening. He paced the manicured grass with the security details at discrete distances, watching as he talked furiously on the phone with the Knesset house speaker, Josef Matursky.

"I left you both with an understanding of everything squared away. What happened?"

"Life's curveball bounced my way, Aram."

Furious, the Prime Minister lets loose.

"Speak English, Yiddish, or Arabic, but none of this mind-twisting crap, Josef. I just got off the phone with that uncultured American President with his aid-withhold threats."

"I'm sorry, Sir. Goram and I are talking with Rabbi Chosky to get to the bottom of this, but we need your help to slow down the Americans."

"How do you suggest I do that without creating the appearance of collusion?........ China manufactured COVID-19 in Wuhan, and I, Aram Marzheim, created Whitemelt in Tel Aviv. That's not going to happen. So, fix it, Josef."

"I will, Prime Minister. I've already made it clear to Goram to help, but not at my peril or the state of Israel's. I need some time."

"Anything else, Josef?"

The Knesset speaker hesitated briefly.

"As I detangle this colossal allaena, we'll be well-served to remember the long friendship with Goram Naphtali and Tanakh Enterprises and the millions donated to the Jewish cause…"

Aram, listening, gradually became furious again and yelled into the phone.

"Cut the shit, Josef Matursky! Fire is engulfing us, and I'm supposed to worry about past beneficiaries when the future is at stake. Call me back only when you have a solution."

He hung up and threw the phone into the flower bed, and the security guards watching him pretended to see nothing.

Days later…

A slew of black SUVs parked behind the large, revered prayer hall announced the presence of a VIP inside.

A long-bearded Cleric in a black top hat walked through the back door guarded by another set of fierce security guards in black suits, whom he ignored.

Inside, the Cleric passed within earshot of two men in the empty Tel Aviv synagogue, whom he also ignored.

Israeli Prime Minister Aram Marzheim leaned on the old podium. "This scorching potato comes with significant consequences if mishandled, Josef."

Josef Matursky, the Knesset house speaker, was frazzled while listening.

Aram continued, "I realize your ties with Goram, but this is beginning to implode."

Josef's hyperhidrosis flared up. He wiped his forehead with a large white handkerchief. Josef was still not talking, so Aram continued.

"Is there anything I should worry about?"

Josef walked closer to the podium, invading his personal space. The Prime Minister reared back a little.

"I'm always afraid of the dark, Prime Minister."

Aram was confused for a second. "What?"

Josef clarified, "These scientific sorts are a complete black box to me."

The Prime Minister stood erect before speaking, "What does your nephew know?"

Josef's handkerchief stopped midair to his face. "Nephew?"

"Avnar Barak. I am the Prime Minister, after all."

Josef Matursky deflated. "He's precocious, but I know nothing."

A security guard walked in and coughed to attract attention. Both men at the podium turned around.

"I'll await your call tonight, Josef. The rude Americans are on my tuchus."

The Prime Minister followed the security guard.

Josef called out loudly to the Prime Minister, holding up his cell phone.

"Goram Naphtali just arrived."

The Prime Minister halted and whispered to his security detail, who walked away while he returned to the podium. Minutes later, Goram Naphtali walked in. The Prime Minister foregoes the niceties of meets and greets.

"Are we in trouble, Goram?"

Goram Naphtali offered his hand, smiling, and they shook.

"Israel is all I have and all I am. Her well-being is the only catalyst for my existence. So, no, we're not in trouble."

Aram sighed in relief and looked at Josef, who still looked constipated.

"Something bothering you, Josef?"

Josef, in turn, looked at Goram's face, searching. "Where does Rabbi Chosky stand on all this?"

The Prime Minister was about to intervene but changed his mind, allowing the two men to continue their conversation.

"Rabbi Chosky was pragmatic, though focused. Therefore, I will handle him."

Goram's words do not alleviate the consternation on Josef's face as he spoke. The Prime Minister noticed.

"Rabbi Chosky sees THE ORDER as the way to glide into Jewish grand eternity—" Goram interrupted, "So do I, and so did you, the last I remembered. What's bothering you, Josef?"

Aram looked at Josef and then at Goram before carefully choosing his words. Then, he stared directly at Goram.

"Promise me you and your group have nothing to do with these global Whitemelt disappearances and reappearances."

"We do not," Goram lied.

No one heard Aram's security detail approach until he coughed.

"Mystery solved. I now have to leave," the Prime Minister declared as he walked away behind his bodyguard.

When the synagogue's back door closed, Josef Matursky was immediately in Goram's face.

"You lied, Goram. Chosky is a zealot and a snake. I will handle him and not you. But, meanwhile, I have to go back to that…," Josef pointed at the back door and continued speaking, "…horrible Prime Minister, to persuade him to stall the Americans. Whatever you're doing, I don't want to know. But stop it, now, Goram."

Goram's silence spoke loudly as his childhood friend and former Congressman walked off, leaving him behind at the podium with a worried look.

"I think I'm in trouble," Josef said to himself.

***

It was a busy night at LAX, and after a successful screening through the TSA gate, Enzo talked with the Colonel on the phone.

"Back to Israel again, but with a huge break on the vanishings to pursue."

"The Tanakh Enterprises angle?"

"Yup."

"Enzo, you're beginning to sound American. I still want you back in Rome."

"I plan to return to the Vatican as soon as we wrap things up, boss."

"Do you keep up with your…"

"Yes. The Psychologist and I have periodic sessions, and it's helping."

Enzo smiled at Berlin, who was passing through the TSA gate.

"I've got to go. We'll be boarding soon."

The Colonel hung up and sat in contemplation at his Vatican basement office.

Enzo, the middle seat aboard the aircraft, confirmed their arrival ETA with Moshe Shula on the phone. He looked up with guilt as the flight attendant signaled again to switch off the phone in preparation for departure.

Berlin, in the aisle seat to his left, was asleep. Enzo hung up the phone, and the flight attendant smiled at him as she walked away. He, in turn, looked at Berlin, smiled, sat back, and closed his eyes as the galley lights went off.

An hour into the flight, Berlin walked the aisle to stretch her forever-aching legs and returned to pore through reports.

She learned of Tanakh Enterprises' meteoric rise, courtesy of the CIA USB, from its humble beginnings, which were started by a tall, skinny farm boy named Goram Naphtali, who became a dotcom millionaire in the early 2000s.

He later founded several companies and many start-up incubators, becoming a Knesset member. The latest success, rumored to be on the verge of a blockbuster Compound via an incubator named NBT–Neshama Biomedical Technologies, led by a brilliant thirty-something American, John Jacobs, Ph.D.

With eyes now drooping, Berlin turned to stare at Enzo beside her, snoring quietly. She giggled lovingly, pulled up his slipped blanket, and pressed the overhead buzzer for a flight attendant.

Chapter 21

Tel Aviv's Ben Gurion airport lounges were buzzing. It was impossible to ascertain if a Jewish or Arab holiday was at hand or just behind.

Moshe navigated the crowd with gamboling children. He spotted Enzo Lupara next to a pretty-looking lady, Berlin Yords. He beckoned to Enzo.

They boarded Moshe's idling car outside the airport, at the arrivals' curbside in a no-waiting zone.

Enzo made introductions as Moshe drove.

"This is SAIC Agent Berlin Yords of the FBI."

Moshe turned around briefly and nodded as he weaved through busy airport traffic.

A vehicle with two men followed Moshe.

Berlin passed a note with an address to Moshe, where she wanted to go.

"We have less than half an hour to get there."

"Are you sure you have the right address?" Moshe asked.

Berlin nodded.

Moshe entered the Barkan industrial park, located the derelict warehouse, and drove behind it to find stacks of old pallets.

Berlin exited the car and commanded Enzo and Moshe to remain behind.

Out of their view, she met with Jueves Abramov, who handed her a large envelope.

She noticed a prominent wound across his throat. He liked that she didn't flinch from seeing the ghastly scar.

As Berlin read the contents, he left.

Moshe thought he spotted his uncle, Jueves, but shook it off.

Back in the car, Berlin commanded.

"Neshama Biomedical Technologies Facility is our next stop."

Moshe became excited, and Berlin stared at him curiously and then at Enzo, who shrugged.

Moshe elaborated. "Chosky fingered a couple of people at the airport days ago, and the people were kidnapped. I witnessed it."

"Why are you telling us this?" Berlin demanded.

"They were Americans."

Enzo was not convinced.

"How can you tell with people trooping out at the arrivals?"

"I just can," Moshe insisted as he cut off a truck.

"Hey, watch it." Berlin admonished.

Moshe laughed it off and dangerously weaved through the busy highway traffic.

Minutes later, Moshe exited the highway.

Leading Enzo and Berlin, Moshe marched through Neshema Biomedical Technologies' entrance without resistance. The boss could not be found.

They toured the offices. The remaining confused personnel struggled to rearrange items and evacuate. The warehouse was in similar disarray.

Driving back, Berlin let her frustrations show. "That was a grand waste of time."

"They cleaned up after taking your guys," Moshe confirmed.

Berlin was mad. "Our guys? They're not our guys. I don't know if they're even Americans."

"I'm sorry, Agent, but someone should have seen this coming."

Enzo interrupted before the fireworks Berlin would bring ignited.

"Guys, where we go from here is more important. Moshe, this is your town. What next?"

Enzo spotted two men in a blue Toyota behind them. "I think we got a tail."

"I know," Moshe confirmed.

Berlin was cynical. "Your friends? Moshe?"

…Days earlier…

Late in the evening, three black SUVs busted through the NBT gate as CEO John Jacobs wound down in his office, packing documents into a briefcase. The commotion caught his attention when a Siren alarm went off. He looked out the window to see an armada of black SUVs race into the facility.

He rushed downstairs to the lobby and saw goons with drawn weapons corral, confused employees trying to vacate the premises back inside.

He spotted Abishak, whose handsome good looks have always camouflaged the ruthless psychopath he embodied, wielding a Luger, and walked up to him only to be ushered back into his office at gunpoint.

"Your cell phone. *Please*," Abishak commanded.

JJ, in agitation, complied.

"Stay put," Abishak yelled as he stormed out of the office and slammed the door behind him.

JJ collapsed onto the sofa and sat dormant in self-pity for a long while. Then, he sat straight up, slapped his cheeks hard, and rushed to his computer.

He forgot his log-on code from fright, tried twice, and stopped, afraid of permanently logging out after too many tries. He leaned back, breathed slowly, settled down, and tried again successfully.

He quickly deleted all incriminating memos, including one sent to a trusted friend months earlier, when he began to suspect Goram.

JJ heard footsteps and hurried back to the sofa before Abishak busted into the office.

Abishak looked around suspiciously and commanded the armed goon behind him to turn JJ's computer system off.

Abishak's marauders splintered into groups and segregated NBT personnel to the basement animal lab, ripping computer terminals and connections off the walls inside animal pens. The petrified workers loaded equipment onto trolleys.

Other raiders ransacked offices to remove file cabinets, desk monitors, computers, and laptops onto trolleys.

Abishak then led his goons and office personnel, pushing laden trolleys through the building into the warehouse behind the office facility.

His crew forced the NBT personnel to unload trolley items onto the floor in the warehouse at gunpoint.

Other goons checked off serial numbers behind the electronic equipment from a list.

Three SUVs backed up to the warehouse loading bay.

Abishak directed his goons to chase all NBT personnel off the facility without allowing them to remove any personal property.

Finally, he returned to the empty, ghostly, and disheveled office building, to JJ's office.

"Let's go, nerd!" he commanded the unresisting, terrified erudite CEO.

Avnar Barak, in a hard hat, oversaw the discreet dismantling of the large manufacturing equipment at midnight.

Animal transport vehicles drove off to relocate the Sows. Heavy trucks and personnel broke down the structures and carted away manufacturing vessels.

The empty facility was power-washed to pristine.

Avnar sat on the passenger side in a black SUV, the last vehicle to leave the now-empty facility.

The truck stopped briefly to chain-lock the gate.

***

It was dawn, and the roads were still dark, but the sun's brightness was beginning to break through this quiet Sunday morning as a luxurious long vehicle turned onto a paved private road. Seconds later, an unremarkable Toyota Corolla followed behind with its headlamps off.

Hoffman Levi owns Kafar Transportations. He lumbered out of the car and walked towards the clubhouse's main entrance. He headed towards the changing room with Abishak Terrel discreetly in tow.

Abishak checked around to ensure no one was about, spied Hoffman sitting on a long bench, and bent to put on his golf shoes. He crept up from behind, slipped out a long, thin stiletto knife, covered Hoffman's mouth, jabbed the knife into his heart without much struggle, and slipped out of the clubhouse.

At the other end of town, at 6:00 p.m. Sunday, Abel Schuster, proprietor at the Genteel Hospital Group, lies dead, head down on his desk as if sleeping with an almost invisible needle puncture wound on his neck.

Frieda Homel slipped into street clothes from the green hospital nurse gown, descending the fire exit stairway. She calmly strolled toward the parking lot.

She dumped the uniform, syringe, and an empty vial of Potassium Chloride into a garbage can, removed her blonde wig, shook her jet-black hair as she got into her car, turned on music, and drove off the lot, whistling an obscure Indian movie tune, "Love in Tokyo."

On Monday, in the city's Northside, Tel Aviv, It was midnight when Avnar Barak, in all black with a balaclava, slipped inside the underground Gaskiya building parking lot, the number one newspaper in Tel Aviv.

He avoided cameras slithering against the wall and eyed a black Bentley, knowing the workaholic hands-on publisher, Mukaiba Golda, would still be working. The lights went out, plunging the building into darkness.

Minutes later, Mukaiba lay dead in his pool of blood.

On the phone, Avnar, Balaclava, was off and drove fast down the highway.

Miles away in downtown Tel Aviv, Avnar jolted to a stop curbside, a hundred yards across from La Alitalia, an upscale Italian restaurant, checked his watch, noticed it was 2:00 a.m., and sighed in relief.

Seconds later, Blau Horowitz, Money Manager and principal at Gefen Capitals, emerged with a tall lady. A cab pulled up for the lady. The taxi drove off. Blau walked down the empty avenue towards a parked black Range Rover.

Avnar exited the car, hurried to catch up from behind, slipped on the balaclava, waited until Blau opened the driver's side door, shot him twice with a silenced gun, and melted into the night.

It was midnight. Night creatures creaked, chirped, and owned the darkness in this grand, manicured compound of a rumored gangster, Abulafia Cardoso. Some would swear he was a lady's man but a committed bachelor living alone.

He quietly but expertly checked all the alarm doors, steady on the green, except the back kitchen door, alternating green and red, which he just missed.

He walked up the staircase to his bedroom. It was 4:00 a.m. on Monday, still dark, in a mansion on the outskirts of Tel Aviv.

A hundred yards from the sprawling home, Avnar Barak, Abishak Terrel, and Frieda Homel, all dressed in black head to toe, carefully climbed into the compound with balaclavas.

Inside, a silent alarm triggered, waking Abulafia up. He peered through the window without turning on any lights or lifting a curtain and saw nothing but suspicion. He pulled a loaded pistol from the bedside table drawer, crept down the stairway into the lounge, and headed to the kitchen, knowing the entry door alarm was unreliable.

Avnar slipped in from the front door and disarmed the alarm immediately.

Abishak entered from the back door and also turned off the alarm.

Frieda climbed through the kitchen window right into Abulafia's waiting gun. He broke her neck instantly and laid her down gently.

Avnar heard scratchy noises from the kitchen area and walked towards it as Abulafia emerged, gun blazing.

A loud shootout ensued, at the end of which Abulafia lay dead, Avnar sustained leg wounds, and Abishak took two in the gut, close to the heart.

A bullet hit the wall alarm console and was triggered at the nearest police station.

Bleeding, Abishak was not much help in carrying the dead Frieda to the car.

Avnar drove off quickly, and Abishak and Frieda were in the back seat.

Several minutes later, Avnar, driving, was talking.

"We caught a bad one tonight, but what a way to go. Frieda wouldn't wish anything else."

Abishak, in discomfort, shivered in the backseat and pushed hard on his stomach to stem the bleeding. It didn't help. His voice faltered as he spoke.

"You ever wondered what light speed gotta do with spacetime?"

Avnar was driving fast, sadly giggling at his friend's delirium.

"No, Abi, I never believed in that $E=MC^2$ shit."

Abishak struggled to force a laugh; blood gurgled from the sides of his mouth with the effort.

"Don't talk, Abi; we'll get to a doctor soon."

Abishak rearranged himself for better comfort and looked at Frieda's dead head lying on the headrest, eyes wide open. He closed her eyes, smudging her face with his blood.

"How can it be that the cosmic time fabric depression will generate perpetual gravity pull…" His voice trailed off as he lapsed into momentary unconsciousness.

"I don't know, Abishak. Gravity and the Theory of Relativity ain't my thing."

Avnar increased speed and swerved dangerously, the only saving grace being the empty early morning traffic. Abishak jolted back to life.

"Gravity? What a load. You can't see or touch it, yet, it fucks with you…" He trailed off again into unconsciousness.

"I agree. That professor Shitface, I mean Ertergu, once told me that 186,000 miles/second equaled a lightyear? What the hell is a lightyear anyway?"

Abishak jolted awake again. "Six trillion miles, dumbass." He slumped over, dead.

"That's a long, long, long way away, my friend." Avnar awaited a crass response from his loquacious friend that never came.

He looked behind the back seat, swerving off the road, when Abishak's dead eyes stared back at him.

"Fuck!"

Both corpses rested upon one another. Avnar burned rubber fast.

Seconds later, an armada of police cars blasting Sirens flew past him, going in the opposite direction.

***

On a side street in Tel Aviv, a tall, bearded man in a black suit with a pinned-on yarmulke walked into a nondescript building next to an equally tall lady in a long black skirt with a headscarf. The building housed the most crucial active espionage professionals outside Mossad's Jerusalem HQ.

Inside, the basement splits into two distinct areas. Jueves Abramov had a small corner desk from which he managed the vast document cache locked in tall cabinets. Mainframe computers and servers are behind the card access gate opposite the records library—Jueves left for the first-floor bullpen.

He briefly surveyed workers affixed to computer screens and spotted an ID badge dangling on a cubicle wall. He discreetly swiped the ID and returned to the basement to access the computer servers. He retrieved Goram Naphtali's first-level records detailing linked business locations, including the pig farm on the outskirts of Tel Aviv.

He looked up at the cameras filming twenty-four hours a day, unworried. He grabbed his light jacket from the coat hanger and headed out.

Jueves Abramov, with earbuds, sat on sidewalks outside a Tel Aviv café, sipped tea, heard Berlin Yords whine, and coped with her background traffic noise.

"Thus far, we haven't sniffed Tanakh Enterprises' aroma. Are we missing something?" the FBI Agent complained.

"Patience, dear Agent Yords, things are sometimes slow in our desert neighborhood."

Berlin, on speakerphone, was upset at Jueves's patronizing statement and looked at Enzo on the passenger side. Enzo calmed her down.

Berlin continued, "Is Goram Naphtali even real?"

"I hate to be rude, Agent Yords. Unfortunately, I must leave this conversation to work on your requests."

Jueves didn't wait for a response. Instead, he hung up, left a tip on the café table, and walked away.

Berlin, angry, called Leeloo. Enzo's body language and speech disagreed.

"You should let the old man do his thing. Europe is not America, Berlin. Things are a little more…" His voice trailed off.

Berlin hung up before the call went through and then completed Enzo's sentence.

"…Laid back. Is that what you were going to say? It's fucking molastic if you ask me, and this is not Europe—"

She raised her hands in defense before Enzo could get a word in. "I know, there's a long history, blah, blah."

"Can I drive?"

Enzo's leftfield request befuddled Berlin.

"Why?" She stepped harder on the gas pedal, to Enzo's chagrin.

Berlin made the wrong exit on the highway heading toward Goram Naphtali's pig farm from Jueves' directives—Enzo rifled through the rental glove compartment for a paper map.

"Why wouldn't Europeans make descriptions as easy as we do?" she complained.

"They're Middle-Eastern, Arabs and Jews."

Berlin flashed a not-so-nice glance at Enzo.

"Really? Do you want to discuss human history and migration with me, Enzo?

"No, I don't, Berlin; take the next exit. There's an adjunct street to get us there. It's a new industrial park, you know?"

"No shit." She smirked in anger.

Enzo burst the tension bubble by laughing out loud.

"I can't believe I'm reading a map in this age of GPS."

"Me neither," Berlin agreed as she banged on the busted GPS equipment on the dashboard.

She took the next highway exit.

Jueves identified Berlin, who was on the phone, struggling to remain calm when arriving at Goram's manufacturing facility.

"This is a real shit show, Sir. There's a tall building, but it looks like it hasn't been inhabited for a while."

Enzo periodically looked at the front passenger side mirror to watch the tail behind. He turned to Berlin, still on the phone with Jueves.

"You know they're still behind us, right?"

The older Israeli spook, Jueves, heard the conversation. He instructed the Americans.

"Guys, don't lose the tail. So many more will be assigned if you do, and you wouldn't be able to keep track of them all."

In befuddlement, Jueves, back in the Mossad basement, stared at his computer screen on Google Maps to see a building he was sure was recently active.

"I'll call you back, Agent Yords." Jueves hung up before Berlin could get a word in.

She was livid. "This is not happening, Enzo. He hung up on me again."

"Let's get the hell out of here. I need to call Rome."

Berlin shot him a look as she headed back to the highway. "Problems?"

"Nah, returning the Colonel's call."

Berlin smiled. "You sound so American. The Colonel was right."

"Shalom," he replied.

"What?" Berlin was lost.

***

Berlin paced her airport hotel room balcony with a drink, awaiting Leeloo's call.

Leeloo was scrambling at the Capitol seeking directives from Barry DaSilva, CIA director, after Goram Naphtali's disappearance and the blatant Israeli government inaction.

It was a little chilly on Berlin's hotel balcony.

Berlin wrapped the blanket tighter, sipped the cognac, and downed the glass, making a horrible face as she stepped back inside and slid the glass door closed.

Watching Berlin, one of the men from the blue Toyota packed up his powerful binoculars five hundred yards from the top floor of a different, adjacent airport hotel and got on his cell phone.

In his second-floor airport hotel room, Enzo poured a drink and then another, massaging his hand.

He sat back on the bed and looked at the ceiling, contemplating whether to hum the Mantra. Then, he slowly began to hum,

"I was a hero to Halimah; I was a hero to Halimah; I was a hero to Halimah...," until he dozed off.

...The man in the olive military uniform had thrashed violently in the Sahara desert, alone in nowhere.

Then, a tall black shadow fell over him. It was Enzo, locking eyes with a wrinkled, white-haired male Aborigine albino grinning down at him...

Enzo, sweating profusely, jerked awake in the hotel bed and heaved. He immediately launched into his Mantra.

"I was a hero to Halimah; I was a hero to Halimah; I was a hero to Halimah…"

Chapter 22

Prime Minister Aram Marzheim, at his hilltop residence on a mild evening, hosted an involuntary meeting with Josef Matursky, Knesset Speaker, to assuage the immense pressure mounted upon him by the US President, Bender Castle, to investigate the only Whitemelt suspect in the books.

The PM of the combative small Hebrew nation now stood at an inflection point between friendship and national security. During Sunday casuals, the influential leaders talked under an island gazebo, protected by secret service lurking unseen but ever at alert.

"You need to get Goram off his destructive path right now. $40 billion of annual aid is in jeopardy, Josef. I need your help urgently."

The speaker leaned forward to talk, "Goram promised me, but I cannot confirm the status now."

The PM's demeanor suggested disbelief.

"Shin Bet will do a better job, Josef, but you don't want me to go that route after one of our own. Do you?"

Josef sat back and sipped a cold drink. "No, Sir, I don't. I, we, owe him one more chance to reconsider."

It's now the PM's turn to lean forward.

"Last chance, Matursky, then the gloves come off."

Aram raised his hand, and two Secret Service Agents miraculously appeared and walked toward the pavilion.

"I have to leave for Europe tonight, Josef. Please convince Goram to stop."

"Yes, Sir." The PM got serious once again.

"Is your nephew involved in all this?"

Josef was taken aback. He stalled before answering.

"I don't know, I hope not." The House speaker is now physically more dejected. The PM didn't spare him.

"I hope the Iran foopah will not raise its head again?" The PM said.

Josef was now visibly upset.

"Sir, I respectfully don't think we should malign my nephew when his name has never come up with all this stuff." The PM backed off a little.

"Josef, if I were you, I would find out before he drags you into it. Being friends with Goram is one thing; family involvement is a different kettle of Gefilte."

Now angry and confused, Josef arose.

The guards led him away from the pavilion. The Prime Minister, in contemplation, watched them go.

Josef left messages from his car for Avnar and Goram, but none were returned. Now, besides himself, he arrived at a hard decision he hated but knew he had to take.

He left a cryptic voicemail for Goram. "Meet me at the 'point' tomorrow morning, or you're alone."

Both men's "point" was their high school gym, where they used to make a "point" against rival basketball teams.

As their coach used to tell them, the point was to win, but not at all costs.

Josef, waiting, saw the gangly Goram saunter into the now-outdated gym.

They sat beside each other at the beginning of the nosebleed seats without talking for a few minutes. Then, Goram attempted to lighten the mood.

"You were never tall enough, even as a point guard, so I had to carry your water, remember?"

Josef was mum, and Goram tried again.

"Without me, you wouldn't have married the most gorgeous girl in school…"

Josef turned to look at him, and Goram shut up.

"What the hell are you doing?" Josef spat out.

Goram's guilty shrug angered the House speaker, who was forced to drive six hours for the meeting.

"What does that mean in the name of Yahweh?" Josef imitated Goram's lame shrug.

"Things happen," crawled out of Goram's mouth.

"Things happen, Goram. What things?"

Goram squirmed a little.

"I can't say."

"What are you, twelve? Spill, Goram."

"I can't get you involved in this, Josef."

Josef flared up, walked down to the court below, and stood at the center; Goram remained seated.

The impasse lasted for minutes until Goram walked down to join him. Josef turned to face him, many inches shorter but determined.

"Do you have anything to do with this Whitemelt thing the PM accuses you of?"

"It's not that simple, Josef," Goram replied.

Josef got further into his face.

"Remember your speech when you left the Knesset? People are still talking about it. If this blows, no, when these blows…" He trailed off.

"Things happen, Josef."

"You keep saying that, and I have no fucking idea what that means. Please, help me understand."

"I cannot say."

Josef had had enough; he walked towards the exit, and Goram called after him.

"Josef, Josef…" but the house speaker neither answered nor turned around.

Goram called Avnar immediately after Josef left the gym.

"Your uncle is on the warpath as expected and is unhappy. We move up the plans as agreed earlier."

"Already done. Doctor Lilly, JJ, and the two Americans are tucked away…"

Goram interrupted, "Not at my homestead, right?"

"No, elsewhere until this blows over."

"AV, this will NOT blow over. We need to accomplish the goal simply."

"How about you, Sir?"

"I'll be fine. You cannot go to your place, either, AV."

"No problems there. The registered ownership is my uncle's."

"All the same, be cautious."

"How long are we staying tucked, Sir?"

"I'll let you know when to return to the orchard."
Goram hung up.

That night, Josef had a Shin Bet Commander at his
home and gave specific instructions to the head of the six-
member emergency task force authorized overnight by the
PM.

"This is a search only, no invasion." The Commander
nodded in understanding. Josef wanted him to repeat what
he had just said.

"It's a search only, Sir." *Good.*

"No one must get shot, or people will get prosecuted,"
Josef iterated.

"Yes, Sir," replied the calm but fierce commander.
"And I don't have to keep repeating your instructions, Sir."

"Do not damage any part of the property. You have
your subpoenas, and your expertise at intrusive entries
without leaving any marks behind is second to none, yes?"

"Yes, Sir."

"And finally, you must also undertake the same process
with Avnar Barak." The commander did a double take.

"Your son?"

"In a manner of speaking, yes, but he's my nephew."

"Understood," replied the commander.

"One last disclosure before you leave. Avnar's home is his by inheritance, but has been registered to me since…" He trailed off. "Hence why the subpoena address was in my name."

"Yes, Sir. I will personally ensure we don't disrespect or betray your trust. We are professionals and will leave no traces of our presence. But your nephew will know. He's ex-Mossad."

With that, the table was set for Josef to extricate himself from an event by which he felt blindsided. He called Goram and Avnar again just as the Commander left, but there was no response.

Six armed Shin Bet personnel in a nondescript vehicle arrived at Goram's orchard early in the morning to an empty homestead, finding red duffle bags and several DVD videos in the safe behind the gun rack. Within minutes of expert search, retrieval, and seizure, they were gone as if they were never present.

The same process occurred at Avnar's, where the surprise was found in the shed. DVDs and red duffle bags were also confiscated.

Goram called Avnar...

"We were raided, and I suspect your place, too."

"They raided the House Speaker's property?" Avnar asked in surprise, and Goram became impatient.

"You now have to accept whether you're with me or your uncle."

"Of course, with you, Sir... but?" Avnar's voice faltered.

"I'm sorry, son, but the die is now cast. You all in?"

Avnar's voice was once again firm. "Yes, Sir."

"Then, get them all resettled back at the orchard; I don't expect Shin Bet to be back."

"It was Shin Bet?" Surprise was laced in Avnar's voice.

"Does it make a difference who?"

"No, Sir. I'll call you as soon as we resettle."

***

Jueves Abramov descended into the basement at the office.

Restless, he paced, sat briefly behind his desk contemplating, arose, and walked upstairs with determination. He knocked on an office door.

He closed the door behind him, arousing the curiosity of Aminata Gottschalk, Mossad's Western Ops sectional head—his boss. She leaned back and invited her old friend to sit.

Jueves confessed as he sat, "You already know I'm assisting our friends across the pond."

Aminata signals him to lock the door. Jueves turned the lock. She stared at him for a long time before speaking.

"Do you know what you're doing?" she interrupted herself before he could respond. "Let me rephrase that… Have you lost your mind?"

"I'm too old to lose my mind. It's already lost, but I must do this," Jueves insisted.

"Why are you assisting the CIA in investigating global disappearances and tagging Goram Naphtali as a person of interest, someone the Prime Minister continued to shield?" she asked in astonishment.

"I'm unexplainably compelled. I have to call in an old favor, Aminata."

She contemplated for a long time before relenting.

"What can I do?"

"I need full access to Goram Naphtali's level seven Bios, which are only accessible by the sectional heads. That's you."

She went quiet, grabbed her purse, left her ID on the desk, and struggled up from her chair.

"I will report my ID stolen if things go tits up."

She walked out on a prosthetic right leg.

Jueves had a twinkle in his eyes and a skip to his steps as he emerged from the nondescript Mossad building onto the Tel Aviv street. He dialed Berlin Yords.

"Take bus 43 from your hotel's south corner in about forty minutes, and meet me at Gossamer's. It's a tiny café twenty miles West of the city. Be careful. The place is easy to miss."

"Can you have another car ready for us when we arrive?"

"Already waiting." He hung up before more questions arose.

Berlin Yords sneaked out from behind her hotel dressed as a maid. Enzo Lupara left as a porter. Per Jueves' instructions, both rode buses to an unassuming café in Ashdod.

Jueves laid an aerial map on the Ashdod café table and traced optional routes from Ashdod to Eilat, Goram Naphtali's orchard. Enzo engrossed.

Jueves sat back, sipped coffee, and watched Enzo massage his right hand. He periodically scanned the nearly empty café for anomalies while Jueves's hand instinctively touched the scar on his throat. Berlin's eyes narrowed, noticing such idiosyncrasies.

"You ducked a nasty one, didn't you?" she asked as she packed the map.

"Almost saved a war with Barry DaSilva."

Berlin did a double-take.

Enzo picked up the car keys from the table and headed for the front exit.

"In the back," Jueves instructed.

Enzo turned around, and Berlin followed. Jueves sipped without looking at them.

Once a biblical desert village, Eilat was now a lush, green valley city, orchard enabled by sophisticated irrigation systems that Goram Naphtali proudly called his ancestral home.

He briefly surveyed the brown-baked mountain that formed the backdrop to the farming locality, with homes traditionally spaced to enable farming acreage.

Neat, four-foot-high cropped shrubbery created a protective wall around the gateless homestead.

Goram's five-generation, modest childhood bungalow home sat in isolation in the middle of the orchard. He was never ceasing to be amazed by the beauty each time he dragged himself away from Tel Aviv for the solemn solitude.

The house was immediately visible from its dusty access road as he heard the vehicle getting closer, knowing Avnar Barak would arrive within minutes.

Both sat inside, with the contents of a nearby briefcase Goram always had with him, and Tara's leather-bound book was on the table.

Goram gave a faraway look to the mountains, fantasizing about a Nobel prize win but wary he'll end up in an orange jumpsuit.

"Are you ready?"

"Not quite, Sir. I want to talk about…"

Goram interrupted, "Not now, Avnar. Walls are collapsing all around us."

Avnar interjects, "That's what I want to talk about, too, but first, I must—"

Goram snapped upright in anger. "Damn it, goy. I already made whole Abishak and Frieda's families. I shouldn't have to tell you that."

Avnar fell into instant remorse, head downcast. "I apologize. I should have known better. It was just that I kept seeing Abishak's face gurgling to death on his blood…" His voice trailed off.

Goram came to his side of the table and patted him briefly on the shoulder. "Soldiers don't come any better than those two."

He stayed quiet for a short spell, then looked up at Avnar, now composed. "Are you ready?"

Goram led Avnar off the deck towards the shed area. He retrieved a key from his pocket to unlock the double sliding gate to the second shed.

Inside shed two, to the left, Sows nestle in four neat pens with antennas sticking out of their heads, monitors against pen walls beeping. Four locked doors dominated the right side.

Goram then opened the first door and revealed an unconscious Doctor Lilly Chen, who was shackled to a hospital bed. Avnar approached her and checked to see if she was breathing.

Goram asked, "What do you think?"

Avnar nodded after scanning the room briefly. "It'd work," the ex-Mossad concluded.

They both walked out of the shed.

Chapter 23

The orchard was quiet, except for nightcrawlers and insects chirping in the night, presenting a picturesque similitude of just another mundane half-moon-lit Jewish evening—except that it was not on this night.

The darkness concealed Berlin and Enzo, watching Avnar Barak sip from a mug on Goram's Eilat farmhouse veranda.

Avnar sensed movements but pretended to be oblivious. He threw out what he was drinking and returned inside. He approached Goram on the phone, who waved to him quietly.

"Is the source concrete, my friend?" Goram inquired.

"Don't be silly. Yes, of course."

"How long do we have, Josef?"

"That's not the question, Goram. Get the hell out of there. You can fight another day."

Avnar grew antsy and wanted to relay something urgent. Goram turned his back to avoid distraction.

"I will not be rooted out of my own home…" Goram began to say.

Avnar lost patience and touched his boss, who jerked around in shock.

"What the hell?" Goram snapped.

"Some people are out there, Sir. I think I saw movements."

Goram responded calmly, the phone at arm's length, "I know. That's your uncle Josef on the phone."

Avnar went to the window and looked through the see-through, white linen curtains without lifting them.

"I have to go, Josef Matursky. Whichever way this turns out, you've been a good friend." Goram hung up and turned to Avnar, who was still peering out.

"Your Godfather warns of a raid." Goram unlocked the well-stocked gun cabinet as they geared up for action.

Avnar, armed, slipped out through the back of the farmhouse towards the shed.

***

Hari Hapa and Lewis Cantor woke up tied up back-to-back in a room inside the brightly lit shed. A yard space separated them so that they couldn't see each other.

Lewis failed to free his hands tied behind his back.

He yelled, "What the hell is this?"

"Relax, you're going nowhere. You killed my sister, asshole." Hari's voice boomed.

Lewis jumped, realizing he was not alone. "It's you again. I told you—"

Hari interrupted and turned himself around to face Lewis's back. "Turn around, idiot."

With disgust on Hari's face, Lewis turned to face Hari after several tries, watching the ineptitude.

"You're one pathetic crook, Lewis. Do you know that?"

"I keep telling you I had nothing to do with your sister…" Lewis went mum as they heard footsteps outside the room that soon faded.

Hari curiously stared at a patch on Lewis' arm with a questioning look. "What the hell is that?"

Lewis tried to shake it loose unsuccessfully. Finally, Lewis began to giggle, looking at Hari's arm.

Hari then noticed the same patch on his arm. "Son of a bitch…" Hari began to say when the door unlocked.

Avnar Barak necked in but didn't notice Hari and Lewis now facing each other. He backed out, locked the door, and walked towards another door.

JJ cowered in the far corner from Doctor Lilly Chen, unconscious on a gurney hooked up to an IV and beeping monitors.

"This is so far off, it's mind-boggling, Avnar."

Avnar walked over to him, slapped the CEO hard, and dragged him to the gurney.

"You need to start the extraction process, JJ, else…"

"I will do no such thing, Avnar. It's against everything I stand for."

Avnar launched a vicious gut punch that doubled the young scientist over and followed with a left hook to the jaw, displaying Avnar's knowledge of boxing.

A few teeth flew out of JJ's bleeding mouth as he collapsed onto the floor. Avnar then stood back to watch the pathetic scene.

With slow deliberation, he pulled the Luger from his shoulder harness and shot the CEO dead.

The gunshot alarmed both Lewis and Hari. Lewis mumbled under his breath, "Fuck, we're next."

***

Enzo held a thin flashlight at a scarcely visible map in the dark. Frustrated, Berlin stuffed it back into her jacket.

"Damn it."

Berlin slowly advanced towards the house.

Enzo skirted around, heading for the shed area.

She crouched near the front steps onto the veranda. Then, all the lights in the house went out, plunging the place into total darkness. She froze in place, listened for sounds, heard none, and crept along.

Goram, armed, slipped out from the back as Berlin entered. She fumbled until her flashlight came on.

The Agent stumbled into boxes labeled *antibiotics*, spilling them onto the floor. She shined the light onto the floor, saw the blister patch fall out of a package, and stuffed a couple into her pocket.

A motorbike engine bellowed from behind the house.

She rushed out the front, ran to the back, and saw the taillight disappearing into the orchard. "Bastard." She gave chase.

Goram slowed down in the familiar orchard, taunted Berlin nearer, and fired shots at her. Berlin ducked, returned fire simultaneously, and hit the bike's gas tank as Goram sped off.

She gave chase, the taillight receding fast. She limped and slowed, favoring her left leg when the leaking bike spluttered. Goram abandoned the bike and labored deeper into the orchard on foot.

Reenergized, Berlin gave chase, stopped, and listened for movements, but heard nothing. Then, sudden gunshots zinged past her head.

She crouched and returned rapid shots to the location of the gunshots.

Goram was hit in the stomach and grazed in the head. He murmured in lament as he fell, "You just don't understand."

Berlin knelt on the ground, listened, heard nothing, remained alert, lay flat in the dirt, and pointed her gun.

***

Inside the shed, Avnar forced Lewis and Hari into the room where John Jacobs lay dead. Hari stared at John Jacobs, still bleeding. "You didn't have to kill him," Hari criticized.

Avnar whacks him in the jaw, and Hari spits blood from the assault. Avnar commanded, "Move the body to the shed."

Hari silently protested, thrusting out his tied hands. Avnar pistol-whipped him more brutally in the face, splitting his lips, then tied Hari's arms above the elbows by the biceps, left enough wiggle to enable more unrestricted movements, and then untied the wrists.

"Now, move the idiot."

Hari struggled with the dead weight.

Avnar watched Hari move the body to a waiting flatbed golf cart behind the shed and then lead Hari back into the room to push Doctor Lilly Chen's gurney out.

Avnar instructed Hari to topple Doctor Lilly Chen's body atop Jacobs' corpse, tie Hari to the bodies, and force Lewis to drive the golf cart sitting next to him.

***

Enzo busted open the shed's front door as the golf cart left from behind the shed. He looked around for a vehicle to give chase, found none, and pursued on foot.

Panting, Enzo kept the golf cart taillights in view but lost fast as the cart disappeared into the orchard.

Hari spotted a low-lit circular clearing ahead of The Circle while working the ties loose. He watched Avnar prod Lewis with the gun to go faster, but he couldn't.

"It was a golf cart with one of them—" Lewis started to explain when Avnar struck him. Lewis began to cry, and Avnar laughed hysterically. Hari glared at him.

The cart arrived near The Circle simultaneously as Hari loosened the tie and jumped Avnar, disorienting Lewis. The cart toppled over. Lewis flew off and landed near the large, wrought-iron bomb shelter-tunnel manhole cover.

The flatbed golf cart and bodies came flying at Lewis. He ducked as Doctor Lilly Chen's head hit hard on the shelter manhole cover and started to bleed profusely. Lewis cradled Doctor Lilly Chen's head in his lap, but could not stop the bleeding.

The sky lit up psychedelically when Doctor Lilly Chen began to bleed out. An alien hyperboloid vessel popped out

338

from the sky. It began to spin with an audible, high-pitched noise. It grew in size by the minute as Avnar and Hari were roughhousing intensely on the ground, oblivious to the cosmic happening.

Avnar's gun went off, and the bullet hit Lewis in the chest, surprising him. He let go of the dead Doctor Lilly Chen and grabbed his bloody chest.

When Doctor Lilly Chen's head hit the ground, the spinning vessel descended below the cloud and was visible to anyone looking up into the sky.

"You shot me," Lewis remarked.

Avnar and Hari continued to wrestle on the ground. Hari yanked off Avnar's gun, which landed near Lewis. Avnar and Hari stopped briefly and looked around furtively for the weapon.

Lewis, in pain, felt the gun near his hand and looked up to see both men staring at him. Lewis lifted the gun and shot Avnar dead without hesitation.

The loudness deafened Hari, who covered both ears in pain, writhed on the ground, ears bleeding, and passed out.

Lewis stared satisfactorily at the dead Avnar and grinned as blood slowly seeped out of the corners of Lewis's mouth as he died.

Lewis's body twitched as the vessel spun faster. Soon, a tentacle wriggled out of the oval welt behind his right ear. A second tentacle followed. The pinnae dislocated, allowing a two-inch, silvery, blue, turquoise-beige exoskeleton to emerge.

The entity spiraled skywards, growing tenfold in size, as it bellowed in a resounding, continuous, hypnotic fashion.

Enzo, gasping, arrived and was immediately transfixed by the overhead magic psychedelic light display, mouth agape.

Berlin, still on the ground, gun-ready, noticed brightness in the sky to the East of her current location. She hesitated and then started to limp toward the bright sky.

At The Circle, Doctor Lilly Chen's head was twitching. Then, a smaller silvery entity emerged with a different red-turquoise-black exoskeleton color variation. It spiraled skywards and grew tenfold, emitting a brisk, continuous, thinner sound.

The call and response continued as both entities slowly entwined in a hypnotic, mesmeric, sensual dance.

Berlin arrived. She was immediately transfixed next to Enzo, gaping at the heavenly cosmic light display and the spinning, gleaming, multicolor hyperboloid craft hovering above the coupling duo in a synchronizing spiral dance.

Everything froze. The vessel and the entities vanish.

Hari awoke. Enzo and Berlin recovered and looked around in confusion as Hari struggled, wondering aloud, "What happened?"

Berlin and Enzo looked at each other blankly, shrugged simultaneously, and spoke in unison, "Nothing."

***

Cosmos

Light years earlier…

In accord, the dead silence of the Cosmic array deceptively masked its immense violence, which soon intruded with the sun's visible Photosphere surface, amassed by a two-thousand-kilometer Chromosphere zone that expels gas fires through the Corona.

The sun's magnetic loop snapped, and giant, violent, explosive flares released massive, destructive solar wind particles that dispersed across the silent, empty abyss.

For millions of years, Myresians from the planet Myresis evolved a highly heat-resistant exoskeleton. Still, the primary component enabling the exoskeletal viability in perpetuity began to crumble and was degraded by the continuous solar shower bombardment of the debilitating ultraviolet spectrum.

The necessary compound to effect a permanent solution was located on Earth, but the Myresians drew angst at an invasion. The planet was forty million miles from the sun, and its landscape showed intermittent skyward elongated poles and domes.

In Earthly terms, the view resembled a collection of inverted golf ball dimples sewn together in clumps with snorkels sticking out of their sides like smokestacks.

A spacecraft no bigger than a sedan glided on the surface of planet Myresis and hovered five hundred yards from the vacuum-sealed stack entrance to the underground habitat. It began a delicate, shape-shift contortion of its hyperboloid architecture to fit and slide down a smokestack.

The Tantalum-Hafnium-Carbide composite exoskeletal vessel was clamped securely onto the wall at the underground docking station. Inside the spacecraft, two oblong-shaped sentries with tentacle extensions at both ends of their bodies attached to the vessel wall and hibernated.

At the Solar observation post on the planet, the sentries scanned the horizon from an impossibly tall panoramic lookout outpost. The quiet was shattered by massive solar flares rapidly approaching the planet.

The sentries sounded the planetary alarm and scrambled into an escape hyperboloid vessel, each enrobed in individual escape pods. They tumbled haphazardly as they barely jetted off planet Myresis.

Above the Nile River, the Alien craft pierced the Earth's atmosphere in Egypt in 1571 BCE, 3,600 years ago. One pod crashed onto the riverbank, and the other exploded on a merchant ship at sea.

The alien on land was embedded into a baby, about to be cast adrift in a basket at the river's edge. The other alien sank to the bottom of the Ocean, embedded in an enslaved person.

Now that events have altered the Myresian procrastinations, the sentries would harvest the specific human DNA chromosome strain necessary for their survival and return to their planet to begin rebuilding toward immortality.

***

Two miles away from Centro Tel Aviv, Moshe Shula, Jueves's nephew, had been chain-smoking in and out of a decrepit coffee house. Moshe was now just back inside when Jueves walked in.

"Been waiting long?"

"Just got here, Uncle J." He lied and signaled the attendant.

A tiny coffee mug with something thick and black appeared in front of Jueves. He picked up the cup.

"The Americans?"

"Still sleeping, I guess," Moshe joked.

Jueves stared hard at him. Then, finally, the smirk disappeared from Moshe's face.

Jueves passed the USB information to Moshe.

"Don't go with the Americans in case things go south. You'll have no immunity. They do."

Moshe starts to protest. Jueves got up and raised his hand so his nephew could be quiet.

"There'll be time for your Macho thing, Liebchen."

Jueves walked out.

Jueves Abramov remained nervous at the Ashdod café, sipping coffee, when his phone rang.

Aminata Gottschalk whispered very softly, "Heavy smoke billowing, friend."

"Who's with you in the office?" Jueves, suspicious, asked.

"No, one," Aminata lied. An impassive Josef Matursky sat across the desk from her, watching.

"How long will it take them to get to Ashdod?" Josef asked, meaning Mossad.

Aminata's voice arose, "Not Ashdod, Eilat."

Josef, now animated, nodded. "Shit. Keep me posted."

He walked out of her office.

Jueves, already on his feet at the Ashdod cafe, failed to catch Aminata's last comments of… "Not Ashdod, Eilat…" as he hung up and dialed Moshe.

"Wait, wait! Moshe Mossad is coming, not Shin Bet." Aminata hung up, swearing, "Goddamnit."

"Hope that helps, Aminata. I'd hate to see Jueves in jail, or worst still…" Josef quipped as he walked out of her office.

Outside, behind the café, Jueves sat smoking against the brown brick wall.

"You in town?"

"Where else could I be with all—"

Jueves interrupted, "Get to them quick, Moshe. Shin bet crew dispatched."

He hung up and redialed as he got into his car.

"Will do," Moshe responded before realizing the line was dead.

"Thanks for nothing."

"We got real problems now," Jueves lamented on the phone as he hurried out of Ashdod to Barry DaSilva, CIA director, who questioned him as he walked into a downtown DC restaurant.

"Are you saying—"

Jueves interrupted, "Yes, yes, yes."

Now it's Barry's turn to interrupt. "I'll call you back in five, J."

Barry hung up and redialed.

***

...It was a night at the Naphtali village homestead as the war raged.

The continuous explosions reverberated inside Menachem Naphtali's nightmare as he tossed and turned fitfully in the bomb shelter at his Eilat ancestral orchard.

His adolescent son, Goram, called, "Papa, papa."

The father woke in a cold sweat and jumped off the bed, only to collapse in pain on the floor. He immediately grabbed his broken left leg in a dirty cast, a souvenir of the

Yom Kippur War that sent him home wounded and now trapped with a nine-month pregnant wife.

"Papa, Mama is sick and vomiting," Goram lamented...

Goram snapped awake in the dark orchard, grimacing in pain. He wiped the blood off his eyes and winced as he got up to hold his bleeding stomach.

He charged in one direction, waving the gun around, only to change his mind and switch to a different approach. Then, in total confusion, he wandered around the orchard, overlooking the cosmic night sky display.

Berlin, Enzo, and Hari headed toward the farmhouse. Berlin's phone rang.

It's on Jueves. "Get the hell out of there now!"

Berlin forced Enzo to drive back to Goram's farmhouse in the golf cart.

"This is ridiculous, Berlin. We must get to the car and get out of here, now."

Berlin jumped out, ran into the farmhouse, returned, lugged a box of unlabeled patches and a silver briefcase, and dumped it in the back seat with Hari.

Enzo took off fast. "Jesus, what the hell was that, Berlin?"

"Something I had to do, sorry."

On the Orchard access road, Moshe, in a small car approaching rapidly from the opposite direction, saw oncoming headlights and flashed, momentarily blinding Enzo, who did not see Goram stagger onto the dirt road.

Enzo struck Goram with enough force to send him flying across the road. Moshe, traveling fast, crushed Goram, unable to stop.

Hari's head banged against the front seat headrest and drew blood. "Fuck!" he cussed.

Berlin yelled, "What the hell was that?"

"I don't know. I think I hit something," Enzo confessed.

Berlin glared at him. "You think?"

Both vehicles stopped yards away from each other.

They hid Goram's limp body in the roadside bush.

Moshe collected all the cell phones, removed all the SIM cards, chewed them to bits, loaded the phones into a bag, slammed the bag repeatedly on the ground, crushing the devices, and threw the pack deep into the bush.

Berlin was left in Moshe's car. Enzo and Hari followed behind in his car.

Moshe saw oncoming headlights and blinkered to the right, alerting Enzo of his intentions. Moshe pulled off the road, hid in the bush, and immediately cut the engine.

Enzo followed suit.

They waited out the police cars and unmarked armada that zoomed past their position.

Minutes later, Moshe sped onto the highway.

The fleet of black SUVs that flew past Moshe and Berlin arrived at Goram's Homestead.

Inside, they found a slew of papers, the gun cabinet open, and a few racks empty.

The Shin Bet Commander spoke with a low, confident voice: "Let's get out there and find something. Touch nothing until the scientists get here. No hero stuff, as hostiles might still be around. Thread carefully until we get lighting here."

As the Agents dispersed, he got on the phone, barking furious orders for several minutes for flood lighting equipment to enable unhindered evidence gathering.

All ten of the Agents fanned out in all directions in the orchard.

Sheba, leaking fluids, was located in the orchard.

Foliage disturbances were identified where Berlin had laid down, shooting any blood spots around where Goram had fallen, and spotted bullet casing positions marked for later collection by CSI.

Minutes later, two vehicles arrived: an SUV with three CSI personnel carrying boxes plastered with menorah symbols and one loaded with lighting equipment.

While waiting for them, the leader outside immediately dispatched them with agents to the field.

At the sheds, samples were harvested along with bagging JJ's body.

At the center, Lewis and Doctor Lilly Chen's bodies were thoroughly examined by the CSI team, ignoring apparent but weird flesh excavations on the victims' heads and upper arms.

The golf cart, Sheba, and other large physical evidence were carted away the following morning.

In the dark morning hours, Moshe slowed down to keep up with the traffic flow, heading to Muwaffak Salti AFB, Azraq, Jordan. The road sign came up with mileage -163 miles away.

Moshe exasperated, "It'll take four to five hours to get there. Shit."

Berlin shifted in discomfort. "That's a long time to sit idle without communication, Moshe."

"I know, but I couldn't risk us being tracked with cell phones, Berlin."

She wondered aloud, "Now what?"

In the car behind, Hari, next to Enzo, reached for the silver briefcase Lewis used to ship Tara's book to Rabbi Chosky. He opened it and found Tara's leather-bound book.

He remained motionless for a beat, removed the journal, returned the case to the backseat, and caressed the leather-bound cover on his lap without opening it.

His eyes welled with tears in the dark.

"You okay?" Enzo asked.

After a long pause, Hari whispered, "No."

At the far end of the Jordanian Muwaffak Salti AFB, A pilot at the Cessna Citation X jet controls talks on the headphones with Barry DaSilva at the CIA communications control center.

The pilot asked, "ETA?"

Barry jumped in. "Couple of hours."

"Yeah?" the pilot confirmed as he calmly tweaked the blinking buttons in the aircraft, which was ready for takeoff, guarded by armed tanks and military vehicles.

Barry watched Berlin and Enzo's cars get closer to the border crossing on a satellite connection at the CIA communications control center. A series of black SUVs awaited, blocking the road on the Israeli side.

A uniformed employee at the controls looked at the CIA director for directions. Barry nodded. The uniform talked on her headset to a drone sergeant miles away.

A guided missile departed from the Las Vegas military drone control center for the Israeli-Jordan border crossing.

Five minutes later, Berlin and her crew witnessed a massive explosion ahead of them, increasing in speed toward the border.

Moshe wondered aloud, "If we'd arrived five minutes earlier, we'd be nothing but pink mist."

"You're morbid," Berlin shot back.

"That's true," he responded, driving like a maniac, then continued, "That's what we homo sapiens do best. Even the dumbest asswipe gets an A in dying."

"You make it sound like a skill," Berlin said.

"It is. Inbred in us all," Moshe replied, pointing at the faraway military base. "We're here."

The Military Base remains dark, with a heavy preponderance of armed personnel visibly placed to reinforce the imminent use of force at the slightest threat.

Berlin, Enzo, Hari, and Moshe are inside Muwaffak Salti AFB. Berlin, Enzo, and Hari climb into the aircraft while Moshe returns to the truck.

The Cessna took off.

***

Bender Castle, the President at the Oval Office, listened to the Israeli Prime Minister, Aram Marzheim, yelling on the speakerphone. ADIC Leeloo Chang, Berlin, and Enzo listened expressionlessly.

Minutes later, Leeloo, at the wheel, drove off through the White House gate, Berlin next to her and Enzo in the back seat.

"Wait 'til I show you the find from inside a Whitemelt reappearance," Leeloo gleefully announced, arousing the curiosity of the sleepy detective duo.

"What? An alien?" Enzo hazarded a guess.

Leeloo smiled and stole a glance at him in the rearview mirror.

Chapter 24

Under the president's directives, the NIH National Institute of Health utilized a task force led by Dr. Romeo Atkins to investigate the two boarding houses in LA and Michigan, Blossom Plaza and Home Away From Home, respectively.

The task force closed down both facilities and forced Homeland Security to release Evans Square, the Blossom Plaza supervisor who tried to save Anna Cantor from Whitemelting.

Hari Hapa was compensated for the death of his sister, Tara Hapa, from the liquidation of Lewis Cantor's bookstore. Hari was then sent to Walter Reed for tests to ascertain the impact of the antibiotics patch Avnar Barak had forced upon him. The outcome of his health would remain inconclusive until he turns 70.

Tambo Gilu of the UN worked with President Bender Castle and retrieved all the Whitemelt returns from Italy, the Count; Brazil, Eugenio Machado; and, along with the Whitehouse Skyfall, the South Korean Park Yu Soon, sequestered in Area 51, with the box of antibiotics Agent Berlin Yords retrieved from Goram's home. The Israeli government also selected scientists who brought the bodies of Lewis Cantor and Dr. Lilly Chen to the United States for further study.

Rabbi Chosky on the lam was captured in Egypt; Knesset speaker Josef Matursky was found guilty of aiding and abetting Goram Naphtali with phone log evidence of him warning Goram ahead of Berlin and Enzo's arrival at his Eilat orchard. He got a twenty-five-year sentence. Erman Erturgu, Goram's Paleontologist, was never found.

Jueves Abramov refused PM Aram Marzheim's commendation, citing his unreasonable actions when he was forced into retirement decades earlier.

His nephew, Moshe? On the other hand, he was reinstated into the Mossad. PM Aram Marzheim lost the next Israeli leadership election.

Enzo Lupara returned to the Vatican and was tasked to find Erman Ertergu.

SAIC Agent Berlin Yords was reassigned to the Arizona border crossing after massive Fentanyl overdose burial grounds were uncovered.

END

Zook Madoo's cushy life in Nigeria ceased from a sudden military coup, resulting in the death of his father, the former state governor.

He didn't have a long, suspenseful wait to ascertain if his freedom was at risk from the junta. That blow came from his inheritance.

The fraudulent bequest from his saintly father was laden with criminal activities and debts he was ill-equipped to service to a nasty collection of international grifters.

With lives now at stake, an ancestral clue surfaced for the existence of a fabled skull with diamonds-studded eye sockets, the Mafidon Head.

Now what?

The author tells big stories that weave international criminal intrigue, exploring the vagaries of human nature under duress and the unpredictable outcome that follows. Those behaviors are not in a vacuum but are often culturally symbolic, straddling the nature/nurture divide.

Yomi Akinode lives in Tarzana, a township North of Los Angeles, California — a West African imbued with decades of the American experience and all the promise she holds.

YOMI AKINODE

THE MAFIDON INHERITANCE

YOMI AKINODE

THE MAFIDON INHERITANCE